Sundown Apocalypse
Urban Guerrilla

Sundown Apocalypse series

Book 2

By Leo Nix

Direct all correspondence to: Leo Nix

Email: leo@leo-nix.com

Web: www.leo-nix.com

Facebook - @LeoNixSundown

Cover illustration: Stephen Kingston

Web: www.wingtipdesign.com.au

A special thank you to: Bruce and Marja for their generous support and the difficult task of proof reading; Peter for his ongoing technical assistance in all things military.

Dedication: to Nulla, a damn good mate.

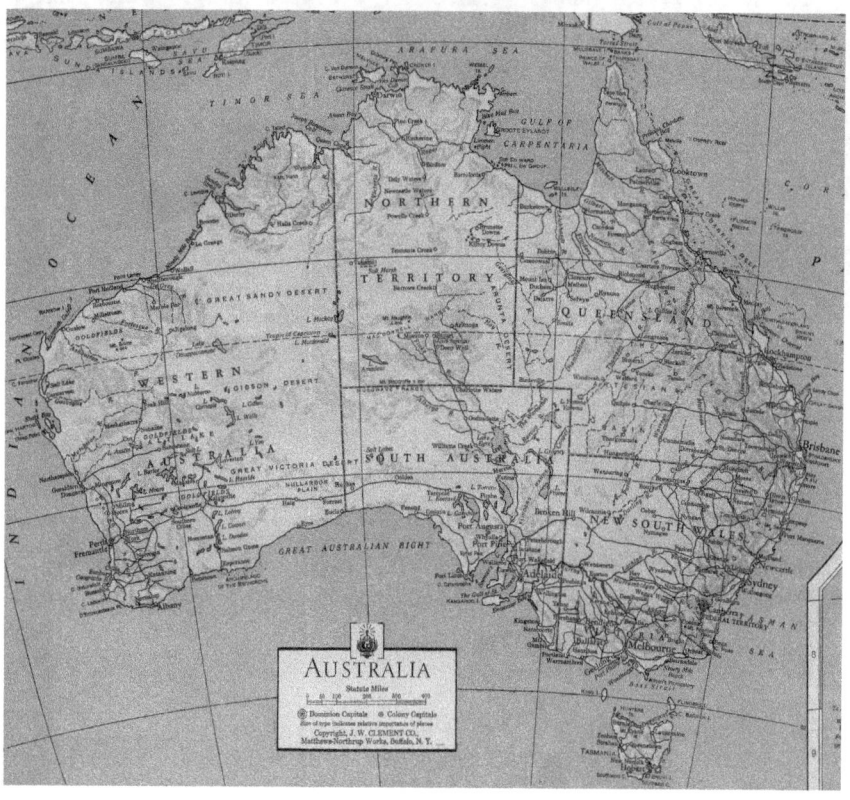

Table of Contents

Chapter 1

Sundown - Flinders Ranges

Even though the weather had cooled a little it was still hard going across the desert sand. Roo pulled up on top of a towering sand dune and peered into the distance. Bongo pulled up beside him. He lowered his handkerchief and spoke. "Roo, how much further to the homestead? I'm pretty sure my fuel is almost done."

Pulling out his binoculars Bongo looked in the direction his silent friend pointed. Sure enough there was a tiny set of buildings a few kilometres away. "I can see some buildings. I hope my bike makes it. I'm running on fumes right now. How are you for fuel?"

Roo bent and looked at his fuel gauge and nodded 'all good'.

"I'll lead just in case I run out. Let's go." Bongo kicked his bike forward in the red sand and slid sideways down the face of the sand dune.

The landscape in this region was sparsely dotted with spinifex and salt bush. Here and there patches of green grass began to show more frequently as they approached the foothills of the towering Flinders Ranges. They rode up to the first shed before stopping.

As they kicked their bike stands down three cattle dogs raced from behind the house barking and growling viciously. Roo whistled loudly and the dogs suddenly stopped, looked at him curiously then gathered around the olive skinned kangaroo shooter to sniff his extended hand.

Finally satisfied he was safe they began wagging their tails. Next the dogs checked Bongo's scent before jumping all over them both. Just then a young man appeared from around the side of the shed, his shotgun pointed directly at them. Roo carefully removed his helmet for the man to see who it was.

"Roo! For shit-sake, I nearly shot you! What the blazes are you doing out here?" the man shouted and walked across to shake the newcomer's hands.

"I'm Bongo, we've come down from Birdsville. We're pretty buggered, it's been a long trip and we need some fuel and a feed," he said as the they walked their bikes into the shed and dismounted their gear. Roo busied himself cleaning grass stalks and seeds from his bike engine. Bongo followed suit while the young man chatted to them catching up with the news.

The farmer introduced himself as Riley, he informed Roo and Bongo of the local situation. "Those terrorists have been shooting up the homesteaders and taking some of them away. Jarl Horsely, said they've got a prison farm or something in Hawker and they're working them as slaves. Strange eh? His missus said the terrorists were religious folks she knew before all this happened and now they've turned crazy. Fancy killing people for nothing? There's no army, no police, nobody can stop them." He pulled his felt hat off and scratched at his head as he wandered off to fill their empty fuel cans. The two men from Sundown's Commando could clearly see a stack of forty-four gallon drums of fuel in his tractor shed.

Riley finished filling the fuel cans then called his family to come out of hiding. Riley's two small children smiled shyly as they stood staring at the two men as though they had never seen a stranger before.

"Have you had any contact with the terrorists?" asked Bongo curious to know what was happening closer to civilisation.

"Not us, we're too far out for them to bother, I reckon. We've holed up here trying to keep our heads down. Sometimes we'll drive around to get some supplies from Jarl, but otherwise we stay away from everyone. They've been to just about every other station though, and collected people, killed some too. They tried to take all the cattle and sheep but they'd no idea what they're doing, so they gave up and left the area, gone back to Hawker we reckon.

"Most of them ain't from around here, they're mostly city folk and don't know anything about the bush or farming. That's why they've taken people from their farms, to work for them. Those they don't put into their prison farms they tax, they take a percentage of their food, cattle or sheep or crops. They call it 'tithing', something to do with the Bible, Jarl said." Katie looked at the two dusty riders as she picked up their youngest, Harry, and balanced him on her hip. The dogs continued to race about sniffing the interesting smells from the boys and their bikes.

Bongo filled them in on their battles with the terrorists and about their commando in Birdsville. He asked where the best place would be to settle in the Flinders Ranges. Bongo explained that they were sent to find a safe haven for their people. The farmer and his wife nodded, shifting their feet a little nervously.

"Arkaroola village is nice, you could probably settle there for a while. Anywhere towards Wilpena Pound would be a good enough place too, but Wilpena's occupied by the Wilson family, they're strange people. Don't go west or south of the ranges because that's where the terrorists have set up some of their outposts and prison farms. They'll capture you and make you work for them. We can help show you some places if you don't mind waiting a day or so. You could help me shift some cattle and sheep around? If you don't mind, I'd really appreciate some help."

He looked at his wife and put his hand on her shoulder, only then did he notice how thin she was. "Poor Katie's exhausted trying to look after the kids and be my rouseabout at the same time. But come inside first and get some tucker into you, then we can look at the map and make some plans."

Riley was one of Roo's cousins on his father's side, his brothers once had properties all over the Flinders Ranges. He was the only one who stayed behind to farm, the rest sold out to live in the city.

"Yeah, Earl lives in Adelaide and Mitchell lives down near Mount Gambier. They hardly ever bothered to visit. Katie and I love the bush, we've survived droughts, floods and bushfires but now we're really struggling. We have to hide whenever we hear a sound, and it's getting on our nerves a bit. We'd sure welcome some neighbours who knew how to fight them Revelationist terrorists. We'd sure appreciate some help with the animals and harvest too. We put in some barley and wheat with the help of a few of the survivors hereabouts. I'm too afraid to start up the harvester in case the terrorists see the dust cloud and come to investigate." Riley was talking while Roo and Bongo hungrily ate his wife's home-made bread with piles of butter, cold meat and pickles.

Through his hot tea and a mouth full of sandwich Bongo asked them about Wilpena Pound and the Wilson's.

"I'm not sure exactly what's going on in there, Bongo. We haven't gone out there since this started, we're too afraid to. There are others like us who escaped the terrorists and didn't get captured, but we stay away from them too just in case they put us in. If they don't know we exist then they can't point the finger at us."

That evening they relaxed, talking and playing with Riley's kids. Bongo was in his element rolling on their kangaroo and cattle skin covered dirt floor wrestling and laughing with little Harry and his older sister, Elle. Katie spent most of her time smiling as she watched her children having a wonderful time playing with someone else for a change. Riley was usually too tired to do much with his kids of an evening and she was flat out helping him and keeping the family fed. Neither had much energy left for their children, she thought, and her eyes reflected her sadness.

The children were put to bed in one of the double beds beside the fireplace and were soon asleep.

Roo indicated he wanted to head off for bed too. Neither of the adventurers could keep from nodding their heads, they were exhausted. Riley told them to throw their swags in the shed, it was the best place to sleep with the nights now getting cooler. Their one bedroom shack was already overflowing and there was simply no room for visitors.

Outside, the moon shone brightly. Roo walked Bongo over to the fences while the dogs walked beside them. "Roo, what say we do some work around the place tomorrow before we do our recon of the Flinders Ranges?" suggested Bongo.

Roo fingered the wire and pointed to the many places that needed mending. "Yeah, I can see it needs a lot of repair work. You want to hang around and repair Riley's fences and do some odd jobs?" Bongo asked, Roo nodded. "OK, why not do a good job of it and spend the week here, shoot a few kangaroos and emu's for them and then go exploring, what do ya reckon?" Again the silent kangaroo shooter nodded this time with a smile on his tired face.

Over the next six days the three of them worked from sun-up to sun-down doing everything from repairing the shed roof to fixing fences and chasing cattle and sheep from one paddock to another. Roo shot four large kangaroos and two emu's and they ate like kings. What they didn't eat they cut into strips, salted down and hung them out to dry for jerky.

On the seventh day Riley said they should go out to Wilpena Pound to meet the Wilson family and have a yarn with them. He warned them not to take their weapons, or to say anything about Birdsville, or their intentions to move here. He said he didn't like the Wilson's much and didn't trust them, no one did.

They left early in the morning riding their bikes along the back tracks. When they finally hit the main bitumen road they were blocked by a large herd of cattle. Two friendly stockmen rode up and invited them to their camp site for lunch.

At the stockmen's campsite was a truck, caravan, and a cook busy making the midday meal. One by one, the cattlemen came in for their lunch. Riley knew some of them and they came over to shake hands and introduce themselves.

"Hi Riley, how have you been mate, not seen you for a while. I thought the Revelationists might have got to you too. How's the missus and the kids?" asked Laurie, a lean sunburned man in his thirties.

"We're doing well, Laurie, how's your family? They safe?" The group yarned for a while catching up on the news and then the conversation turned to current events and the terrorists.

Laurie spoke up first. "They've got control of the entire country, mate. They tithe ten percent of everyone's cattle and sheep too. They like us here but only because Jack's a Wilson, and they don't touch the Wilson's. They've got a prison farm on the other side of the ranges, and have taken most of the farmers in the region to work there. You'd better watch yourself, Riley, because they'll take you and Katie too if they find you.

"Our Jack's not as bad as his old man but try to avoid him if you can. He doesn't come around much but he's here today, just keep your head down and be polite. You never know what he'll do. He's got four arseholes who run the property for him - psycho's they are, avoid them if you can. They've got connections with the Revelationists and do their dirty work for them. They act a bit like those Nazi Gestapo."

Riley looked at Laurie and the small gathering around the camp fire. A few of the heads nodded in agreement with Laurie. Cookie came over and added, "If Jack finds out yer here with these two strangers there might be trouble, Riley. They're after more cow hands so just finish yer meals, and leave, boys. Don't make a fuss of it, just jump yer bikes and head back where yer came from."

Again those same heads nodded.

The meal was almost over and the stockmen began preparing to move back to their cattle just as Jack arrived in his four wheel drive. He got out and walked over to the three trail bikes, then wandered over to the camp-fire with his four henchmen and sat down.

"Riley, nice to see you, mate, it's been a while. Brought some friends with you?" Jack called across the fire.

"G'day, Jack. You might remember my cousins Roo and Bongo, on my father's side. They're up from Yalpara ways, been working the cattle stations and harvesting wheat. They dropped in to give me a hand with me cattle and repair some fences. How's things with you, Jack?" asked Riley, amicably, but his eye's watched Jack's carefully.

"We're busy, as you can see. We could do with some extra hands though. You boys ride a horse and muster cattle, eh?" he called to Roo and Bongo. The boys both nodded.

"If you've finished working on Riley's property, I'll take you all on. We're light handed right now and could use you today..." The large man thought for a moment his eyes shifting from one of the newcomers to the other. "How about I send some of my boys over to help you, Riley, they could speed things up a bit with your repairs? The sooner we get some extra hands with the muster the better."

No one spoke for a half minute. The uncomfortable silence was broken when Bongo spoke. "That's nice of you Jack, thanks for the offer but we're only here for the week and today was our last day. Riley wanted to show off the beautiful Flinders before we headed back." He watched the man opposite, waiting for his reaction.

"No sweat, boys," Jack said but he didn't sound pleased, "If you want full-time work just let me know, good workers are hard to come by. Things have changed in the world, boys, so bring your families if you want, we can put them up as well. We're a family friendly company and you'd all be welcome." His eyes had gone dark and he looked away from the three as he stood up. "Right lads, back to work. Riley, nice to meet you again, take care now, boys."

Within seconds the gathering dispersed and the only ones left were the three from Arkaroola and the cook. Bongo could hear Jack speaking with his four henchmen beside their bikes. It made him feel uncomfortable.

"Boys," said the cook softly as he collected the cups and plates, a smoke hanging from the side of his mouth, "I suggest you take him up on the offer. He's got a nasty streak and no one gets away with saying no to him."

"Why? What could he do?" asked Bongo, curious.

"What could he do?" The cook laughed. "He'll kill you."

Riley looked at the cook then at Roo and Bongo. "We'd better get back to Katie, I don't like this." He stood up to leave.

As he did a voice called from beside the bikes, "Hey, nice bikes you got there boys. I tell you what, you do a days work with me and I'll let you have them back." It was Jack's voice and beside him stood his four bully-boys. They each had side-arms strapped to their leather belts.

"No sweat, Jack." Bongo called back politely, "Roo and I can hang around for a few days and can give you a hand if you need us that badly, sure. But you'd better let Riley get back to his missus and kids, they'll be frightened something's happened to us."

"We don't want to keep Riley from his kids," replied Jack. He looked at Riley and said, "Piss off, Riley, we'll probably drop in some time and invite you back here." Then he turned to the two Birdsville lads. "Grab yourselves a horse and join us. If it's adventures in the Flinders you want, we've got plenty. Leave your gear here, it's safe, I guarantee it. Cookie will make sure no one touches anything."

Bongo thought just how fortunate it was that they'd left their rifles in Riley's shed.

The two worked with a will which impressed Jack and his bully-boys. Roo was an expert horseman having learned to ride horses, camels and donkeys since before he could walk. Bongo was still a bit of a rookie but he did a good-enough job. By nightfall they had joined the muster gang for dinner and sat around the camp-fire chatting and drinking the Wilson's beer.

Bongo was watching the four bully-boys like a hawk. He knew that at any moment one of the them would challenge either Roo or himself, he'd seen their likes before. They were drinking like cattlemen did after a hard day in the saddle. He noticed how the four enjoyed their positions of power, openly bullying the others when it pleased them.

"Hey, boy! Rooster, or whatever you call yourself. How'd ya learn to ride like that?" called the tallest, Brad.

Roo looked at him but didn't speak. Bongo felt the heat rise inside him when Brad's mate, Joey called Roo a 'dumb prick'. Bongo felt his outrage rise and knew that the four were looking for a fight.

Joey called out across the camp fire, "I didn't know the special school taught retards to ride." The four of them laughed, no one else did. Jack sat in his directors chair silently watching, his cigar smoke drifted lazily into the night air.

There was dead silence, the only movement came from ten pairs of eyes switching between Joey, Roo and Bongo. All that could be heard was the crackle of flames from the camp fire.

Thinking quickly so that he could protect his silent mate, Bongo stood up and called out in the growing silence, "Why don't you just go fuck yourself, Joey, you arsehole."

Bongo smiled knowing he'd taken the heat off Roo. He had a soft spot for his quiet mate and there was no way he would let anyone bully a mate of his. The younger man knew that if he started the fight before the boys were truly drunk, there was a chance someone would step in before it got out of hand and someone was killed.

"You prick!" Joey's face flushed bright red in the firelight. He threw his beer can at Bongo who easily ducked. The bigger man walked stiff legged around the camp-fire and with a big wind-up took a wild swing at the new boy.

Bongo rocked back on his heels and then cracked his right fist into Joey's chin sending him flat on his back. Joey shook his head and groaned as he tried to stand. He wobbled on his hands and knees then vomited. He collapsed to the ground, curled into a ball and began rocking back and forth holding his broken jaw.

The cattlemen stared in shock, they couldn't believe it. Bully-boy Joey, flattened with a single punch by the new guy. Jack Wilson smiled quietly, he was enjoying this. The three bully-boys looked at each other and as one came around the fire and threw themselves at Bongo. He didn't stand a chance against all three.

Roo stood when he saw them charge Bongo and kicked the legs out from under the closest. As he stepped in to protect his young friend, Brad flattened him with a swinging king hit from behind. Roo didn't get up, the punch laid him flat on the ground beside Joey.

Laurie stood up and cried out, "Why don't you lot fucking grow up? Every time we get a new boy you have to beat the shit out of him!" But he didn't step in to help, no one did.

Two of the bully-boys held Bongo by the arms while Brad started punching. "Hold him still, Ferrie. Greg, grab his arms, tighter!" He smashed a fist into Bongo's face opening a cut along his cheek, blood sprayed with each blow.

Soon Bongo was unconscious and had to be held upright as Brad exhausted himself. Brad stepped aside to allow his cousin Greg to use Bongo as a punching bag. Greg had a reputation as a fighter and relished every opportunity he got to use his fists.

"You smart-arsed prick." he said kicking Bongo's prostate body as it lay on the ground. "You Yalpara boys think you're better than us, eh? Next time you want a fight just call us Wilson boys, we'll show you how we fight in the Flinders." Greg turned and smiled at the frightened faces of the other cattlemen looking on in horror. He wiped some of Bongo's blood off his knuckles and reached for his beer.

"Anyone else want a flogging? Anyone here think you're better than us? Come on, stand up!" When no one stood he raised his voice and laughed, "You gutless bastards, you're all just pieces of shit that God has placed for us Crusaders to use to glorify our Lord, the God of the Revelations. Amen!"

The cattlemen sitting around the camp fire squirmed uncomfortably. Some turned away, others just stared into the fire. Laurie put his face in his hands and shook his head.

"Don't any of you bastards here think you can challenge us. Try it and you'll end up like these two." Brad nodded to his mates and they resumed their drinking. Jack smiled smugly having had a ring-side seat to the excitement. None of them bothered tending to Joey who was still rocking and sobbing on the ground.

After a few minutes Cookie saw that it was now safe to step in. He dragged Bongo across to his trailer and washed the blood off his face. Then he carefully applied ointment to his cuts and bruises.

"Leave him, Cookie," called Jack. "He started it, let him wallow in his own blood. It'll teach him that it doesn't pay to upset the Wilson's." But Cookie ignored him and continued to administer to Bongo. He then brought in Roo who was now beginning to stir. Cookie looked at Joey sobbing quietly on the sand with his broken jaw, and left him there.

The next morning they were kicked awake by Brad and Joey. "Get up you yokels, time to pay for your meal." Joey's face was well wrapped in a bandage and his eyes were black. He was in a foul mood unable to eat or talk. The bully-boys were about to kick Bongo but suddenly stopped when they saw the violent look on Roo's face.

"What the hell did we get ourselves into, Roo?" said Bongo trying to stand up. Bongo had a livid cut on his swollen cheek. It was red and inflamed and the combination of swelling, lumps and bruises clearly showed that he'd been in a fight and lost badly.

Neither did anywhere near as well as they were expected that day. They stoically bore the brunt of the Wilson boy's bullying and jokes. By late afternoon Bongo realised that Greg had disappeared with three others of their pack. He was sure they were on their way to Riley's place.

"Strewth, Roo. I hope Riley gets his family away in time. I know what them bastards are going to do if they catch them." Bongo began to shake in rage and fear. He adored kids and had fallen in love with Riley and Katie's two children, he felt he would die if anything happened to them.

An hour before dusk Roo and Bongo found themselves alone on the very edge of the gap which was the only way out of the compound. Roo looked around then whistled to Bongo, lifted his chin and galloped his horse towards a break in the rocks, Bongo took off after him. They were free and no one noticed. Neither of them knew the Flinders Ranges well enough to make their way to Arkaroola. They knew it was best not to return by the route they took coming in though.

After an hour of hard riding they came across a detailed map on the tourist road leading into the ranges. They studied it for a few minutes. Finally Roo looked at Bongo and nodded. Bongo knew Roo had a photographic memory and trusted his mate's keen sense of direction. Roo pointed out the route they would take on the map and Bongo nodded. Mindful of their injuries they climbed back on their horses and headed towards Arkaroola.

It was a hard ride through the rugged ranges. They had to detour via some of the deserted farms to gather water and food for themselves and their horses, and that added another day to their trip. The two pushed hard only stopping for short rests so the horses could catch their wind and ease their backs. Bongo kept hoping against hope that his new-found friends were safe. At times he found himself crying – he wasn't sure if it was from pain, fear or exhaustion.

They sat and watched Riley's homestead for an hour before Roo nodded that it was safe to ride down. They saw no dust clouds and no sign of vehicles or horses since they had escaped. Of course Jack would know where they were headed. But on horseback, in desert country, he wasn't bothered too much. Jack knew he could pick them up whenever he wanted.

As they entered the yard, Roo stopped his horse and jumped down, wrapped the reins on the timber fence and scanned the ground. He pointed out fresh truck tracks and foot prints.

"Four men's foot prints going into the house and only one coming back. There's multiple drag marks and these patches look like blood. What do you reckon, Roo?" said Bongo beginning to hyperventilate. He then let out a keening moan when he saw more blood on the ground as they approached the front door.

Roo swung the door open and the two entered. Bongo gasped deeply and pointed to the wall where a shotgun blast had plastered blood and what looked like an eyebrow on the whitewashed stone wall. There were bullet holes in the walls and empty cartridge shells on the floor.

"Riley must have ambushed them when they walked inside." Bongo continued his dialogue, "It looks like he took out one at the front door... one inside just here with his shotgun and that's his face, or what's left of it, on the wall there." He pointed to the eyebrow and Roo nodded. "Then they opened fire with their automatics. Oh hell, Roo. Riley, Katie and the kids might be dead outside the back door." He started to sob when he saw more blood and a shotgun blast-sized hole in the open back door.

Roo put his hand out to stop his friend. He then stepped out carefully looking at the ground and reading the tracks. He crooked a finger at Bongo and grunted. Bongo stopped dead in his tracks and looked squarely at his normally silent mate. That grunt was the first sound he had heard coming from Roo in all their time together. Roo then held up his hand for Bongo to stop and observe.

A master tracker, Roo bent down to read the signs on the ground using the sunlight to highlight each footprint. He pointed to the bent grasses and prints which spoke to the initiated of the story of the fire-fight

Bongo began talking again to calm his nerves. "So..." he began, "Riley then ambushed the next one as he pushed the back door open. That's the blood there and it looks like he then ran across to his truck in the carport." Bongo stopped and Roo pointed out the small tracks made by a pair of bare feet.

"That's Katie's tracks," said Bongo. "OK, she must have got out first with the kids. But where's the children's tracks, I can't see any." His voice went up an octave as he started to fret again.

Roo pointed to the roll and variations in depth in Katie's tracks. "So that means she was carrying one on each hip?" asked Bongo, Roo nodded.

He then pointed to Riley's footprint covering part of Katie's. "OK, got it, he followed her. I can't see any of the bully-boys footprints though, does that mean they didn't follow?" Again Roo nodded and pointed back to the door and the drag marks.

"Yep, I can see it now. The last Wilson was too afraid to come out. So that means Riley and his family got away? And one of those Wilson boys escaped, taking his three dead mates back to Jack. That means he'll want revenge."

Roo grunted a second time and stood up, they walked to the carport. Again he bent to study the tracks and pointed to the back cattle grill. Together they walked over to the fence line and the cattle grating separating the enormous paddock from the house block.

"They got away, thank God, they got away!" Bongo smiled and then hugged Roo. Roo smiled and even returned the hug, briefly.

"Roo, we've got to find them and help them. We're not going back to Birdsville until we make sure they're safe."

Roo smiled, a tiny grunt escaped his lips one more time and he nodded - it was exactly what he was thinking too. They ran back to the shed and recovered their weapons, collected what gear they could pack onto the now exhausted horses, and began to track Riley's truck into the Arkaroola wilderness.

"Roo," called Bongo walking his tired horse, "did I really hear you talking to me just now?" He was smiling, in fact he realised that he was feeling darn joyful.

Roo looked at him, looked away, then back again and nodded. It was late afternoon and he wanted to put some distance between them and Riley's homestead before dark. He looked back at Bongo and grunted. It was a soft, lighthearted sound, then he smiled broadly. He too had been afraid for his cousins and was overjoyed they had escaped.

Chapter 2

Nulla - Luke and Simon's Apocalypse

A panicked voice cut into the static on their CB. "They have infiltrated my unit! All personnel, be advised, terrorists have infiltrated 1st Armoured. We are compromised and ineffective. I repeat, we have been infiltrated by terrorists planted in our units. I repeat..." They heard a loud bang followed by an ear splitting scream. The voice was replaced by static.

Simon turned to his mate, "Wow! Luke, did you hear that, terrorists have infiltrated our army units, they must have killed that guy. This is starting to freak me out." They set their CB back to scanning the radio frequencies hoping to discover more but all they could pick up was static.

The two teenagers had been listening on their hobby scanner all morning. News stations broadcast of hundreds of synchronised terrorist attacks across the globe. The 'Crusaders Of The Revelations' had been threatening to bring down the Apocalypse of the Bible for what seemed ages. Their numbers had exploded after they ran a brilliant, world-wide recruitment campaign earlier in the year. Turning on their CB scanner they listened to the police and ambulance calls with escalating anxiety.

Simon was in the habit of listening to his CB scanner when he woke before dawn almost every morning, but this was different, very different. The radio and TV told of power outages, poisoned water supplies and people dying by the millions. Internet news footage showed images of the

Crusaders cutting down civilians in broad daylight. They saw people dead and dying, lying in the streets, poisoned by their municipal drinking water.

In the USA, Asia, India and Europe reports came in describing how the crusaders had also released a biological weapon, similar to the SARS virus. It had a mortality rate close to 90%. It was predicted that it would travel around the globe infecting billions. News reporters went off the air as they too succumbed to the poisoned water and infection.

By midday there were no more news broadcasts, no more TV or internet and no more mobile phone service. Then there was no more electricity either. The poisoned water caused people to die in their homes and on their way to work without even knowing what had struck them.

In Simon and Luke's neighbourhood people began to congregate outside in the street. They gathered in confused and distraught groups as they sought to understand what had happened. Many people simply dropped and died in front of their own homes. Whole families began to collapse to the ground in agony. Simon heard screaming coming from his neighbours house. He was frightened and gathered up his scanner and the backpack he and Luke prepared earlier. The boys decided to escape the city.

It was almost midday and the two teenagers could now clearly hear the approaching sound of gunfire. They guessed their army was fighting in the suburbs as they were forced back towards the CBD.

"Come on, Luke, those terrorists will be here soon, we'd better move. Our parents are probably already dead or

captured by now and it's just too dangerous to stay here."
The distant gunfire was moving closer. Simon kicked his dirt
bike into gear and pushed forward with his left boot. Luke
did the same and their bikes leaped into the now quiet and
deserted street.

There was only enough space in their packs for a few
days food and water. With much regret, Simon left his
remote control helicopter behind. It cost him every cent he'd
earned over the entire year. Luke told him they could go
back for it when things settled down. Many things were left
behind the day of the apocalypse.

As they rounded a bend in their suburban street they
almost ran into an army truck filled with armed soldiers.
Desperate, hard faced men leveled their rifles at them. The
boys pulled up sharply and put their hands in the air. The
bikes coughed and stalled, silent.

"What the hell are you two doing out here? Get back
home and lock your doors!" came a booming voice and they
watched as an officer jumped from the front cabin of the
truck. He towered above them with his hands on his hips,
looking tough but his red, sweaty face betrayed his fear.

His voice softened somewhat as he said, "Boys, there
are terrorists right behind us. Get out of here right now or
you'll be caught in the middle when we set up our ambush."

"We're heading up into the Adelaide Hills, sir," said
Simon. "We heard on the army UHF that the terrorists had
infiltrated our military units, some of our own soldiers are
terrorists, sir. They might be in every unit. The radio said the
military were compromised."

Sweat flicked from his face as the officer's head jerked back with the news. Simon thought to himself, '*You didn't know did you*.'

Right at that moment the deafening staccato drumming of automatic rifle fire sounded beside them. Simon swung his head around and witnessed a soldier firing short bursts of his Steyr assault rifle, killing his comrades in the back of the truck. Bodies jerked and slammed backwards from the force of the fire. The uniformed traitor then swung his rifle towards the officer and the teenagers.

Simon and Luke reacted swiftly. Kicking their bikes into life they leaped forward speeding rapidly through the gears. Luke looked back to witness the officer savagely flung backwards as he was hit by the terrorists burst of automatic fire.

The teenagers rode like maniacs through the streets and then into the hills on secret dirt tracks they knew so well. They didn't stop till they could look down on the city itself an hour later.

At one point they had ridden past a terrorist road block as rifle fire cracked around them. Terrified, they put on speed to escape, ducking their bikes behind parked and stalled cars to avoid being hit.

As they neared the top of a bush covered hill they slowed, then stopped. In front of them was a group of civilians sitting beside a Greyhound coach. They appeared lost and disheveled. One explained they were on a holiday tour when the terrorists struck, the driver headed into the hills for safety. A woman called the boys over and asked them what was happening in the city.

"Hi boys, we've been watching you ride up. Can you please tell us what's going on down there. Did our army kill the terrorists and is it safe to get back to our tour?" she asked, her face moving closer to Simon's, almost pleading for good news.

"Lady, things are not safe down there, please don't go into the city. The Revelationists are there, everywhere. We saw them kill an entire truck load of army guys and their captain - right in front of our eyes. We only made it this far on luck," Simon told her.

Some of the other civilians asked questions and it was obvious to the boys that many of them struggled to believe that their army no longer controlled the city. One even went so far as to abuse the boys for telling lies.

"You think we're lying? Go down and see for yourself then!" replied Luke, he wouldn't be called a liar by anyone. The man shut up and put his head in his hands, rocking silently.

"What about all the dead people?" asked one of the women. "People are dying everywhere. The driver said he saw dead people in the streets and in their cars. I'm terrified. Do you boys know what's going to happen."

"I told you before, Marian, it's been on the news. The Crusaders Of The Revelations have finally done it. They're killing everybody like they've been preaching for years. Isn't that right, boys?" a middle aged man called out to them.

"Yes, that's right. It's on the news and CB radio, that's exactly what we've heard. They're saying that the water in every city has been poisoned right across the world and we shouldn't drink the tap water." Simon turned to the lady. "I'm sorry, miss, but things are really bad out there. The terrorists have taken control of the part of the city where we escaped from. They've set up road blocks and they're killing everyone they see."

He looked up to see the crowd moving in closer to listen. "We got out by sheer luck. I wouldn't go down there, but if any of you want we can let you listen to our CB?" The teenager began to set up their mobile CB set from the rack on the back of his bike. Luke sat on the ground and turned up the sound.

"I'll scan our police channels and see if anything has changed. This morning we heard the armoured cavalry on UHF open channel, warning everyone that the terrorists had infiltrated their units, they were killing everyone. We can't usually listen in on the military frequencies because they scramble their transmissions, but this time was different. They must've done it on purpose. The civilian channels can sometimes come up with something useful like that." Luke tried to sound hopeful for these clearly distraught and struggling people.

They crowded around but the news was all bad. Reports of army reversals came in from all points. They heard orders passed back and forth between police units, it sounded like the entire countryside was in a total shambles.

One piece of good news was that some of the 1st Armoured Cavalry still held out in the Adelaide Hills. Although they'd lost control of one cavalry squadron the other continued to fight against stiff opposition. They heard a broadcast for the police to organise transport and ensure civilians did not block the roads.

Sadly, few civilians survived. One police report stated that 75% of the population were either dead or dying after drinking the water. The police fared no better than any other service. The report said that the police were barely functioning with a skeleton staff. The only force in any strength was the terrorists.

"Those damned Revelationists killing everyone. I always knew they were doing the work of the Antichrist." sobbed one woman, others soon joined in.

The woman that called the boys forward said to Simon, "I would get out of here if I were you. Just pack up your set and go into the countryside. Stick to back roads and tracks. Just get out of the city for God's sake." She looked at them and stepped back into the crowd.

Simon nodded as he and Luke began to pack up their gear. "Miss, I hope you get away safely." Turning to the group he said, "Good luck everybody, I hope you all find somewhere that's safe from the terrorists, and the army comes to find you. We need to go now, good luck again." Simon kicked his bike alive and waved. He sped off along a path that he and Luke knew from their years of riding in the hills.

Simon and Luke decided they should try and contact the armoured division higher up in the mountains. They picked their way along back tracks then headed towards a service station off the main road. Their bikes sat on empty and they needed fuel.

The boys arrived at the station but everything appeared too quiet. Suspiciously they climbed off their bikes and took their helmets off. They looked around but noticed nothing out of the ordinary. Sitting out front was a battered station wagon which made the whole place look quite normal, but that added to their sense of dread. Just then Luke pointed to a figure in the window. It looked like old Mr Thornton sitting in his rocking chair, just like they'd seen countless times before. They made their way carefully towards the open shop door.

Simon waved hello but the shape in the window didn't return the wave. He pushed at the front door to the store and called out greetings but still no answer. Stepping inside he almost tripped over the two bodies lying on the floor. Luke followed and then gasped in shock. Simon stared at him with a questioning look on his face.

"What is it?" he mouthed.

Luke pointed to the hunched figure beside the window. Seated in his rocking chair was the elderly owner. His eyes were closed and his mouth open. He didn't seem to be breathing, he looked dead.

"Hello, Mr Thornton? Hello? It's Simo and Luke. Are you OK?" Simon called out as he took a tentative step towards the aged body in the rocking chair.

The old man made no movement and uttered no sound. There was just a slight rocking of the chair accompanied by a 'creak creak' as it gently moved back and forth.

There came a deep, shuddering gasp, as the old man dragged life back into his lungs. Simon and Luke's heads snapped upwards in shock. The withered figure suddenly opened its eyes.

"Shit!" yelped Luke and he looked to run outside.

"Oh, boys, sorry, I was just taking a nap." He grinned his usual grin. "What is it you want today? Some fuel for your bikes?" came his slow, reedy voice.

"Are you all right, Mr Thornton?" asked Simon, he looked at the dead bodies on the floor and then slowly back to the old man. Beside his rocking chair they spied an aged sawn-off shotgun.

Mr Thornton noticed their glance. "Oh that, it's fine boys. Those two are just some roughnecks who wanted to rob me. They won't be doing that again now, will they?" He sucked his gums as he chuckled wetly. "These out-of-towner's should know better than mess with an old man and his shotgun."

"You shot them yourself?" asked an incredulous Luke.

"Sure did young fella. I heard on the news this morning that terrorists are trying to take over the city. The world's gone crazy they said. I know what happens when terrorists are on the rampage and scavengers come out of the woodwork. Saw it in South America during the sixties. So when I got out of bed this morning I prepared myself with the old shotty. When these two came in demanding money, I told them to bugger off. One of them made the mistake of pulling out a pop-gun." He rocked back and forth as a smile formed showing his bare gums.

He saw Simon staring at the pistol in the hand of one of the dead bodies. "If you want that pistol, just grab it. Go ahead, search his pockets and take what you want, he won't be needing anything now." He paused for a second. "Do you know how to use a pistol? No? OK, point it to the floor away from your feet, and pass it to me handle first. Now watch carefully."

Mr Thornton then explained the mechanism and action of the weapon. It was a 'Saturday night special', a snub nosed .38 commonly used in armed robberies, he explained to the fascination of the two boys. He spun the chamber.

"Only one bullet so it looks like that's all they had. Poverty's a bitch ain't it? You can check their pockets and their car outside there for more bullets. Huh, hmm, well, use it wisely and don't waste it. What are your plans for today then?"

Over the dead bodies lying on the floor they discussed the situation from their experiences and what they'd heard on TV and their CB. Mr Thornton had no idea things were so bad. He told them to fill up their bikes, grab as many fuel cans as they could, and strap them down as they'd done many times before.

"Hmm, that plan to find the armoured cavalry may not be such a good idea. They're in a fight for their lives right now. Listen, you can hear the rumble of shell fire every now and then. If you're dead set on finding them make sure you identify yourself first, and be careful it's ours and not there's. Don't show anyone you have that 38 either, just in case they aren't who they say they are. And keep it safely in your pocket until you're absolutely sure you want to use it. A 'special' is a deadly weapon close-up. Remember that, a .38 bullet at close range just might save your lives one day."

The boys were back on their now heavily loaded bikes and riding towards the sounds of battle. Simon had the .38 in his trouser pocket, his hands kept wanting to take it out and handle it. He was fascinated with the weapon and thought it an object of absolute beauty.

They experienced no trouble finding the cavalry, they just rode their bikes towards the rumble of gunfire. It was fortunate that they came across a sentry who didn't fire first, then ask questions. Teenage boys on trail bikes still look like teenage boys, and this saved their lives.

An armed sentry stepped in front of the boys as they slowly rode up the fire trail towards the firing.

"Stop right there boys and off with the helmets," he called, his Steyr pointed at the ground in front of them. The boys obeyed and kicked down the stands on their bikes while they took off their helmets.

"Are you the cavalry?" asked Simon. "We escaped the city and want to join up and do something useful. We know how to operate a CB unit. Look, we have a mobile one we use." He jabbed his finger at the CB set strapped to the back of Luke's bike.

The sentry shook his head. "You boys must be bloody mad coming up here. Can't you tell this is a battle zone? There's ordnance flying all over the place. The terrorist army have pushed us almost back to the city itself." He continued to shake his head at them as he spoke into his mic. Turning to them he said, "Sit down and wait while my superior comes down. He'll only be a few minutes."

A stern-faced man loped down the dirt track towards them. He looked them over then said firmly, "Boys you can't hang around here, we're about to push off again and if you stay you'll be killed. The terrorists don't take prisoners. Go home and stay indoors, it's not safe out and don't drink the tap water, whatever you do, its poisonous."

Simon looked at the sergeant major and said, "Sir, we just escaped the city, we saw a truck load of soldiers executed by a terrorist dressed in uniform, our uniform. We've seen dead and dying people everywhere. Our own families are probably dead by now too. We don't have a home to go to and we can't go back if we wanted. All we ask is for you to give us a job so we can help fight these terrorists."

The weathered warrior stood there, his mouth opened then closed. He then looked them over with an experienced eye. Eventually he spoke. "Well I'll be," he half whispered, "how old are you fella's?"

"We're sixteen, sir," said Luke.

"Sixteen, you want to die for king and country and still in nappies. What a mad world we live in. OK, bring your kits with you." He turned to the sentry, "Private, call up Captain

Ridges and tell him we have two new recruits. Tell him I'll bring them up now." He waved his hand at them and they trotted their bikes behind him. They dared not start their engines for fear of stirring his wrath.

Blackened, bloodied and smoking bodies lay everywhere: soldiers in jungle camouflage and terrorists in black shirts with strange white writing. They walked past a damaged APC, it was surrounded by twenty or more bodies. Just below the top of the hill they could see what must be headquarters. A shell exploded down the hill and the boys flinched.

"Stick right next to me, boys, don't wander off because there are mines about." At that they stuck to him like blu-tack. The sergeant major pointed, "Put your bikes and gear there, walk behind me and don't say a thing unless you're spoken to, and don't ask any questions, got that?"

He turned and looked directly into their eyes. They nodded their heads nervously. As they walked into the tent the sergeant major bawled "Attention!" it frightened the daylights out of the boys and they quickly snapped to attention.

He explained the boys presence to the captain then stepped back and folded his hands behind his back. Captain Ridges looked at the two boys. "Well your parents should be proud of you offering your services to fight for our country. Unfortunately, we are in a bad situation, we just don't have any positions for you. In any other situation, at any other time, I would be able to offer you a cup of tea and a chat before kicking your backsides back down that hill and all the way home." The officer pinched the bridge of his nose with his thumb and index finger wearily.

The lines in his face and the black rings around his eyes suggested extreme exhaustion. He shook his head and continued. "I'm sorry boys but I can't keep you here, it's just too dangerous and your deaths would be a sheer waste. I'm going to send you back down the hill with one of my most experienced men. He'll escort you back to a safe place. I suggest you get back on your bikes and ride as far away from here as you can. We're being pushed back inch by inch and we still don't know if we can hold Adelaide, or any other place for that matter."

"Sergeant Major, grab Private Nulla for me please." He turned back to the boys still standing at attention in front of him. He rubbed the bridge of his nose between his thumb and index finger again. He sure looked tired, thought Simon.

Turning back to the boys he said, "Relax, stand easy, your hands can go in front if you and you spread your feet a bit. That's it, it's more comfortable." He looked at them and thought for a moment.

"Seriously boys, we don't stand much of a chance the way things have turned out. We're completely unprepared for this. I don't want to see either of you dead, not here nor anywhere. Private Nulla will take you to a safe place even if it takes a month or two. I admire your spirit but not today. Take your time and be warriors in other ways. Save what you can and fight guerrilla style. Fight the terrorist's with your brains. Don't take risks and always retreat to fight another day. Right, here comes your escort."

The captain extended his hand and Nulla shook it firmly. "Private Nulla, consider yourself reinstated to Sergeant. You are sectioned off to escort these two warriors to a safer place. I don't know where that is or how long it will take. Take a weeks rations, ammunition and anything else you may need. Sorry, but I don't have a spare trail bike, but I'm sure these boys will double you." His head bobbed up and down as he closed his eyes to think.

Captain Ridges looked up, his voice firm. "Nulla, go country and set up a civil resistance, guerrilla style. I don't expect we'll be an organised army by the end of the week so do what you can, and that's an order. Questions?"

"Sir, I am to escort these two scoundrels to safety even if it takes so much time that the war might be over. If things go to the proverbial then I am to go country and engage in covert action against our enemy, guerrilla style." He stood to attention while speaking. Simon and Luke watched in amazement at the formal military display.

"Correct ,Sergeant. And nice work with the ammunition truck this morning, well done." They shook hands like old friends. Captain Ridges stepped back, they saluted then he turned on his heel and went back to work. The solidly built aboriginal sergeant did the same and turned to his fellow sergeant.

"Sar'n major, am I to allocate weapons to these boys?" asked Nulla.

"Hmm, best not to, they might shoot someone." He scratched at the stubble on his chin then said, "Belay that Nulla. Yes, A3 Steyrs with ammunition. They're of an age and they want to fight, they had the courage to come up here and offer their lives for their country. Collect what is lying around and get them some gear. Then get the hell out of here. You have ten minutes before we move out, better start moving as soon as you can."

Surprised at how things had turned out, Simon and Luke felt like they belonged in the army now as they shook the large man's out-stretched hand.

"Good luck, lads. Nulla, may we meet again in better times." The sergeant major turned to the boys then said firmly, "Attention! About face! Dismissed!"

Then they were alone with their escort.

"Well boys, looks like it's you lot and me against the whole terrorist army. Do not move from this spot until I call you," the well muscled, aboriginal sergeant said firmly. "When I call I want you to bring your bikes over and we'll get moving. Do what I tell you and we might just get out of this trap alive." Nulla went off to get his kit, supplies and two standard issue A3 Steyrs for the boys.

Luke didn't know whether to laugh, smile or wet his pants he was so excited. This had turned out better than he could ever have hoped for. He could not imagine anything better in life than having his own assault rifle.

"I was hoping we'd get to ride in the tanks, darn it." said Simon as he pulled a sad face. They were like wide-eyed kids in an ice-cream shop as they watched the soldiers preparing to move out.

Chapter 3

Charlene - Heidi

When Charlene woke it was dark. She hurt all over and the blood soaked into her clothing made it feel sticky and cold. The pain was something she wasn't ready for and it knocked her down when she tried to sit up. Putting her good hand to the ground she sought out a nicer place to die. Her left shoulder was on fire and she heard herself cry out when she tried to move her arm. It had been a hot day, but it was proving to be a scorcher of a night in Adelaide city as the terrorists continued with their killing rampage.

Charlene knew she was in trouble. She was in severe pain, thirsty and had a slight fever. Her arm and shoulder were swollen and inflammation had already set in. She couldn't straighten her left arm nor could she move her hand. Her torso appeared to be untouched but her shoulder was numb and each pulse beat was like a hammer pounding into her.

'My shoulder must be broken. I need to move or I'll die here,' she thought. Charlene knew that if she didn't get treatment soon, her arm would become infected and she would die a slow and painful death.

The young woman tried to stand but fell back, her head spinning. Trying again she had the same result. But Charlene was never a quitter so she tried again and again until she could sit up without the world spinning inside her head. She finally stood and staggered back to the now quiet and darkened supermarket.

The back doors to the bakery, where Emma shot her a few hours previously, were open. She tottered through, not registering that this was the scene of her violent assault. Charlene looked down at the dark stain and shuddered as she recognised it was her own blood there on the concrete.

In a haze Charlene forced herself back inside and crouched behind a counter, listening. She heard no sounds of movement so she stood up, and, on unsteady legs, she wobbled into the aisles. There she found an empty shopping basket and began to fill it with food, bandages, pain killers and bottles of water, as much as should could carry in her one, useful hand.

The pain in her shoulder almost made her pass out so she sat down and crawled over and leaned behind a cash register to rest. That was when she heard sounds, voices, female and male, punctuated by sobs of terror and sadistic laughter.

She shuddered in pain and fear as she hunched down as far as she could into the cubicle, trying to be as quiet as possible. The voices started again and she recognised the three who shot her. Her breathing was so rapid she feared they would hear her. Peering through a gap she saw her assailants and began to shake uncontrollably.

"Get over there, all of you. You too. No, stand there. You, stand still, no one is going to hurt you." His voice was pleasantly smooth but authoritative. "We've chosen to send you all to paradise, to cater for our Crusader heroes waiting there for you. They have greater need of your services than we do here." She heard a stifled cry and a slap, then more crying broke out. Tears coursed down her cheeks remembering how that same cruel voice had spoken so reassuringly to her.

"Get on with it Jabba, we have to get back. Just friggin' do it." That voice was Larry, she recognised how his voice cracked and went up an octave when he got excited.

"No, let them suffer, we don't owe them nothing!" That was Emma. "On second thoughts, my arm's getting tired holding this damn rifle. Come on Jabba, give the order and let's just do it so we can go get some food, I'm starved."

There was a voice calling from outside the mall telling them to hurry up. Jabba spoke hurriedly, "OK everyone, I'm sorry that I can't formally send you on your way with a prayer, but if you could just close your eyes, this won't hurt a bit."

There were bursts of automatic gunfire, louder than Charlene could remember, fortunately it was over in seconds.

"Fuck it!" came Larry's livid voice. "This fucking gun keeps fucking jamming!" he yelled again, his voice breaking and jumping up several octaves. "I'm telling you, when we get back to camp I'm gonna get a new one! This is just a piece of shit!"

Charlene could hear him screaming and their voices receded as they left the mall.

'*They might come back,*' she thought to herself.

Her body was shaking again but she forced herself to look at the victims. '*There may be survivors and they'll need my help,*' she whispered to herself unconsciously.

There was a row of bloodied still forms on the floor beside the wall. They were tumbled together, like puppets left for kids to play with in the morning. One squirmed and cried out. Charlene didn't know what to do, she froze. Her natural instinct was to run over and help but she was deeply afraid that it was a trap, and she'd be shot again. The bloodied young lady was stuck in a no-man's-land of indecision.

Her morality won the battle. Leaving her basket of groceries, she staggered as quickly as she could to the struggling girl on the floor.

"Are you OK?" she asked sitting down beside her in the spreading puddle of blood. She took the girls hand in her good right one. A frightened face looked up at her.

The young woman's eyes were wide with wonder as though reborn. Seeing the blond haired beauty above her she was confused. "Are you an angel? Am I in heaven?" said a voice so soft that it perfectly matched her fine-boned face.

The teenager held tightly to Charlene's hand as she sat up, she didn't let go. "I thought I was dead," she said simply, "why am I alive?" The girl seemed to come out of a trance as she shook her head then checked herself all over.

It was then she noticed the bodies. The teenager stopped all movement and stared around, some were her friends, they were lying dead beside her. Something snapped inside, she shuddered and began to scream.

"Zombies! Argh! Zombies!" She tried to scramble to her feet in panic. It escalated into a full-blown panic attack and she started hyperventilating. Her feet failed to grip in the pools of blood beneath her and the teenager slipped and fell on top of Charlene, causing her rescuer to scream in pain. That caused the young lady to take stock of where she was and her surroundings. Closing her eyes she calmed her breathing and came back to reality. Once settled she carefully examined herself for bullet wounds.

There was blood on her clothes but when she ran her hands over her body she felt no pain or sign of injury. All of a sudden the flood gates opened and she began to cry. Regardless of her own pain Charlene drew the teenager to her breast and they clung to each other on the floor amid the bodies and the blood. Charlene felt something rise inside her, an excruciating warmth and affection for this gorgeous girl - it frightened her as much as it thrilled her.

After what seemed an eternity the teenager pulled herself away and looked at her rescuer. She did a double take when she saw how badly wounded Charlene was.

"Oh, I'm so sorry, I need to get you to a doctor... or something. You're a mess," said the young lady slipping easily into action mode. "Stay still, I'll get some things together and come back here. Please, don't move." With that she scampered off running down the aisles gathering bandages and medicines adding to what Charlene already had.

When she returned the girl said, "I'm taking you to my house. They've already searched there and it should be safe. Come on, I'll support you. I promise I'll look after you." As small as she appeared she was incredibly strong and together they fled the carnage of the mall.

"I'm so sorry, my name's Heidi, what's yours?" That was how they started their special friendship, struggling across the main road in the early hours of the morning.

The two young women made it across the main road and into one of the side streets. There was a half moon and enough light for them to walk by. They had to stop many times for Heidi to swap the grocery bag to her other shoulder and to allow Charlene to rest. It was slow but after a half hour she announced that her house was the next one. Charlene was dizzy and feverish, she couldn't have cared less, she was nearing collapse.

Without warning a truck engine roared, it was heading straight towards them. Heidi carefully eased Charlene onto the nearest front lawn and behind a screen of shrubs just as a truck of civilians and their guards raced past. They lay still and quiet together on the grass. Heidi held Charlene in her arms protectively, like a big sister.

"That was close. Here grab my hand and I'll help you inside. That's my house just there," said Heidi as she now held out her hand to her new-found friend.

Heidi helped the staggering Charlene into her house. Exhausted, Charlene fell on the bed and was soon asleep. With practiced ease Heidi quickly pulled the blinds closed and draped spare blankets over the windows. She then came back to strip Charlene of her bloodied clothing.

By the light of several candles she cleaned and bandaged her wounds. Charlene moaned and tried to fight her off in her fevered state but she was weaker than a kitten.

Heidi had the job done and was preparing food and medicines within an hour of their arrival.

The days went by in a haze of fever for Charlene. All she could recall afterward was the throbbing pain and the sweet taste of water dripped into her mouth. Sometimes she tasted soup followed by tablets and more water. Many times she woke herself up by the sound of her own screaming. Nightmares appeared too real and she lost all sense of time and reality. She was no longer Charlene, just a floating ball of pain and fever.

The weather was getting hotter and with her fevered mind the nightmares never seemed to stop. She relived each bullet striking her shoulder spinning her around and around. Sometimes she felt herself floating on the ceiling observing herself lying on the bed. At other times she relived memories of her childhood.

Then there were the waking nightmares when she saw dead bodies with Jabba, Larry and Emma in the room with her. Charlene could clearly see their leering faces as they fired their bullets into her weakened body.

Each day Heidi fussed over her, talking and chatting away trying to keep her spirits up. It helped to keep her own spirits up as well. Heidi was afraid that Charlene would die and leave her alone - that was her nightmare, to be alone among the terrorists. To be tied up and forced to lick the vomit and urine off the floor of the prison cell, was her other nightmare.

Heidi remembered that there was a time when she hadn't a care in the world. All she had to do was go to college and play hockey, that was a happy, carefree life. It was all gone now, never to return.

One morning she noticed Charlene open her eyes but there was something different to them. Her eyes stayed fixed on hers and didn't float away like they had over the past six days.

"Who are you? Where am I?" Charlene asked but having exhausted her energy in those few words, she sank back into the bed and fell asleep.

The next time she woke Heidi was there waiting. "Hi, I'm Heidi and I brought you here from the supermarket," she explained slowly. "You were very badly shot up by terrorists and now you're recovering. We need to be very careful and very quiet because they could come back any time." Heidi stood up and continued, "I'm going to leave you for a few minutes while I make you a cup of special herbal tea, and I want you to drink it, OK?"

Heidi held the cup to her friend's cracked, dry lips . Charlene drank it down until it was all gone. She then closed her eyes and drifted off to sleep. This time she actually slept the best part of the day without waking in a hot sweat or screaming from her nightmares.

Her young rescuer breathed a sigh of relief. "I think you might live my dear friend, Charlene," she said softly.

It wasn't long before Charlene could walk to the toilet unaided and even sit outside for a while under the back porch. Heidi explained that whatever the terrorists put in the city water might still be there and they had to be careful. The bucket beside the toilet had the city water in it and was only to be used to flush with. There was rain water in assorted bottles and bottled water from the shops, that was all she was allowed to drink.

In the heat of late spring Charlene drank a lot of water and ate soft foods, mostly soups and stews made from tinned beef and vegetables. The fruit trees were covered in blossoms and small immature fruits, they wouldn't be ripe to pick for another few months.

Every few nights Heidi crept to the supermarket and gathered bags of dried fruits, nuts and vegetables of all descriptions and brought them back home. Sometimes she made two and three trips each night to build up a store of supplies for later on. Charlene told her she was amazed at what Heidi had done in such horrible circumstances. Even down to the candles and buckets of water for the toilet.

Every morning Heidi was up before dawn straightening the house to disguise it to look unlived in. She cleared everything to look as untouched as it had been before she'd returned with Charlene. She explained that if the terrorists came again, they would hide under the house and wait until they'd gone. To that effect Heidi had cut a trap door in the corner of the spare bedroom, it led to a hideout under the floor containing water, food and bedding. There she put some torches and a bucket to use as a toilet if needed. All she had to do was drag the spare wire-framed bed over the trap door and that would hide them.

Heidi even had two packed bags with water, dried fruits and nuts ready for an emergency escape. There were two other grab bags secreted under the house and two hidden in the garage. *'This is one well-prepared girl,'* thought Charlene, *'and I am so lucky to have found her.'*

It was mid morning when they heard noises in the street and then the sound of gunfire. Several voices called out followed by the sound of someone slamming their front door closed. They had no time to move as the sound of speeding footsteps meant someone was racing into their kitchen. The two young women stood paralysed in fear.

Heidi had already finished her pre-dawn clean-up but neither of the girls were ready for the tall youth crashing into their kitchen panting for breath. He looked at them in disbelief. They stared back in shock.

The boy could barely speak, but after some moments he panted, "Help me, Heidi, the soldiers... they're chasing me and my mates... we spread out but I reckon they'll... search house by house... until they find and kill us... help me hide, please." He was shaking as he desperately attempted to get the girls to understand the danger. Almost as an afterthought he added, "We all need to hide or get out of here... they'll be onto us in a minute. I think they saw which house I ran in to."

Heidi's mind clicked into action and she reacted immediately. "Arthur, go with Charlene into the spare room and both of you get into the hideout. Now! I'll follow as soon as I tidy up here and disguise things."

Charlene took the youth by the hand and led him into the back room and then pointed. "Quick, down you go. I'll follow but be careful of my shoulder, it's sore."

They'd just pulled the trap door up when they heard the front door being bashed open. The two looked into each others faces in fear. "Pull the bed over the top of us, hurry, then close the trap door. It's too late for Heidi, I'm sure she'll do something."

Heidi heard the crash of the door and knew immediately that she wouldn't make it to the hideout in time. She ducked into the pantry, softly closed the doors behind her, and waited. There was the sound of objects smashing and shouts, but then her heart froze.

"Hey, take a look at this, guys," called a voice from somewhere in the house. "Someone's living here. See this, in the toilet, a candle and a bucket of water." There were other voices and more movement, the sounds of beds being upended and cupboards opened. Heidi had no choice but to move now or be caught. She was under no illusion, being caught meant rape and execution. Having survived one and escaped the other, there was no way on God's earth she would ever let it happen again.

She peered through the slit of the cupboard door, saw it was momentarily clear and walked softly into the kitchen. The sounds were coming from the bedrooms down the hallway, so she sneaked to the back door. Heidi opened the door with haste, but was careful not to make a noise. She then raced into the garden fearful someone had seen her. She panicked, what should she do next?

An excited female voice from inside the house interrupting her thoughts, "Hey! Over here, guys! Woot! I think we've found a rat's nest. Anyone got a grenade?"

Heidi was both grateful that the terrorists were still in the house, but horrified they'd found the hideout and her friends. She knew that there was no protecting Charlene and the runaway now. Racing behind the garage she climbed over the back fence and leaped into the yard of the house behind her. Then she kept running and hid in the bushes, hoping the terrorists wouldn't bother looking beyond her house.

Funny, she thought to herself, she had just been thinking about setting up a safe house in the next few streets, but hadn't quite got around to it. She sure wished she had now.

An explosion shook her to the core. It was followed by gunfire and laughter.

"Oh no," she cried, "they've found Charlene." She shook all over then broke into a deep, body wracking sob. *'I've just lost my best friend, what will I do?'* thought the small boned teen, and she cried into her hands as the terrorist's rifle-fire and laughter continued.

Chapter 4

Charlene - Arthur

By the time the terrorists found their hideout Charlene had led the frightened youth under the house to the side exit. He carried both escape packs as she led him along the escape route to the back of the garage. It was obvious that Heidi's plan stopped there, because there was no way Charlene could climb the fence in her state. Even though she had regained a lot of her strength, the shattered bones in her shoulder had yet to fully heal and any movement still caused excruciating pain.

The boy looked at her, then at the fence and shrugged. He stepped forward and kicked at the rotten wooden palings. '*Why didn't I think of that?*' Charlene asked herself as she crouched down to ease herself through the gap in the fence.

It was only then that the young man noticed that the pretty, straw-haired girl had limited movement in her torso, and her left arm was in a sling.

"My name's Arthur," whispered the youth as he held her good hand and guided her towards the front of the house behind Heidi's. "Thanks for helping me to..."

He was stopped suddenly by an explosion that shook them both to silence. Pieces of glass and timber flew through the air. There was gunfire and laughter. They both froze in fear thinking they were the terrorists targets.

Arthur glanced around frantically for an escape route. He spied a small, female figure squatting in front of them in the shadows, and tugged at Charlene's jacket.

"Be quiet," whispered the figure, "say nothing, follow me and do exactly what I do." With a sigh of relief they saw it was Heidi, she was back in command doing exactly what she did best, using her smarts.

Heidi signalled for them to wait quietly among the bushes while she reconnoitred the street. Giving the all-clear she ran across the road to the house opposite. Arthur and Charlene followed. She did this until they were three blocks away in a neighbourhood she knew well.

"That's my best friend's house, she's dead now and so are her parents, all of them. I saw them executed." she said matter-of-factly. "We'll move in until I work out what to do next." Heidi led them to the back of the house and in through the back door.

It was spooky being in someone else's house without anyone home, without being invited. Charlene felt like a burglar, it was an alien feeling. Heidi went straight to the blinds and curtains to close them. Secrecy and security were top priority and she had a knack for it.

The kitchen still had saucepans in the sink and bowls of porridge were sitting on the table. The three stopped moving and looked around the kitchen. All of them shifted uncomfortably feeling like intruders at this ghostly family breakfast.

"We should be safe here." Heidi spoke softly breaking the spell. "Just be quiet and keep the escape packs ready. If we were followed be prepared to leave through the back door, and we'll do the same thing we just did - run. If we ever get separated again, we'll meet three streets away, in the same direction, and the same house number. Got it?" The two nodded silently though still quite fearful of the spooky house.

A few hours later Charlene was still sitting silent and subdued in the lounge room. Her shoulder throbbed and she was close to fainting. Soft groans escaped from her as the shock and pain increased. Wicked hallucinations formed and faded as the pain ebbed back and forth. In a panicked voice she called, "What about the water... it's poisoned... we need to get out..."

Arthur and Heidi noticed her face was as white as chalk so they sat beside her and helped her drink from their bottled water supply. Suddenly Charlene vomited and promptly passed out on the lounge. Heidi found some sheets and arranged her into a more comfortable position then she cleaned up the mess. Waving her hand to Arthur she motioned for him to come with her into the kitchen.

Standing all of five foot five inches to Arthur's five foot ten she stood on tip-toe staring him right in the face. "Why the hell did you go and place me and Charlene at risk by coming into my house?" Heidi stormed at him, she was livid.

Although she managed to keep her voice down and her temper under control she was steaming mad inside. "Hell's-fire Arthur, you better start using your brains from now on. No more goofing off like you did at school. This is the real world and any tiny mistake you make can cost us our lives." Arthur cringed and stammered an awkward apology.

After she settled down Heidi started to go through the cupboards and shelves of the pantry in her friend's house.

She turned to Arthur, "Well you might as well tell me what you did to make them chase you."

Arthur was still red-faced from the dressing down, but with some pride, he began his story. "Me and my mates set fire to their trucks with petrol bombs. We knew where they parked their trucks and Jeeps and things, and early this morning we bombed them. We took out eight of them, it was quite a bonfire too, Heidi." Arthur smiled to himself remembering that sweet, short moment of triumph.

"We had a rough plan of escape, but as you always said, never listen to Swampy Watson. He's a first class dick head. He was supposed to hide our bikes in a shed but it took us ages to find them, he put them in the wrong spot. By the time we found our bikes they were after us." He stopped and looked upwards, remembering. "We were trapped on all sides so we rode right through the middle of them. It was pretty awesome, but they fired and Swampy fell, then Lyons. We just kept riding and dodging as best we could." Arthur stopped talking. He thought of the mates he'd lost that morning and knew what would be happening to them right now, if they had survived.

"I can't go back to our hideout either. If Swampy or Lyons were wounded and taken prisoner they'll squeal, prisoners always do. We watched once what the terrorist do to prisoners. After that I've never let myself watch again. I still see it in my head at night. I hate them." Heidi put her hand on his shoulder and he turned to her.

"Arthur, you can stay with me and Charlene if you want," she said gently. "Just remember to behave yourself though." Heidi lifted her finger and held it in front of his face like a school mistress. "I'm warning you, if you ever do anything without asking me first, I will cut you where a man scratches himself." She then softened her face, "Just don't put us in harms way ever again. You can help me prepare this place the same way I did in my own house. It'll take a few days, maybe a week. Then we'll go out collecting food and water together, got that?"

Arthur nodded, he was more than pleased to be with Heidi again. His face brushed her hair and his throat tightened as he caught her female scent. He felt a desire as something primal awakened inside him.

"I'm scared Heidi, I think we should all stick together." His voice cracked as he tried to hold back his emotions. It had been a genuine race for survival and he was still in a heightened state of distress. He pulled Heidi into his arms and hugged her tightly, he closed his eyes to hold back his tears.

As he bent to bury his face in her hair she lifted her face upwards and whispered his name softly. Her eyes spoke a promise he yearned for and he bent to kiss her. Heidi held his kiss and he pulled her closer to him. She then took Arthur's hand in hers and led him to one of the bedrooms so they could consummate their reunion.

Even though they experienced no more drop-in's they all knew that eventually they needed to find a safer place to live. Somewhere they could stretch their legs and enjoy life again. They felt safe enough but it was like living in a cave, any outside activity had to be done at night.

They managed to collect some of the early ripening fruit from the trees and vines around their house but it was difficult in the dark. A variety of fresh fruit abounded in Adelaide and they looked forward to enjoying fresh vegetables as well. Apricots, peaches, plums, apples, cherries, nectarines and figs all had to be squeeze tested and that bruised them. Heidi preserved some of the excess fruit in jars she'd collected from the empty houses surrounding them.

Arthur went with her on her house-hunting trips now. The dead bodies were beginning to mummify in the hot, dry atmosphere and they frightened her. Heidi started to have nightmares of zombies. She became more afraid of zombies than the terrorists. With Arthur by her side she resumed entering houses to collect food and other necessities - but remained wary.

The three became good friends, but Heidi and Arthur were closer than friends. Charlene felt left out and a little jealous when the lovers went off to bed together.

Charlene felt that Heidi was her special friend, she'd rescued her, not Arthur. She was uncomfortable when the two shared moments of intimacy in front of her. That was when Charlene realised she had developed feelings for Heidi and it confused her normally, well structured sensibilities.

Ever the practical one Heidi had stored enough condoms to service an army so there was little chance of pregnancy. They all agreed that falling pregnant was definitely not a good idea given the situation they were in. Heidi never did anything if there was the slightest chance of failure.

Charlene remained jealous of Arthur, so she busied herself reading books they found in the empty houses, and several evening visits to the local library. She wanted to understand the psychology of terrorism and read everything she could find on serial killers, mass murderers, psychopaths and war criminals. As an undergraduate student of psychology she knew what to look for.

Her shoulder didn't heal properly either, and she wore a sling to keep her arm immobile. There was a constant ache in her shoulder and the bones knitted poorly, limiting all movement in her arm. It was fortunate that she was right handed but her sleep was still disturbed with nightmares and the constant pain. Charlene found her left hand had some strength but was generally useless.

Nights were the worst but she no longer cried herself to sleep, a blessing for the others she thought. One thing she continued to grieve was not saying goodbye to her family. Her older brother might still be alive. He was in the military, somewhere, and she prayed that he was safe and fighting the terrorists right now.

Over the months the terrorist activity quieted down. Although it wasn't safe to walk the streets, day or night, there were no more house to house searches. There were fewer sightings when they went in search of food and water at night. By now the poison had dissipated from the water system but they were always careful. It appeared that the

Revelationists had forgotten about the city dwellers or 'house rats' as they called them, and probably considered them a zero threat.

A house-dweller's network had developed, as small groups gained knowledge of each other. No one really trusted the others though, capture meant betrayal. It was commonly accepted that once a member was captured the entire group would move to a new safe-house. There were now very few dwellers, those not killed or imprisoned by the terrorists remained well hidden or escaped to the countryside. The survivors lived by night and slept when they could, which limited their opportunities to form a community.

To keep their spirits up Heidi, Arthur and Charlene would sometimes talk of escaping to the countryside, possibly the Flinders Ranges where Heidi still had family. That helped, a little.

Chapter 5

Nulla - safe house

Nulla led the boys back down the same track they had walked up. The sentry came forward and wished them good luck then faded back into the bushes. Their rifles were heavy, so too the ammunition. The two young men felt both proud and overawed.

"Righto, boys, we'll ride from here and you follow my lead in everything. Your lives, as well as mine, depend on your immediate action. You, young fella, Simon is it, right, get on behind me. You, Luke, keep up. If we get hit by enemy fire we go bush regardless. If I go right you go right too no matter what, got it?" Nulla kicked the bike into life and took off at speed. Luke was hard pressed to keep up on the rough dirt track.

They spent the next fifteen minutes on the track when Nulla unexpectedly took a right turn straight into the bushes. They bashed through thick scrub, the branches whipping painfully against their uncovered hands, necks and chests. They continued for a full thirty minutes then stopped. Nulla switched off his bike and indicated for Luke to do the same.

"Righto, watch me like hawks and do what I do. Listen, observe, then act. We should be safe here for about a half hour, after that we are in real danger. I mean that fella's because we just dodged a terrorist patrol back there. Righto, let's get this done." He pulled the Steyr off Simon's back and placed it in his lap. He slowly explained the mechanism for loading, unloading; what to do if it jams and finally how to aim and fire. Then he explained what to do if attacked and how to react. He kept repeating, "...just watch me, listen, observe, then act."

Feeling a little more prepared for war the teenage boys jumped back on their bikes and Nulla again led the way. They didn't leave the safety of the bush for another few hours. Time meant nothing and it seemed to stand still since that morning when they found the world had gone to hell.

They rode almost to the bottom of the mountain when Nulla stopped the bikes at a fuel depot to fill their tanks.

"Righto boys, time to eat. Luke break out the tucker in the pack and help yourselves. Not too much though 'cause it could make ya crook. Go easy on the water because we don't know when we'll get safe drinking water again."

They finished refueling and sat with their backs to the depot walls and ate what the boys said was '*darn good food.*'

Simon stared at Nulla and said enthusiastically, "Nulla, there's nothing wrong with this army food, it's delicious."

"Not when you have to eat it day in, day out it isn't. Righto, fifteen minutes kip. Luke, get yourself up on top of that shed and keep an eye open for baddies. If you see anyone driving a vehicle of any description, call out to us." Nulla then rolled himself a cigarette, smoked quietly then closed his eyes and directed Simon to have a short sleep too.

But Simon was too excited to do much more than stare around him. He watched in fascination as Nulla skillfully rolled, smoked, slept and keep his wits about him all at the same time. In fact he was sure that if he had to write an essay he could add that to his repertoire. He tapped Nulla's leg, "Can I go up on lookout too? I'm bored watching you sleep."

Nulla chuckled to himself, he had been given the keys to the kingdom. No officers, no one to tell him what to do, and he had the freedom to run his own war. He could play at being warlord if he wanted, that was basically what the captain said, he assured himself.

After some minutes there came a cry from the lookout, "Nulla!"

He opened his eyes and peered at the two excited faces. "What?" he called back.

"The hills are on fire, up where we came from, it's all smoking, looks like a bush fire. You can hear the thuds too. They must be bombing the terrorists," called Simon.

Nulla got up and looked. "Yep, you're right. I would say there is some heavy fighting going on up there. The terrorists captured a lot of our heavy weapons and we're trying to get them back. We know most of them aren't as well trained as us but they had the advantage of surprise, numbers and they took a lot of our good lads out in the first few hours. Our soldiers are trying to take control. Sadly the poisoned water business has devastated not just the civilian population but our troops too." Nulla called the boys back down and they kick-started their bikes.

"Follow me, Luke, and keep up. We need to find a safe place to hole-up tonight and I think I know a good place. It's only an hour away. If you see anything let me know. Luke, just toot your horn, Simon you tap my shoulder. Let's go."

Just before dark they pulled into an average looking house in the outer suburbs of Adelaide. Nulla walked up to the door and knocked. He signalled for the boys to take the bikes around the back, secure them and to collect their gear ready to go in through the back door. He knocked again then kicked the door in. He called for the boys to enter via the back door.

The house was empty. Nulla met them in the kitchen. "Boys this is my mob's safe house. Beauty isn't it?" He chuckled when he found a gas camper stove in one of the rooms and began to boil water from their water bottles.

"Boys, be careful what you touch, they had drugs dumped all over these benches last time I was here, and I really don't want you getting high on me," he laughed. "This was my retirement set up. Damn useless now ain't it. Oh well, it has everything a man could want except a woman, eh boys," he laughed again. Nulla was happy and he was free.

"You're going to be my soldiers while I'm going to be your lord and master. How does that sound?" Once again he laughed but this time there was a wicked gleam to his eye.

"Nulla, what are you talking about? Soldiers? Lord and master? Are you going crazy on us?" asked Luke as he piled their gear into a corner of the lounge room.

"Sorry boys, I'm just mucking about. There's no authority now, none, no police, no law and order. We can do whatever we want, to anyone we want. Don't you boys get it?"

The older man turned to them with a serious look in his eyes. "What do people do when they believe they'll never get caught?" He paused to let the question sink in. "They do whatever they damn well please, that's what they do."

Opening the fridge door he said, "Blast, the power's off and the beer's warm. Looks like we have to drink the lot then. We're gonna party tonight!"

Together they examined their weapons and equipment. They looked on as Nulla stripped their Steyrs down. He walked them through once more how to load, unload and then took them outside to fire off a magazine each. When Nulla was satisfied they wouldn't shoot themselves he brought them back inside. They stripped the Steyrs back down, oiled and cleaned them under his supervision. When they finished they did it again and again, until he was satisfied they had the basics down pat.

That evening they cooked their meal and sat back and drank the beer left in the fridge. Nulla kept an eye on the boys, making sure they didn't drink overly much. He did, however, want them to have their fill, to know what it meant to be hungover. Nothing tempers teenage drinking than a solid hangover, followed by a firm hand the next time it's offered.

It was bed time, but boys will be boys and they asked a lot of questions, the alcohol loosening their inhibitions around this intimidating warrior.

"Who are you really, Nulla, and what's this you said about drugs and lords of the universe you keep talking about?" asked Simon as he began to sway slightly.

"Righto, looks like I must give you the 'Cook's Tour' of my life before you'll go to bed. Worse than my own kids yez are. I was born under a coolabah tree on the Hay plains and spent my humble youth horse breaking throughout southern and central Australia. I learned a thing or two about hustling when working in the circus with old man Jimmy Shannon. I joined a biker gang at seventeen and been a patched member since."

He rolled another cigarette and leaned back into his lounge chair. "In those crazy years I did some drug running and delivery. I even did some protection and even a few hit jobs. I was what they called a 'soldier'. Unfortunately I wasn't smart enough to avoid getting caught up in the justice system. I had a choice: do something with my life or go the way of many of my brothers and a life in and out of prison. I chose the army.

"The army gave me a routine and I enjoy routines. They gave me a gun and I like guns. They gave me power and I love power. Then they demoted me for fighting. See my shirt, those faded marks there, that's where I hand stitched me proud stripes, when I had them." He winked at the boys and rolled a smoke for them to share.

After some coughing the boys weren't so keen to find out more but Nulla hadn't quite finished. "This here safe house isn't actually mine, it belongs to my bike gang. We only use it when we lie low. Today we needed to hide nice and low, just in case. But that thing about the drugs, that's true, so don't go licking the benches."

At this he sent the boys to bed and sat up thinking. He had a lot to think about.

The next morning the boys didn't get out of bed. Nulla stepped over last evening's dinner lying in a puddle on the toilet floor. The smell of vomit spread through the house. He let them sleep it off while he tuned in their CB set. Every broadcast he heard just made him more depressed.

He managed to chat with some HF guys who lived on a remote outback station and was very careful with what he said and what he allowed them to say. There were others, mostly CB enthusiasts travelling around Australia in their four wheel drives. Some he spoke with lived in cities and one called Charlie lived in Sydney. The situation reps were all negative. No good news, losses and retreats by the army and Sydney Charlie reported massive death tolls and an exodus out of Sydney for those who managed to survive. The situation was catastrophic.

Nulla tried to set up regular times to chat with these people but the signals were repeatedly jammed. Eventually he gave up and went inside to make lunch. Most of the food had already disappeared from the fridge. He sorted out what needed to be eaten now and what could be stored away for later, and what had to be thrown out.

At midday he tried to wake the boys but they wouldn't budge. Nulla knew what to do.

"Righto boys, hands off cocks and on with sox. Everyone up for lunch or I get to use your face for a toilet." Sometimes there is only one way to get a teenager out of bed.

The sound of his zippered fly brought an instinctive urge for the boys to leap up and start dressing. As primitive as it sounds it certainly worked, in fact this method never failed, not in Nulla's lifetime.

"Oh my head, my stomach, I feel terrible." Simon staggered into the kitchen and slid down into a chair at the kitchen table. He tried to look at his bacon and eggs but his stomach revolted and he ran to the toilet.

Luke wasn't as badly off as Simon. He hadn't had as much beer nor smoked as much of the cigarette, he tucked into everything on the table. He called out to Simon, retching in the toilet, that eating might make him feel better. Luke managed to finish everything Nulla placed before him. Later, Simon ate a little dry bread and sipped on a cup of black tea.

"Righto, lesson number one for today: what did you boys learn about the pleasures of smoking and drinking?" he smiled broadly. A hard lesson but an important one he thought, the same lesson his father gave him many years ago. 'Not that it worked,' he reminded himself.

"Don't drink or smoke, ever," came Simon's droll reply, he wasn't feeling well and his face was still a shade of gray.

"Luke?" smiled Nulla enjoying himself.

"If you drink and smoke expect the worst. I guess another lesson is not to trust your elders who've been in the army and belong to bikie gangs." He looked up and smiled right back at him. He clicked onto what Nulla was up to.

'He catches on quickly, that's good,' thought Nulla.

"Righto, today we talk, train and go on a shopping trip. I don't have to remind you boys that we are in deep trouble.

Humanity seems to be hell bent on destroying itself and our goal is to survive." Nulla looked at his charges. They were smart, willing and quick learners. Above all they had a desire and a hunger to learn everything he showed them.

"We also need to find better lodgings, establish a few other safe houses and develop a network of survivors. All of this must be done with security in mind. No silly behaviour and always tell someone what you plan to do before you do it. And you also... what do you do when you're out with me?" he looked at them expectantly.

Luke grinned and said, "We watch, listen and then act immediately." His chest puffed up when Nulla patted his shoulder.

"Yep, perfect. Now look around and tell me what you see that might tell you more about what we'll be doing today. Take your time and then report." He'd placed their three back packs on the floor, their weapons by the back door, and maps on the table.

"Simon, what do you see?"

"Hmm, three Steyrs with ammunition belts, maps on the table, food and water in the backpacks and boots on the back steps. I guess we are either going for a run and weapons training, or do some map work?" came his reply.

"Correct on all counts except one. You forgot cleanliness. After you clean the toilet and the vomit on the floor, get yourselves ready and we'll start." Nulla told the boys to dress in the fatigues lying on the lounge which he'd found in one of the rooms.

They started with their weapons. He made them clean and oil their Steyrs, again watching everything they did. The boys had to talk through what they were doing at each step.

"Map orienteering next. Stand at the table here and let's get this place checked out. Grab that street map too. The first things we want to locate are shopping centres, why?" he pushed the boys at every chance.

"Shops is where people would go?" ventured Luke.

"Yes, and?"

Simon said, "People need water and food and with no electricity their food is starting to go off?"

"Yes, and?"

"People need to be told what to do and we can tell them?" came back Simon.

"And?"

"We can form an army of civilians and fight the terrorists?" Luke said.

"Hmm, let's think about that one." Nulla wanted no illusions or fantasies. "Why would we be careful with civilians? What would we do and not do when we meet them?"

"Geez, maybe don't give them weapons... or... maybe we should?" said Simon whimsically.

Luke offered his thoughts. "People are generally stupid and think of themselves first, they might try to control us?"

"Righto, good replies. I now have you thinking so this is your homework for today. First of all: are there any civilian survivors? If so how many? What are their immediate needs? What are they struggling with? What are they thinking of?

What will they be struggling with in a weeks time, a month or a year?

"The answers to these questions, my lads, will guide your actions when you meet them. Civilians are not our enemy, but they pose very definite threats to our safety, and to their own. Part of your homework is to work out what these threats could be." Nulla finished rolling his cigarette and offered the tobacco pouch to Simon and Luke. They both declined and went slightly gray in the face.

"I want you to think about those questions. Now we need to go for a run into town to find some suitable clothing, footwear, more backpacks, hats and anything else you think we might need. We might also meet civilians, if there are any left."

"Oh, and Simon, I just pulled my bike from the garage so you aren't my passenger today. Let's roll." Simon's eyes lit up, he was starting to feel a little more human now he had something inside his stomach.

Chapter 6

Charlene- Zombies, Phil and Fatima

Not long after moving to their new safe house, Heidi and Arthur decided to explore a different shopping centre not too far from the ones they had been visiting. This was larger, and appeared to have more options for their supplies, and fewer scavengers. In fact the only people they found there were dead ones. There weren't any goods strewn on the floor like most of the looted shops in their own area.

"Arthur, you go in first, shine your torch over there so I can see if there are any zombies." Arthur was accustomed to Heidi's fear of the dark and what he thought was an irrational fear, zombies indeed. But he never criticised her or said a word about how silly it was to fear dead people. He shined the torch around the walls and aisles as she directed.

"OK, it's all clear," Heidi stated. "You go down the frozen food aisle and see what you can find that's not gone off, and I'll head down the health snacks and dried foods aisle. If you hear anything make sure you come running over - all right?" She looked up at him with both fear and hopefulness, Arthur nodded reassuringly.

"Of course I'll come running," he said calmly and tried to smile. It was dark and it was scary now that Heidi had him spooked with all that talk of zombies.

Arthur remembered that ever since they'd brought back some zombie comics from the local library Heidi began to have nightmares. Everyone had seen their fair share of dead bodies, and in fact they were as common as house flies. But Arthur knew about her experience in the shopping centre, surrounded by the bodies of people she had known. Even Arthur could tell it affected her though she wouldn't talk about it.

The two separated and their torch beams made the shadows play chase across the floors and walls. Heidi felt uncomfortable, like she was being watched. She had a shopping trolley in front of her and began quietly stacking supplies into it. She slowly relaxed losing all sense of time and place, becoming fully absorbed in deciding which items they would take back with them. Forgetting her fears she was on autopilot working quietly and efficiently.

Without warning a zombie body leaned towards her and she screamed at the top of her lungs. She let go of the trolley, dropped her torch and raced backwards only to be stopped by another zombie creature. She tripped and fell to the floor screaming.

Arthur raced to her aid, his baseball bat in one hand and his torch in the other. He saw Heidi curled on the floor among a scattering of giant, furry toys. She was gasping for air and in a faint, her heart felt like it would burst inside her chest.

"Arty, Arty," Heidi sobbed as she slowly regained some of her composure when she saw the toys illuminated by Arthur's torch. "I thought they were fucking zombies!"

"I thought you were being attacked. Don't ever do that to me again will you." He was struggling to calm himself as he sat beside her and held her tightly in his arms. The teenagers suddenly sat up in alarm when a moment later they heard a voice calling from just outside the store.

"Hey, you people in there? I'm coming in for some food, please don't hurt me," called the voice.

Arthur nearly vomited in fright. Heidi somehow managed to reply to the lone voice. "Who are you?"

"I'm Phil, I live near here, I won't hurt anyone. I just need to collect some food for my wife and I. Can I come in, please?" His voice sounded old to the two youngsters, it echoed in the huge store and they relaxed a little.

A torch beam cut through the darkness and as the voice approached they shined their torches towards him. They saw an old man dressed in baggy cargo pants and a long-sleeved khaki shirt. He wore glasses and carried some green shopping bags. The old man came up to them and sat gingerly beside them.

"Hi, my name's Phil and I live near here with my wife, Fatima. I call her Fati." He gave a snort and a chuckle. They liked him immediately. "I hope you don't mind me asking but what was all that screaming about? It sounded like you were attacked by terrorists but I've been here for two hours watching and I haven't seen anyone besides you two enter. What happened?" he asked, his eyes blinking in the bright torchlight. They politely lowered their torches.

"I, I ah, I touched some soft toys, these ones." Heidi pointed her torch at the toys that lay jumbled on the floor around her. "I thought they were zombies," she giggled realising how silly it sounded. She looked at him and smiled.

"My name's Heidi and this is Arthur, Arty. We're pleased to meet you, Phil."

"It is a pleasure to meet you too." They all shook hands. "I sometimes have that feeling too," he said, "especially coming out at night. I saw a dead body the other day, in a house, and it was standing up. Can you believe it, someone died standing up and then they dried out in the heat, and now they look just like a real zombie. It scared the bejesus out of me I tell you. So don't think you're the only one to freak out at these zombie creatures. But soft toys," and here Phil turned his head to the side and smiled mischievously, "now that's funny." As he smiled his face wrinkled even more than it already was. He liked these two kids with their easy and honest manner.

"When I've finished gathering some food, why not come back to my place and meet my wife? She hasn't seen a living person since this horror began. She'll make a meal you can only dream about. She's the best cook in the country," he said that last sentence with glowing pride.

Arty and Heidi looked at each other and nodded. "Yeah, we'd love to, Phil. I can't remember the last time I had something that wasn't out of a packet or tin," said Heidi. "We do have a friend back home who'd love to come along too. She's got injuries that stop her coming out and if we went without her she'd feel betrayed. Is it OK if we bring her too?" Heidi looked at Phil and she saw his face melt.

"You have a friend with injuries? Sure, do you want me to help you bring her? Can she walk? Does she need a wheeled trolley of some sort? I can build it if you need one."

He was talking quickly and thinking to himself about how he might help.

"If we go with you now, and learn where your house is, we can bring Charlene with us tomorrow night. Is that OK?" asked Heidi.

"Yes, of course. I have a few herbs and spices to pick up for Fati. And some rice and lentils and maybe some dried mushrooms, if I can find them out the back, and then we can go."

Phil's house was a little further than they thought but at least it was in the same direction as their own. Once they got their bearings, Heidi and Arthur were confident they could easily walk Charlene there the following night.

Even though it was past midnight Fatima was absolutely delighted to see the two young people. She was so starved of company that she hugged them and wouldn't let them go until they'd eaten and shared some of her fresh, home-roasted coffee.

"Oh my goodness, you two are so thin, are you sure you couldn't eat any more? Here, I'll wrap this up and put it in a bag so you can take it back for Charlene." She chatted away fussing over the youngsters. Arthur thought she was just like his own grandmother who had sadly passed away some years ago. He warmed to Phil and was especially excited when he promised to show him his workshop and the projects he was working on.

"And dears, please bring something to change into because we'll have a feast tomorrow night and then you can sleep over. Nothing fancy but we do have spare bedrooms you know." She looked at her admiring husband. "Phil is going to help me clean the place up. When you come over it'll be like a holiday." Her face beamed with delight. In fact, thought Heidi, she looked like a young girl for a moment.

"We'd love to, Fatima, thank you. We'd better get moving, it's close to daybreak and we need to get back before first light. We'll meet you here before midnight, OK? We'll bring Charlene too. Thanks for everything." They prepared to leave.

"Don't forget Charlene's breakfast." Fatima pushed a parcel that needed an extra bag to carry, it was so heavy. "Enough to feed an army," she said with a giggle.

They chatted all the way home barely aware of the danger of being caught outside by a terrorist patrol. When they arrived, Charlene was sitting up waiting, her eyes rimmed in red and a worried frown on her face. Heidi saw immediately that her friend had been fretting. Normally they would be home by three in the morning but dawn had already broken by the time they came in through the back door.

"Hi, Charlene," said Heidi as she leaned over and hugged her, "guess what we did and who we met last night?" she said with a smile and handed the parcel over to her.

Charlene was silent as she opened the parcel and its aroma wafted towards her. She stopped what she was about to say and looked at the wrapped items. One contained a curried meat pie made the old fashioned way. It was still warm and she ate ravenously not realising how starved she was.

"Heidi, I was scared something had happened to you. I didn't know what to do so I just sat and waited," she mumbled as they sat drinking tea. "I was worried that you'd been taken by terrorists."

"I'm sorry, Charlene," Heidi replied putting her hand on her friend's knee, "but we now have new friends and surely that makes up for it?"

"Well yes, I guess so." Charlene yawned and the three headed off to their bedrooms. They needed to get some sleep before preparing for their trip to Phil and Fati's house that night.

They packed a bag each and headed off. Arthur rode his BMX bike with the bags filled with fresh fruit and jars of preserves that Heidi and Charlene had made. It only took them twenty minutes to get there.

Fati met them at the back door, hugging them all tightly. She fussed over the blond-haired Charlene careful not to touch her shoulder. "My dear girl, please let me have a look at that and see if I can do anything for the wound. Oh, it's still weeping? I've got some salves that might speed up the healing." Fatima fussed some more until Phil arrived to usher them into their large lounge room and helped Arthur unpack the bag of preserves.

"My goodness, Arthur, did you make these yourself?" Phil chuckled and Arthur went a bright red. "Only joking! When we get sorted out here I want to show you my shed, what do you reckon about that?"

"Yes please, Mr Phil, I'm not much good at anything, I can't cook or make things, I can't even use a screw driver.

I'm pretty useless." His head hung down and Phil looked soberly at the young man.

"Artie, call me Phil, just plain Phil. Now if you can't do anything then maybe I can teach you? How about that?"

"Would you really do that? I can help you make things and maybe I can have my own set of tools." Arthur's face lit up.

"Take the boy outside, Phil, and show him your trolley and help him build a basket for his bike too. That old thing he's got tied to it will break any day now. Go on, shoo, I'll call you when dinner's ready." Fatima turned to the girls and sat Charlene down ready for some treatment on her shoulder. She started Heidi in the kitchen stirring the stew. Fatima had thought that a day like today would never come. These were real living people and she was overjoyed.

Arthur was mesmerised by Phil's handiwork and ran his fingers over some of the pieces of furniture in the shed. He picked up some of the tools on Phil's workbench and asked, "What's this? What do you use it for?"

"It's a plane, it's what you use to make pieces of timber smooth before you sand it down with those pieces of paper there." He lovingly ran his hands over some chair parts he had lying in neat rows on the garage floor.

"This leather is old so I'm going to freshen it up by rubbing oil into it. I can take just about anything I find, pull it apart, then fix it and put it back together." He beamed with pride as he watched Arthur's eyes open wide in admiration.

"Is this the trolley Fati mentioned?" he asked.

"Yep, I found some babies prams in a shop in the mall. I pulled the wheels and axles off and brought them back here. Then I brought back a decent shopping trolley and replaced the wheels with these big ones. Now I can put bigger items in and not have to worry about the stupid thing trying to run me off the footpath when I push it."

"Wow, that's amazing. What's this thing for?" Arthur was holding an old hand drill and spun the geared handle.

"It's a hand drill. I found it in a second hand shop that's got all sorts of junk. But it's not junk any more is it? Some of the hardware stores still have useful hand tools we can use without power. That's where I spend a lot of my spare time, wandering around hardware stores, antique and second hand stores. It's amazing what you can find in them." Phil pointed to the walls of his shed. Arthur followed his torch beam to see dozens of tools hung up in orderly rows according to their use.

"Wow, you've got everything." He didn't say much more but spent his time before dinner touching tools and Phil's odd jobs and asking questions. Phil was delighted to have an admiring audience to show off his work.

At meal time they all chatted away about the apocalypse, the terrorists, what they did before the 'end of days' as Fatima called it, and about how they had survived.

"I can't imagine God agrees with what these Revelationists have done," said Fatima. "They're killing and raping and God's knows what and it's all against what it says in the bible."

"Now dear, please, don't go on about it. If God were here he'd zap them all with his lasers but he isn't, he's on holidays somewhere and forgotten all about planet Earth," said Phil.

"Don't you go on about holidays, Phil. One day God will call us all to answer for our deeds, and these terrorists will find they'll spend eternity in damnation for their evil ways." Fatima said over her shoulder as she collected the empty plates. She asked the girls to help her serve up their dessert.

"Phil always says there's no God, the heathen. I think he's spent way too much time with his head in history books and not enough on preparing for his finals, his day of judgement," she said it loud enough for Phil to hear.

"I heard that," he called out from the dining room.

Heidi and Charlene looked at each other then broke into laughter as they realised that this was a game the two played.

"He makes it so hard for me, I have to pray twice every night, once for me and another for his lost soul. Bah, but who cares, these Revelationists think they know everything about God and religion but they're just murderers. They'll get their comeuppance one day, of that I'm certain."

Fatima handed Charlene a large spoon to pour a delicious caramel sauce over her fresh baked orange and plum pudding. The aroma was pleasant and to the malnourished youngsters it was almost overpowering. Everyone was so thin from their forced diet but Arthur still managed seconds and then ate Charlene's left overs.

The beds were all made, but before they were allowed to head off to sleep, Fati and Phil showed them how to take a shower. The three were shown a simple pulley, roped to a bucket with a shower head.

"It's dead simple folks," explained Phil. "Just fill the bucket with warm water, pull the rope and wrap it over this hook, twist the tap and voilà, a hot shower. Arty, I'll help you make one to take back with you." They had no trouble getting the three youngsters showered after that simple demonstration. With an entire city of spare sheets, blankets and towels, Phil and Fati's house was a veritable motel.

They slept soundly until mid afternoon waking to Fatima's cooking, another stew with lentils, chick peas and dried mushrooms. It was heavy with spices, home grown potatoes and sprinkled with fresh parsley.

"You kids eat up now, when we finish we want to sort out a visiting program so we can do this once a week, we need to stay in touch so we can help each other." Fatima then turned to Arthur and said, "Phil says he wants to teach you how to work his tools. One night he wants to take you out to the hardware to get a collection of tools for yourself."

Charlene had been quiet for most of their visit, unsure how to contribute and feeling self-conscious of her useless arm. Fatima had rubbed a warmed oil with herbs and spices into her shoulder and wounds which helped soothe the pain. They had chatted a little then but now that it was almost time to leave she had clammed up.

Heidi looked across at Charlene to see if she wanted to say anything but noticed she had withdrawn back into her shell. It was time to head home, she thought.

"Thanks Fati, thanks Phil," said Heidi looking at each in turn, "we'd love that. I have a few ideas too but we can wait till later, this is too nice to talk over." She tucked into her meal not looking up again until she'd finished.

When they returned to their own home the three slept like they had never slept before. Little did they know that their adventures were just beginning.

Chapter 7

Nulla - Glenda

Nulla and his new recruits took the back streets into town and rode around for a while to orient themselves. They couldn't help but notice the dead bodies and smashed cars, their drivers huddled over their steering wheels as if asleep. The sweet stench of death pervaded everything.

They pulled up in front of the supermarket and Nulla told Luke to stand guard over the bikes. The warning signal was to first call out and if no response to then fire two rounds with his rifle. Luke found a shady spot against the wall and sat down with his Steyr held upright beside him.

Nulla and Simon carried their backpacks into the store and looked around. They saw a small group of people standing inside. The group quickly huddled together when they noticed the weapons and Nulla's military uniform.

"It's OK, we're on your side. Anyone with military experience here?" Nulla called to them. No one moved, but then a man pushed through to the front.

"I have some experience, navy medical corps, retired. These people are afraid and confused, do you know what's going on?" He looked like a solid type. Nulla called for the group to 'gather 'round'.

"It appears that you are basically what is left alive in this town. Unless you know of someone else it's basically you lot. We rode around the town and saw nothing move. The tap water's poisoned across the entire city so don't drink it, use bottled water, rain water or surface water. The poison should dissipate but give it a week or two before you try the tap water. Grab as much food as you can and store it. Work together as a team and support each other, that's about all you can do right now."

"Are you from the army?" asked a nervous voice.

"They'll contact you as soon as they can. I'm a forward scout sent to organise a civil resistance but I need your cooperation. If any of you are prepared to join us please step forward. For the rest of you I suggest you stick together." He stopped talking and looked at the small, frightened group, "Go tribal folks, live in the one big house and organise routines and cooking, protection, that sort of thing. So, is anyone interested in joining a civil resistance?"

Nulla looked at the retired medic but he waved his hand and disappeared back into the crowd. Just as he did a hand shot up.

"I will," called a sweet sounding female voice. A young Eurasian woman stepped to the front of the group. "I have no one left here, my partner and family are all dead. I'll join if you'll take me."

"What's your name?" asked Nulla staring at her, she looked to be in her mid twenties.

"I'm Glenda and I might look fragile but I can do anything a man can. I can kill if I need to." She gave the answer that Nulla's simple question hadn't asked.

"We're pleased to accept you, anyone else?" He looked around but no one moved. "I'm Sergeant Nulla of the 1st Armoured Cavalry, this is Simon, the fellow outside is Luke. We'll drop in on you when we can but it is up to you to sort yourselves out. We'll keep contact via messages we put in that bin there." He walked over to a bin, tipped it upside down, rubbish fell to the floor. "This is now our mail box. Write your messages and leave them here. I'll do the same. I can make no promises when we'll be back but we'll try. Any questions?"

There were mumbled questions between group members and then the questions started to come fast and furiously. The cavalryman answered them as best he could. Simon looked sideways at the woman, she was pretty he thought.

"So you're Simon? My name's Glenda, nice to meet you." She put out her hand and they shook. Simon liked the feel of her soft skin. He was dumbstruck, he didn't know much about talking to girls.

"Umm, here's a spare pack, would you like to help us gather food and water?" he offered.

"Sure, I think I know what we'll need. Come on." She led him into the food aisles.

They gathered as much as their bags would carry. Nulla eventually joined them and asked her if she could drive. He wanted to take one of the four wheel drives he saw in the car park.

"Yes, I can drive." She tilted her face up defiantly. Nulla went slightly weak at the knees, he thought she looked like a model. Simon noticed too.

"Simon, relieve Luke and send him along. Walk with me Glenda." They stepped out through the side doors and into the car park. Nulla pointed to a black Nissan Patrol. A woman's body leaned out of the driver's window. "Which one do you like?"

"So... I have a choice?" she came back at him. "Actually, I'm not too keen on sitting next to dead people, is there another?" she queried.

"Sorry love, no, I want that one. Hang on a sec." He turned to find Luke. "Luke!" he called in his best parade ground voice. "Get yourself here, now!"

Luke, yelped and raced over. He dropped his Steyr, turned and raced back for it. Glenda giggled behind her hand.

"Here, boss!" yelled Luke as he stood to attention in front of Nulla. Red faced he glanced at Glenda then did a double take when he noticed her breasts dangerously stretching her low cut top.

"Luke, eyes front! See that four wheel drive, the black one with the body hanging out of the window? Tidy it up for the lady here, go gentle on the body, she was once someone's loved one." Luke looked at the new girl again and smiled at her. "Now, if you don't mind," continued Nulla.

Luke walked to the Nissan and began examining how to respectfully move the stiffened woman's body out of the window and onto the ground. He was stumped. Its torso was stiff and fluids dripped down the outside of the door.

Nulla spoke to the girl. "Do you think you could help him? I know it's not nice but you're going to be doing things that aren't very nice if you want to join us." He looked at her carefully, measuring her will.

"OK," she said politely and walked slowly over. "Hi, I'm Glenda, you must be Luke?"

Death at close range can be quite confronting but together they managed to move the body then wiped the stained SUV with rags as best they could. The odour made them gag but they needed a solid work horse and this was just what Nulla wanted. Glenda sat in the driver's seat and started the engine. With all windows down she drove carefully over to Nulla.

"Ready, Nulla," she reported.

He directed her to back it up to the double doors and then into the centre itself. They loaded more stores including clothing and other gear for the boys as well as for Glenda. They took a lot of bottled water they found stored in the warehouse still sitting on pallets waiting to be packed in the store shelves. By this time it was almost dark so he directed his troops back home.

It was near midnight and Nulla kept talking. They had been at it for hours now. Nulla made them take short breaks to walk together in the dark and then back again. This was all part of assessing their strengths and weaknesses.

"This strategy comes from the Japanese infantry manual of 1941: when you stop you might as well sit down; and if you sit down then you might as well eat and drink something; and if you have time for that then you take off your shoes and dry your feet; while you dry your feet you might as well check the condition of your skin, toes and boots... get the picture?" He sat back and drew on his cigarette.

Glenda asked, "What about toilets, what do we do if we're outside and there's no toilet?"

Nulla choked and smoke appeared to come from every orifice in his face. "Pfft! Well you got me with that one, Glenda!" he gasped and coughed once more.

"We apply the same strategy," he managed to say, "and you two boys can stop smiling because that's a good question. If we've time to sit down we've time to piss, I mean pee. And if we have time to pee we have time to poop. Make sense?"

He turned back to Glenda who was glaring at the boys. She said, "But what about toilet paper, Nulla, what do we do about that? I mean, it's going to smell down there if we don't look after ourselves. You know, hygiene is important."

Turning to the giggling boys he said, "It's important for us to examine these issues, fella's. So what do you boys think?"

The boys stopped their smirking, "When we were in the bush we'd always use a rock or a leaf or something like that," said Luke having done as such when out riding with Simon.

Simon said, "I think we need proper toilet paper, girls do anyway. Maybe we should all carry toilet paper in our pockets?"

Nulla nodded, "Glenda?" he turned back to her.

"Yes, girls have special needs, thanks Simon. Carrying paper in our pockets would work. So where do we go? In the bushes? Do we dig a hole?" She really wanted to know everything about guerrilla toilet protocol.

"Boys?" Nulla spun it over to his young troopers again.

"We dig a hole if we have time or just poop where-ever we are if we have to. I guess it depends on time. Hey, isn't that what the Japanese manual is all about, how to manage time and activity?" Nulla could see Luke's brain light up.

"Good points, Luke, and yes, correct, we do what we can given the situation and time. Glenda, I suggest you should always take paper in your pockets and choose your opportunities as they present, like Professor Luke here says." He looked at Luke, smart lads, he thought.

"We try to learn from history, there are lessons in everything and everywhere. Sun Tsu said as much, when we get time we'll go through some of his points. OK, time for bed." Nulla stood up and looked at them all.

"Glenda, you did well today. I am proud of you and I think your family would be too. Boys, you are turning into rock solid warriors, keep your mind on your tasks though. Soft minds lose lives. OK, bed, up at dawn, last to the table is our toilet cleaner for the week. And boys, there is a lady present. Watch where you water the horses and put the toilet seat down. Good night."

Just before dawn Nulla woke everyone up, no one tried to stay in bed this time. They ate quietly, anxious, knowing that something bad was heading their way. They watched Nulla's body language like hawks. He didn't speak.

Silently they packed their gear for the day and then set about breaking down, cleaning and assembling their weapons. They left at sun-up. Nulla doubled Glenda on his Norton V4. The boys following behind. They rode into the hinterland outside the suburbs when Nulla finally pulled over at a fuel station.

"I spent some time on the CB last night," he spoke for the first time that morning. "The terrorists broke through my old unit and they're headed towards the city suburbs. They'd already broken through in other places. My squadron pulled out and are now on their way north looking for a suitable lay-up position. Looks like we need to get up to speed a bit faster than I expected." said Nulla frowning.

His three troopers began working the small electric fuel pump filling their bike tanks as a matter of habit. Nulla nodded for Glenda to walk with him.

"Glenda, I need you to get up to speed as quickly as possible. I've got a weapon for you in my bag, a shot gun. We're going to do a bit of target practice this morning then head into town for more supplies and find more civilians. Are you ready to handle a weapon?"

Glenda looked sideways at Nulla. She felt drawn by his self assured manner as much as by his rugged good looks. "I said I was ready to kill if I had to. Sure, give me the shotty."

He pulled out a well used sawn-off shotgun. Glenda noticed how he handled it like he owned it. As he showed her how to use the safety switch he said, "Keep your safety on at

all times unless you're in the process of killing someone."
Her eyes grew large at that but said nothing.

After her first shot almost knocked her off her feet she
learned to hold it as tightly into her shoulder as possible.

"I hope you didn't think I'd give you a toy gun did you?
This lass kicks like a wild woman on speed so treat her with
the respect she deserves. Hold her tight, caress her trigger
like a..." He stopped, stumbled on a bit, "err, like a umm, just
be damn careful where you point it and always remember
the safety." He turned to the boys to avoid her seeing his
embarrassed look.

"Boys, check your weapons. Glenda, you too, we're
going to engage those targets. Fire when I give the order."
Nulla set up a few bottles twenty metres away and told the
boys to fire single shot first. "Use the sights Simon, don't just
expect the bottles to step in front of your bullets."

"Luke, slowly, don't jerk your trigger finger, you don't
need to rush it. Don't forget your safety switch. Use it all the
time when you load and when you stop to check the target."
When they'd emptied their magazines he called a halt.
"Stop. Safety on, all of you, you too Glenda. OK, let's check
our score shall we." Not one of the bottles had been touched.

When they reached the bottles he asked, "What have
we learned today?"

Luke spoke first, "We're crap shots."

"Simon?"

"We are definitely crap shots."

"Glenda?"

"I'm as good as the boys, just plain crappy."

"Righto, those were accurate assessments of your performance. What can we do about it, suggestions?" He was starting to enjoy himself again after the upsetting news of his unit's losses and withdrawal.

Luke said, "I guess we should practice more?"

"Correct. Any advances on practice?"

"Read up on how to fire better?" said Simon stabbing in the dark.

"Hmm, yes I suppose that might help, Glenda?"

Glenda wasn't sure what to say so she shrugged her shoulders and said, "Mmmm?"

"Good answer my dear - it's just not that easy is it? Looks easy on TV but in real life it's not. We'll do more target practice when the opportunity arises. Righto, on your bikes, follow me and observe, listen, act immediately I do. Got it?" They all nodded and climbed onto their bikes.

They parked away from the main town centre and walked the ten minutes towards the shops. The closer they got towards the town centre the more bodies littered the ground. Some had started to swell and decay but a small group appeared to have been shot recently. The blood was still wet. Nulla stood beside the bodies and called his troops over.

"Seems that we might have terrorists here or perhaps they're scavengers. I see four recently murdered people here, that's not a good sign. Load your weapons, one up the spout, safety on, be prepared for an ambush. Don't walk too close to each other or we might all be taken out in a single burst of automatic fire." He made this last comment deliberately to make them realise this was now the real thing.

They started towards the shopping centre car park and saw a four wheel drive being loaded by a group of people. They wore black leather and the sparkle of chains and jewelry glittered in the sunlight. One held a rifle by the barrel and began to lift it to a firing position when he saw them approaching.

Nulla pulled his troops behind a row of parked cars, out of the line of fire. "There's four of them, armed and they look like trouble don't you think? We can take them out but we need to be disciplined and use our brains." He spoke softly, as if to himself.

Nulla looked at the young woman beside him chewing on her thumb nail and said, "Glenda, I want you to stay here and guard our retreat back to the bikes." He gently touched her hand and went on. "I didn't say that to keep you out of the fight. I need someone to protect our escape route. Besides, a shot gun has a limited range and it's useless against that bludger's rifle."

Glenda nodded, she understood.

"Luke, you go right and stay behind those cars right there, see them? Simon, you go left to those ones there. Try not to be seen and do not go any closer or else you'll be shooting into each others position. Can you see that possibility - shooting each other?" he asked them, they nodded.

He went on. "Your role is to distract the enemy. Fire when you get a chance, don't do anything stupid. We don't know how many weapons they have. It looks like there's just these four but there may be more of them inside. Be careful and watch your backs as well."

He looked closely at the boys, judging their mood and state of readiness. He saw nothing to worry him, they were staunch.

"I'll go up the middle and assess the situation. If they fire then we fire. Use short bursts, three round bursts only. If I think it's too dangerous we go home. Watch what I do and copy. If I fire then we fight and you two join in." He raised his eyebrows, they nodded.

"If it's a fight just annoy the crap out of them so they lie on the ground to escape your bullets. I'll do the rest. Stay behind cover as best you can because their bullets will kill you. If either of you do anything to disobey my orders, I will take your weapon off you, got it?" His face was serious.

"Yes, sir!" they said in unison. Nulla knew that losing their weapon would be the worst punishment he could ever hand out to these two lads.

"Repeat to me what I just told you." The boys and Glenda each recited clearly what he had just told them. He nodded once, pointed the boys in the direction they should go, nodded at Glenda. "If all hell breaks loose disengage and get back to the bikes. If one of us goes down we leave them and make our way back to the bikes. We regroup then head back for recon and rescue. Got it? Repeat everything again please." They did, perfectly.

No sooner had Nulla walked to within fifty metres the firing began. A bullet whined off a car bonnet beside him and he leaped behind a one ton truck. He cursed but he was excited, he needed action, violent action.

The boys had crawled stealthily into position. Simon opened fire first then Luke. They fired a series of short, three round bursts. Simon's fingers closed gently around his Steyr's trigger and they did their thing without him thinking. The four scavengers ducked behind the cars surrounding them.

The scavengers fired back and both Luke and Simon were forced to fall flat on their stomachs as bullets went right through the cars they were hiding behind. The two teenagers tried to melt into the ground as they huddled behind the wheels of the cars in terror.

Nulla stood, took aim and fired then he quickly ducked back down. The bullet almost severed one of the scavengers legs. He screamed so loudly the whole township could hear him. The two girls already yelling abuse increased their chorus. The air turned blue with their creative word-smithing. He aimed again and the girl crouched over the wounded man stopped swearing and was flung backwards. Nulla aimed and fired again and the man on the ground stopped his screaming.

He couldn't allow the screaming to weaken his troops resolve, not on their first blooding. The sounds of the screaming wounded sometimes traumatised new recruits ruining any chance of them becoming first class warriors.

The scavenger's rifle fire then turned on Nulla. They must have had at least one automatic. It sounded like an AK47, thought Nulla. He ducked as bullets sprayed into the truck he was hiding behind. The sounds and smells of battle made him shiver and added to the thrill of killing, it was what he had trained for all his life.

He stayed down, '*let the boys do something, time to turn these boys into men,*' he thought somewhere at the back of his mind.

They did exactly as he expected of them. As soon as they heard the screaming they knew Nulla was firing and scoring hits. Both of them opened back up and the man with the rifle collapsed. The other girl screamed and cursed. She stood up holding his automatic rifle in her hands so Nulla put a round between her breasts.

It suddenly fell quiet, very quiet. The sound of a crow cawing in a nearby tree could be heard above the sighing of the wind. '*This is so peaceful, so right,*' thought Nulla. He blinked his tired eyes and leaned forward pondering his next action.

Luke squinted through his Steyr's magnified scope when he saw one of the men turn towards Nulla. The scavenger lifted his rifle to his shoulder and fired. Luke saw the rifle kick, heard it crack and the scavenger's body moved back a bit. He quickly swung the Steyr scope towards Nulla and watched as he crouched behind a truck.

Luke heard a sharp '*brrrip*' of Simon's Steyr and swung back to watch where he hit. Simon's rounds hit the vehicle in front of the scavengers and sparks leaped into the air. Luke saw the four enemy fall to the ground in panic and wriggle about as they sought to locate where the fire was coming from.

He snapped off two bursts of three rounds each himself. Through his magnified viewer he saw his rounds ricochet off the ground and among the scavengers. A round hit one of the men's shoes and tore a piece of leather from his heel. He fired another burst but it hit the wheel of a nearby car ripping out a chunk of rubber. Its squeal was loud in the silence between the bursts of rifle fire.

Luke's breathing came sharp and sounded harsh in his dry throat. His chest heaved as he tried to breathe more oxygen into his lungs. His head spun dizzily with the noise and a rising panic. He didn't notice the scavenger crouch and aim at him. A patter of bullets ripped into the car that he was crouched behind. They bounced off the bonnet and into the air - some went right through both doors. They made a whining sound and Luke recalled sounds of ricocheting bullets from the war movies he and his father liked to watch together.

Instinctively he ducked his head. Luke checked his Steyr sights and saw one of the scavengers squirming and screaming at the top of his lungs. A growing pool of blood beside him. His leg lying square to his body looked as though it was a piece of play-dough stuck there by a child's hand. One of the girls crouched beside the man on the ground. '*I hope she doesn't get shot,*' he thought to himself.

Nulla didn't have that same thought. Through his scope Luke saw the girl flung backwards as though hit by a truck. She flew back to slam into the car parked behind them. She slid into a sitting position and didn't move. He heard the crack of Nulla's Steyr again and the man stopped screaming.

Adjusting the focus on his sights to see the girls face, he watched as her eyes fluttered slightly then closed. Both fascinated and sickened he was drawn to watch in morbid fascination, he finally jerked his eyes away.

The other man moved into a crouch and opened up with his assault rifle. Luke looked back through his magnified sights and saw him. 'Right in my line of fire!' he thought and pulled at his trigger with short excited jabs. His breathing had stopped completely and he had to gasp raggedly for more oxygen.

The bullets flew wide and whined off the car bonnet where the scavenger was hiding. Then the man fell, his head jerked to the side and one half exploded into the air. Luke went into mild shock, 'I missed him, surely I missed?' he thought.

He then saw the other girl reach down and pick up the man's rifle. 'Put it down, put it down!' Luke breathed in a panicked sob, 'you'll get yourself killed too.' He clearly saw the bullet strike her in the chest. Blood sprayed out of her arched back as she appeared to trip and fell against the same car her friend was lying against.

Luke was sickened and sad but couldn't stop himself watching her through his scope. She wore a chain that curled from her nose to her lip. It looked cute on her, but when her eyes glazed into nothingness, he snatched his rifle up and looked away. Luke shivered in the burning sunshine then looked across at where Simon crouched. He tried to erase the sickeningly vivid image from his mind.

"Stand down! Cease fire boys!" yelled Nulla. "Don't move, stay in your positions. Check your surroundings!"

He waited a few more seconds then stood up but remained covered by the truck. He leveled his Steyr, through his scope he could see all four bodies spread out on the ground, none moved. He scanned the area behind to check if there were other scavengers. He expected they would have done something by now if there were.

Fifty metres of open ground lay between himself and the four-wheel drive where the scavengers lay still. He wasn't keen on leaving his cover. "Boys!" he barked, "Pull back to the bikes, make sure you use your cover. Now!"

They did as they were told, fearful of losing their coveted weapons.

Once together Nulla led them back to their bikes. "Well done all of you. We'll go back to the training ground from this morning and debrief."

Chapter 8

Nulla - debrief

Back at the park they'd left only a few hours earlier Nulla brought them together around the picnic table. He told them to eat and drink. He kept his eye on them for signs of distress. They all sat and ate their army rations without speaking.

"I want each of you to tell us what you did, your every movement, every shot you fired and what you observed. Don't leave anything out. You first, Glenda."

They each told their story. Nulla explained that this helped make sure everyone saw the contact from a full 360 degree perspective.

"Today you started out as novices, and now you've experienced a real firefight. You learned what it's like when someone shoots back at you. It's not nice is it?" He didn't wait for a response. "Those folks were scavengers and they would have killed us if they'd had half a chance. We should have done several things, and I'm to blame for that. I should've withdrawn and reconnoitred properly first. I didn't because I was in a bit of a rush to blood you lot. It paid off, but I want you to know that it's always better to reconnoitre your contact. Can someone tell me why I pulled us back and didn't follow up?"

The three looked at Nulla then at each other. Luke said, "Because there could have been more inside the shopping centre and if we went to the scavenger's vehicle

they could ambush us?" The others nodded. Nulla waited but
no one added anything.

"Yes, that's right. We'll head back tomorrow, just
before sun-up. We'll take the Nissan. Glenda you drive and
Luke you ride shotgun with her. I'll take my Norton and
Simon you ride shotgun behind me. Righto, why will we
approach a new target, the new shopping centre, this way?"
For Nulla everything was a lesson. He needed his troops to
be battle-smart and ready, he didn't want followers, he
needed leaders.

Luke wanted to answer but he let Glenda speak first.
Nulla nodded for her to go ahead.

"I think it's because we'll be taking the weapons the
scavengers left behind and their four wheel drive as well.
Plus we save fuel by cutting down on extra bikes." She
smiled up at him and Nulla found himself thinking of other
things. He closed his eyes briefly and focused his mind.
'Calm down you old fool,' he said to himself.

"Ah hmm." He cleared his throat which had suddenly
grown tight. "Correct, I think we just might make good urban
guerrillas after all. We'll take what we can and that includes
their four wheel drive. We'll also run a patrol through the
shopping mall. It's big and we'll need all four of us to check it
out. I think the automatic the scavengers used was an AK47,
the best terrorist weapon on the planet. Glenda, that's
yours," he added. "We'll be moving house soon so anything
you need grab and throw in the Nissan. There's another safe
house closer to the city centre. We can set up base camp

and run our guerrilla operations from there. We're just about ready to be a real pain in the butt for those terrorists."

He stopped speaking for a moment then said, "Boys, how do you feel about killing that scavenger, are you OK? I want you to talk about it. Glenda, what was it like to be on the outside watching and not able to help?" Nulla pushed them along.

Glenda spoke first. "It was horrible listening to the screaming. I was terrified, I wanted to run away. It reminded me of my partner dying and his screams. I feel a bit weird and shook up still."

Nulla nodded but didn't add anything, he looked at the boys expectantly.

"I don't feel anything, I don't even know if I hit anyone. So much was happening, so much noise and the recoil of the rifle. I concentrated so much on doing the right thing, trying to slow my breathing and aim properly. I kept hearing your voice in my head to breathe, remain calm and fire short bursts. The incoming fire was scary, I felt frightened then." His eyes widened as if it were still happening. "I discovered that a car isn't the best place to hide behind, the bullets can go right through the doors. I'm still running it all over and over in my mind, it won't stop. Those scavengers shouldn't kill innocent people, they deserved what they got." Simon spoke clearly and carefully. He stopped and turned to look at Luke, so did Nulla and Glenda.

"Well I feel pretty horrible. I didn't know it would be so sickening to watch someone die. I watched all of them die through my sights. I'm glad I didn't shoot those girls too, that'd be pretty hard to live with. And Simon, you took out the second scavenger, I saw it. All I hit was one of their shoes and a car tyre. I'm still a crap shot." He looked at the three watching him, smiled briefly and resumed eating his cheese, ham and tomato sauce sandwich that he'd found in his pack from the day before.

"Righto, Glenda, you're up for lookout, choose your spot carefully and watch the road in both directions. Run and get us if you see movement. Righto boys, time for us to clean and oil our weapons. Later we'll do some weapons training and look at the map for tomorrow's trip." They cleaned their Steyr's without Nulla's help, then loaded their empty magazines.

When they finished the cavalryman sat with his back against a tree and said, "Boys, close your eyes and go to a nice place in your imagination. I'll teach you how to train your mind when we get the time. For now, find a nice place, like the beach or a tropical island, and go there, like in a day dream. You'll need it after today." Nulla then pulled out his tobacco pouch and rolled a cigarette. He sat quietly smoking, his eyes closed.

That afternoon they trained in how to select strategic positions for an ambush followed by target practice.

"A pinning strategy only works if you don't fire in the direction of one of your own blokes. Just imagine if Simon and Luke stood opposite each other this morning. Any bullets that didn't hit the cars or targets would hit their mate. What if Simon or Luke went to a different position instead of the one I told them to go to this morning? They could have put themselves in the line of fire for me, or each other. That would mean they compromised the assault and I would have had to call them back.

"It's important we take orders, listen, observe and act. We always think of safety, of ourselves and of our mates in every contact. What if someone crept up behind you while you were busy firing at the scavengers? How would you ensure your own positional security or that of your mates?" Nulla drilled them over and over and then directed them to take command and place the other three in positions and then to explain why. It was a full day of fight, kill, train.

They got home just before dark. He made them approach their house as they would a contact. He went through their movements and positions over and over repeating everything he taught them earlier. Each took their turns to be the commander. When they finished they collapsed exhausted. It was Simon's turn to cook the evening meal and clean up. As expected it was simple: cereal and bread sprinkled with curry powder and tomato sauce with layers of cheese.

Nulla made them wash daily in the big bowl they found on their previous trip. It wasn't big enough to sit in but they could stand and splash water over themselves. They didn't have much water for washing and Nulla drilled into them to conserve everything, especially water. By mid evening they sat around the table under candle and torch light, to plan for their trip tomorrow. That night they slept like logs until Nulla woke them for breakfast.

They were up well before dawn and breakfast was the first item on their agenda.

"I don't want coco pops, I want something that'll stay there all day. I'll make some porridge if anyone else wants some?" grumbled Luke. "My mother always said porridge made big boys and girls." He twirled his spoon in the air and poured some hot water on his bowl of dry porridge. It turned into a stodgy mess.

"I don't care as long as it's food," said Nulla doing stretches in the lounge room. "I've eaten rats, cats and saddle bags so porridge is as good as anything else. Count me in, you're the cook for today, Luke."

Simon and Glenda, still half asleep, ate what was on the table: coco-pops with powdered milk and boiled water. Glenda finished her bowl and first cup of black tea.

"I just can't get use to this dried milk business, Nulla. Can we get a cow in here some time soon?" she called as she squeezed past Luke on her way to do her morning ablutions.

Breakfast gave them time to wake up and socialise. The boys enjoyed having Glenda with them. For the pubescent males she was nicer to look at and more fun than Nulla and his endless lectures.

Simon left the table and came back from his bedroom with the snub nose special .38 in his hand. He handed it to Nulla.

"Where'd you find this little beauty?" said Nulla. He stopped his stretching and curiously held the pistol up to the candle light and checked its mechanism. He spun the cartridge chamber. "Nice action but pretty useless in a fire-fight. Only the one cartridge? Got any more ammo?"

"Nah, just the single bullet. We took it off a dead body up in the hills before we found you cavalry guys. I just remembered it was in my bag. Do you want it?" Simon stroked his nose with the back of his hand and raised his eyebrows.

"Yeah, thanks. We'll take it with us and see if we can find some bullets for it. Handy in a close fight or sneaking around." He finished his stretches then said to the group. "Remember, we discussed what we should do when we met some civilians?"

The boys nodded and Glenda looked blank.

"Well, now that we've met civilians what do you think?" he asked.

"I think we need to know more about every group we meet, we need intelligence. Each one is different and we shouldn't have expectations they are good or bad," offered Luke.

"We should approach civilians carefully and prepare for the worst like we have so far. Some are safe and some are dangerous. Otherwise we risk getting caught with our pants down in the middle of the road," said Simon offering one of his one-liners.

"Yep, now you know. We take every civilian contact on its merits. Righto, let's get ready to move." said Nulla.

───┤▬▬▬

By the time the sun was rising they'd infiltrated the shopping centre and made their way to the car park entrance. They could see the carnage of yesterday among the parked cars. Nulla made them squat until their legs burned with the effort.

"Pst! Pssst!" whispered Simon in Nulla's direction until he turned and frowned at him. Simon pointed towards the cars. They all followed his pointed index finger. In the growing dawn they saw a pack of dogs rummaging among the scavenger's bodies. It looked like they were eating them.

"Nulla, they're eating the dead people," came a strangled whisper from Luke. They heard him make a choking sound and up came his beloved porridge.

"We hold our position until it gets a bit lighter, then we'll check the bodies." Nulla nodded at Simon. "Simon, you partner Glenda today. Make sure you both support each other like in your training."

As the sun rose above the horizon he lifted his arm, pointed to them, and then with his whole hand pointed in the direction of the bodies. Next he pumped his arm up and down.

Simon ran to the shopping mall's main door and waited while Glenda ran out to the car. She stopped, crouched and nodded to Simon. She raised her shot gun to her shoulder to bring it to bear on any would-be attackers. Simon ran up to her and scanned with his Steyr scope. He gave Nulla the all clear sign.

Nulla sent Luke to secure his position closer to the bodies. The dogs stood stiff legged and growled at him. As

Nulla stopped beside Luke, one of the dogs approached, growling low in it's throat. Nulla shooed it off. Reluctantly it turned back to feed with the pack.

Luke used his scope and reported that he saw nothing other than the dogs. Simon and Glenda also gave the all clear. Nulla stood with Luke and the two made their way to the scavengers bodies on the ground. The dogs growled and some stood their ground until Nulla walked closer, swung his boot and landed a solid kick. The mangy dog yelped and ran off. The rest followed, but stopped a short distance away, snarling menacingly.

Simon and Glenda came up to join them. Simon asked Nulla, "Why aren't these dogs dead like the others?"

"They must be outside dogs who didn't drink the poisoned water or eat any poisoned dead people? Or maybe the poison's gone from the dead bodies already?" suggested Nulla, his three troops nodded.

"Can we keep one?" asked Luke.

Nulla looked at him and screwed up his face. "These might be wild dogs, can you see any collars? Besides once they taste human flesh what's going to stop your pet eating us while we're sleeping?" He looked at Luke and shook his head.

Luke initially had the sympathy of the other two, but as soon as they heard that, they shook their heads in agreement.

Each of the scavengers were torn in places showing where the dogs had been feeding. Flies began to settle on their open wounds. It smelled of death. The four collected the weapons: a .22 semi automatic and an AK47. Nulla handed the AK47 to Glenda and showed her how to handle the safety switch and load it. They quickly packed up the Mitsubishi four wheel drive with what the scavengers left lying on the ground.

Luke stood there for a long minute staring at the girl with the nose chain. Flies walked on her opened eyes. Nulla watched as the teenager went to an open car and brought back a cloth to place over her face.

"Are you all right, Luke?" Nulla asked softly.

"Yeah, I'm all right. I just said sorry to her." He stood quietly for a moment then said, "People stop being pretty when they're dead. If she'd given up she could have been one of us. She could have been one of our friends."

Totally oblivious to Luke's morose mood, Simon called out, "Hey, Nulla, can we use the dogs for target practice?"

Glenda's head jerked up and she snapped, "No way Simon! What sort of monster are you? That's cruel!"

"I thought they might attack, look at them snarling at us." He kicked the car tyre next to him, his face was red.

Nulla spoke before anyone could say another word, "No one is going to shoot the dogs for target practice, so everyone just settle down. Righto, I saw an army surplus store inside. They should have binoculars and night scopes." He picked up his Steyr and sent Simon and Glenda ahead. "Scout ahead while Luke and I take the Mitsubishi around the back and put it next to Glenda's."

They spent the next few hours going through the mall collecting gear and packing their four wheel drives. Inside the army surplus store they found a nice collection of night vision goggles, scopes and a lot of useful camping gear and clothing.

As they prepared to leave Nulla stretched the street map over the car bonnet and walked them through the plan for the day ahead. They now had to make their way through the city, avoiding the terrorists and find their next safe house.

"We stick close together, you boys will be riding shotgun. Shoot anything that looks nasty. Got that?" Now everyone was nervous as hell.

Chapter 9

Charlene - gas bomb

The Dwellers, as they called themselves, began to meet up at midnight inside the supermarket where they'd met Phil. For Heidi and Arthur it was a reasonably short walk and under the cover of darkness it didn't pose much of a safety problem. They lived in an old suburb with established trees and bushes that almost covered the footpaths. There was always somewhere to hide on the rare occasion the terrorists went on patrol.

On this particular night Heidi, Charlene and Arthur met with the regular dwellers. There they met up with Stacy and Abraham, a middle aged couple who'd lost their children to the poisoned water. They were always sad and depressed and Heidi tried to help them as much as she could. Then there were Lucy, Tony and their daughter Annie who brought a smile to everyone's face. Heidi liked to bring a special gift for Annie each time they met up.

The only other people they knew were Fatima and Phil, who were more comfortable with the apocalypse than everyone else. These dwellers appeared to be the only survivors in their area. There had been others a few weeks back but they seemed to have either been caught by the terrorists, died from illness or just drifted off.

"Hi Annie, I brought you another book from the Pony Club series. Do you have this one?" Heidi handed over a battered hard copy she'd found in one of the houses.

"Thank you, Heidi," said Annie shyly. "I have three of them and this makes four." She smiled from inside her jacket as she huddled into its warmth. A cold midnight wind was blowing across Bass Strait and in through the shattered doors of the supermarket.

"Fatima, I found a cook book for you and a book on how to make and repair tools for you, Phil." Heidi handed over two books that she knew they'd enjoy. Although finding fresh meat was difficult there were times when Fatima brought them curried possum, rabbit or pigeon and rice in plastic containers. She was a magician on the gas cooker and Phil had a knack for trapping animals. The dwellers learned that he was an academic but now he turned his hand to trapping, gardening, wood working and any handyman jobs he could find to keep himself busy.

Abraham shrugged his jacket closer around his neck and said in his gruff voice, "What do you all think about the gas bottle situation? I've run out of butane canisters and I'm having trouble trying to fit the LPG gas bottles to my camp cooker. Can someone come over and give me a hand?"

Heidi and Arthur had been to Abraham and Stacy's house a number of times to help them manage. Their depression always lifted when they saw the two teenagers. Stacy tried to mother the youngsters, she even invited them to move in but Heidi fiercely defended her independence. There was no way Heidi would move in with anyone now she was enjoying the freedom of running her own household.

Cooking gas was a problem for the dwellers. All the camping stores had been ransacked and gas canisters were always the first to disappear. They could find no more butane canisters and full LPG gas bottles were scarce. The other problem was that no one knew how to work the enormous LPG gas tanks at the fuel stations. They hadn't tried too hard, fearful they'd blow themselves up. But now there was no other way, they had to find an answer before winter.

Each group had moved into houses with a fireplace where they did most of their cooking. They never lit their fires during the day in case the smoke gave them away. As soon as it was dark they would light their fires to cook their meals, ready for the next day. Firewood was not a problem, they each had their own coveted caches from around the neighbourhood. No one ever bothered to ask for firewood because they knew what the answer would be. It was survival of the fittest and the best resourced, and resources for survival were jealously guarded.

Sometimes they would all gather at Fatima and Phil's house for a meal, each bringing something for the pot. They would arrive after their shopping trips just before dawn. Fatima would finish cooking as the last family arrived and they would usually eat around breakfast time.

Fatima suggested at their first meeting they should all stay over till the next evening, to avoid possible detection. Phil and Fatima even went so far as to collect all the necessary bedding, sleeping bags and pillows, as well as expensive sheets and woollen blankets, for the group. The idea to bring gifts began with Heidi.

The families tried their best to support each other but it was hard. Little Annie had no idea why she couldn't play outside in the parks during the day and was always restless. Tony and Lucy relished visiting Fati and Phil's if only to give themselves a break from Annie's demands for attention. As much as Heidi and Fatima wanted to take her for a holiday in their own homes, they knew that if something went wrong, that precious bond between them would be broken.

It was Charlene who brought up the idea of how to fill the gas bottles from the large depot tanks. She'd watched her father fill their barbecue gas bottles many times. Although apprehensive, Charlene thought she could recognise the special gas tank key and remember how it was done.

Everybody was sitting around Fatima's dinning table at one of their weekly visits where they discussed how they could resolve the gas bottle problem. Fearful of saying the wrong thing, Charlene always tried to avoid making suggestions. Her traumatic experiences had dampened her enthusiasm for adventure, even the thought of foraging was too much for her.

She spoke up just as people were finishing their stew of heavily spiced possum on a bed of saffron rice and stewed peaches. Fati's possum stews were always heavily spiced to disguise its sometimes unpleasant flavour. There is a well kept secret about possums and it's that they'll eat anything. Their flesh tastes like their last meal. The dwellers knew there were plenty of dead humans for scavengers like possums to eat. Fortunately only Fatima and Phil knew the details, not wanting to upset their guests they kept the secret to themselves.

"I think I know how to work the gas tank at the depot," said Charlene softly.

They all stopped what they were doing and looked at her. It was so unlike Charlene to offer her thoughts on matters other than psychology.

"Go on?" said Tony, careful not to sound like he was rushing her.

"I've seen my dad do it a few times and I think I know what the special key for charging the gas bottles looks like." She'd said enough and now waited for their reactions.

"You must be talking about that big gas tank at the service station around the corner? That one we looked at last time we spoke about the LPG gas bottles?" Arthur piped up licking his plate clean then placing it back on the table.

"Yes, it's not the same one my father used, but it looks the same. I'll need to check it out, but if someone comes with me to help...?" her voice drifted off.

"Goodness girl, what do you take us for, Numbats?" Abraham turned to the group. "How about we each bring some empty bottles on our next trip? Heidi should stay behind this time and Arthur can take the little trolley he made with Phil. I'll go with Stacy and I imagine Tony will be the first one there with his gas bottles lined up like nine pins."

"Let's organise as many bottles as we can handle and all meet at the depot at our usual time, midnight. There, it's done!" It was Tony, Charlene was grateful for his support. He always did that on the rare times she ventured an opinion or idea.

"I think that'll work, yes. Is tomorrow night too early? My shoulder pain is bad with this cold wind and if I don't do it soon, I mightn't be able to go out for a while," said Charlene, gaining in confidence.

"OK, let's do it," said Abraham turning to their host. "If Fatima doesn't mind another stay over, since your house is the closest. If you don't mind, can you stay at home too Fati, and mind the house with Heidi, Lucy and Annie? The more hands the better but safety and security should be our main concerns, I think." He turned and smiled with delight at Charlene.

They decided to meet at the depot at exactly midnight. The long, low whistle with a twist upwards was their signal Heidi had decided upon. They were each to bring as many empty gas bottles as they could carry. When filled they were to store those they couldn't immediately carry, inside the station itself, and return each night until they were all filled and brought home.

With their plans set they cleaned up their communal meal, washed and dried the dishes then prepared for bed. It was Arthur's turn to do the rounds for security and while he was out they gathered their pillows and bedding onto the floor of the lounge room. Lucy read a bedtime story for Annie and they all listened like little kids. It had become the dwellers ritual when they had a sleep over. Eventually the dwellers fell asleep one by one in front of the now cooling fire.

The following evening the dwellers collected their empty gas bottles and brought them by their various routes to the service station. Arthur and Charlene had arrived a few minutes earlier. While Charlene was searching the office for the gas tank keys, Arthur set himself as lookout.

Phil and Tony came out of the bushes and placed their gas bottles beside the enormous LPG tank with the markings, HIGHLY FLAMMABLE, written in big letters. Stacy and Abraham arrived soon after, they too placed their bottles in a row. Arthur kept watch for roving patrols and the rest waited quietly in the shadows for Charlene to show them what to do.

The wind blew scudding, dark clouds in the moonlight and they stamped their feet to keep warm. A sudden rain squall made them all huddle inside their jackets, they felt miserable standing there in the pale moonlight. It just as quickly eased off to a light sprinkle then stopped. No one spoke.

Finally Charlene appeared with something in her hands. By blinkered torchlight she unlocked the cage and released the gas tank hose calling softly for Abraham to bring the bottles one by one. She had no strength in her left hand so she quietly showed him how to screw the hose into the gas bottles. He kept getting it wrong until she pointed out that the thread went in an anti-clockwise direction.

The first bottle was filled but not without loud liquid screams from the loose connection until Abraham learned that he had to screw it in tighter. Everybody cringed hoping no patrols could hear the noise. Stacy helped Abraham fill while Phil placed them inside the station using his hand trolley.

Just as their last bottle was filling a noise startled them all. Arthur gave his warning whistle, Phil and Tony immediately raced into the bushes. Stacy was in a state of panic as she tried to help Abraham unscrew the hose and hide the bottles. Abraham panicked and dropped the bottle. The noise was enough to wake even the dead bodies lying on the ground around them.

A voice called out, it was answered by several others. There came the sound of footsteps running towards them. Torchlight beams cut the cold midnight gloom and reflected eerily off the rain-drenched concrete.

Abraham grabbed Stacy's hand and they ran into the fuel station building and hid behind the counter. Arthur raced to Charlene and whispered, "A foot patrol. Just drop everything and run."

Charlene looked at his frightened eyes and then at the swinging torch lights approaching along the road. They took off along their prepared escape route.

Gas was leaking from the open bottle and the hissing hose connection and they knew they had to put as much distance between them and the bottles as possible. Phil and Tony carried a full bottle of LPG gas each and ran off, hobbled by their precious cargo.

There was a rifle shot, then another. It was followed by a burst of automatic fire that ripped through the tree branches above the running figures. Some of the bullets screamed as they ricocheted off the metal gas tank.

"Stop! Stop or you're all dead meat!" came a shouted order and they all knew what that meant. Phil and Tony reluctantly threw their full bottles of gas into the bushes and ran for their lives. They split up and headed in opposite directions as agreed upon.

The terrorist patrol had yet to notice Arthur and Charlene. As Charlene turned to look behind her she saw the patrol approaching the gas station firing at Tony and Phil over the top of the gas storage tank.

"Oh no, no, the gas tank is going to explode and we'll lose all that precious gas." She almost cried with rage when she heard more automatic fire. Bullets now whined off the tree trunks and rained leaves over her and Arthur. They pressed on into the gloom even faster. Charlene cried out to Arthur again that the gas tank could blow up at any moment.

Arthur nodded and led her behind a house then cut through another. Their escape routes had been carefully planned by Heidi the day before, they knew the suburb by memory even in the dark, especially in the dark. They knew that only a speeding terrorist could ever catch them. But tonight it wasn't the terrorists that worried them.

The voices became louder and rifle fire ripped into the air, the two dwellers could hear bullets pinging off the metal tank. This was followed a few seconds later by a thunderous explosion as the gas tank detonated knocking the dwellers off their feet, instantly incinerating the terrorist patrol and the service station next to it. A giant fireball shot up into the night sky lighting the ground Charlene and Arthur were standing on like they were at a night football match.

Stacy and Abraham had chosen the worst possible place to hide and were vaporised along with the terrorists. The blast completely knocked the station over, flattened it to the ground as if hit by a giant mallet.

Tony didn't realise he was flying until he hit the wall of the house he was next to. It knocked the wind out of him and his ears were ringing. *'Holy crap, the gas tanks gone up. Those bloody idiot terrorists! I hope they went up with it,'* thought Tony as he picked himself up. From experience he knew that retribution wold soon be on its way, so he hurried as best he could back to Phil and Fatima's house.

Phil wasn't so lucky. He hadn't gone quite as far as the rest and was thrown off his feet and high into the air. When he came down he landed violently on his leg and felt it give out from under him. He lay on the ground confused and slightly concussed for some twenty seconds while he got his mind back into some semblance of order. On trying to stand he fell back down and that was when he realised his leg was either broken or badly sprained. His knee was on fire and he couldn't put any weight on it. In considerable pain he managed to crawl over to the nearest house and hid in the bushes.

'Blew themselves up didn't they, damn terrorists wouldn't have a brain in their damn heads. I'd better hurry up and hide, those sods'll be here soon and they'll scour the neighbourhood for a mile.' He crawled up to the next house and decided to hide inside. The first few shattered windows

he tried were stuck firm, his anxiety began to build. Eventually he came across one that gave way. Crawling through he let out a loud cry as his knee banged on the floor.

Phil knew he was in trouble and recalled Heidi's story of what they did to her house when they chased Arthur. The terrorists had thrown a grenade into the hideout below her bedroom and then tried to burn the whole house down. She said that they had gone through every house for a hundred metres trashing everything firing wildly into every cupboard and possible hiding place. Yes, he thought to himself, this might be his last day. That started him worrying about leaving his beautiful wife and the sadness it would cause her.

Charlene and Arthur had fared better than Phil. They'd made it behind a house before the explosion shook them off their feet, it blew broken roof tiles and glass onto the ground around them. They remained unhurt but shaken and their ear drums throbbed.

Arthur looked at Charlene and checked to see if she was OK. Charlene couldn't hear a thing and told him so, but he was deafened by the blast too, so they both gave up trying to talk. Arthur pointed the way ahead and they staggered off knowing that at any moment more terrorists would be on patrol with trucks, grenades and spot lights. They had to find a safe house quickly.

Every creature for a radius of thirty kilometres heard the explosion. The terrorists based in that region responded quickly and had a dozen patrols heading towards the area within ten minutes. It was enough time for Arthur and

Charlene to find a safe house, but it wasn't possible for Phil to relocate to any of them.

Charlene and Arthur were safely hidden in a very normal looking garage. All signs of entry were disguised and there was no sign of life. Heidi and Arthur had spent many busy nights creating a network of safe houses and building hideouts under the beds complete with trap doors and carpets. Several had their hideout in the garage under a car parked innocently inside. It was in of these that Charlene and Arthur now hid.

The survivors were worried for their own reasons. Tony was still on the move towards Fatima's house and worried about his wife and daughter. Would they think he'd been killed? He was certain they would have heard, and felt, the explosion - the whole of Adelaide must have.

His main fear was that Lucy might give up on life and do something silly. Her depression hadn't lifted and in fact it grew worse day by day, this might be enough to tip her over the edge. Tony shivered with that fearful thought and prayed to a God he wasn't sure was listening. Hoping to get back to Phil and Fatima's house before the patrols hit the streets, he pressed on faster.

Phil was in serious pain. His knee had swollen to twice its size. When he finally sat up he pulled out his torch and noticed the room was in a mess. He also noticed the rank smell of death.

On the walls were prints of rock stars and electric guitars, he recognised an expensive music system on the desk. Clothing and CD's lay all over the bed, the floor and computer desk. It clicked, this was a teenager's bedroom.

He tried to stand but the pain knocked him down and he rocked onto his back clutching his knee. Phil tried again and managed to stand on his one good leg long enough to see the body lying twisted on the bed. The old historian shuddered, its face was contorted in a mask of confusion and pain.

'Shoot, a damn zombie, just what I wanted. I am so done with this world.' Phil whispered to himself but continued to process exactly what he needed to do to stay alive. It was simple, he needed to stay alive for his Fatima. He couldn't imagine leaving her alone in this damned world.

Phil sat down on the edge of the bed careful not to let the body roll towards him. He'd seen enough bodies these past months and they no longer shocked him. It was fixed in his mind that the terrorists would raid every house in the vicinity of the explosion and fire indiscriminately into every possible hiding place.

'But they might not bother with this room, not with a stinking body right here on the bed.' Phil thought to himself. It was a long shot but it was about the best he could do given his situation. It hit him that he could be here for a few days so he went looking for something to wrap himself in. He had to be prepared for the long wait until he was out of danger. Three days was what the dwellers usually considered long enough for the terrorists to leave an area.

Phil found a doona in the teenager's cupboard and he carefully extracted it, placing it under the timber-framed bed. He slowly and painfully wrapped himself and his knee and was soon fast asleep.

After sleeping past dawn Arthur wasn't going to stay hidden inside a dirty hole for any longer than he needed. He wriggled and squirmed in the tiny space until Charlene eventually told him to go and climb on the roof and keep a lookout – or something. She threatened him with blue murder if he was seen and said she would tell Heidi if he was.

He smiled down at her as he slid out from under the car and climbed the garage rafters. By peering through the cracks in the timber he could see directly up the driveway and could watch the street for patrols. It wasn't perfect but it was safe. He pulled out a pack of cigarettes and lit one, 'this is going to be a long wait,' he thought.

The sounds of roaring trucks and crashing gears, explosions and the frequent bursts of automatic fire came to their ears for the next three days. Each dweller was thinking the same thought: 'if they find me will I betray my friends?'

It was a slow few days. For the dwellers in their safe house with Fatima, and those in their hideouts, they all lived in fear once again.

Chapter 10

Charlene - Phil's lovers

Eventually Phil decided he could no longer stand the smell of the dead body lying directly above him, so transferred his sleeping gear to the main bedroom. It was painful and took longer than he wanted, but he managed to drag himself under the bed in the main bedroom. He wrapped himself in the doona and, in a light fever, he fell asleep, exhausted from the effort.

He was still asleep when the patrol came down the street. They went from door to door firing and throwing grenades into each house. It took them most of the day to reach the house Phil was hiding in, but by that time they'd run out of grenades.

The old man was shivering both from fear and the summer heat, he was also running a fever. His leg was swollen and inflamed. The pain of his injury had run him down and he was physically and emotionally exhausted. Phil was hungry and dehydrated it was almost a full day since the gas tank explosion and he had no food or water with him.

The truck driver had her feet on the dash board as she listened to the rap music blaring in her cabin. Her feet were tapping and she seemed to be having a good time. Captain McCarthy had ordered his platoon to enter each house and destroy everything that might harbour the 'house rats' as the terrorists called them. He was smoking a joint and passed it to his driver. They were both tapping their feet to the music.

The captain didn't care what his troops actually did, no one seemed to these days. They had their orders and did what they were told. If they jumped to it they were safe enough. Missing prayers, failing to turn up to training or when a task was left undone, always led to some form of punishment. It didn't happen often because this army group had been training together for years and knew what to do to stay out of trouble. Executions happened frequently in the other three army groups.

Captain McCarthy finished his joint, tossed the butt out of his window and flicked his drivers ear lobe. The captain nodded at his waist, undid his belt and lay back in his seat. Might as well enjoy this lovely sunny day while he could, he thought.

Holly and Allan had the same idea. They found what they were looking for: a house with closed blinds and a clean bed. The two leaped at each other as they bounced on the bed quickly ridding each other of their uniforms. There were no rules on sex in their army group, as long as you didn't fall pregnant you stayed. If you fell pregnant then you aborted or died in the attempt. It was a simple rule and it worked reasonably well.

Holly cried out as Allan entered her and clawed at his back in a rising ecstasy. It had been days since they'd had sex and were now driven by the raw passion of adolescence.

Phil was woken by the girl's groans and awkwardly shifted his body as the pair bounced above him. In his half crazed mind, sick with fear, pain and fever, his imagination went wild. In his mind's eye he saw a crazed terrorist raping an innocent young girl, and he struggled to unravel the doona wrapped around his body to go to her aid. His mind was racing, he wasn't awake and he wasn't asleep and he wasn't successful.

The girl screamed and her moans came faster and louder. A male voice soon joined hers and the noises climaxed, only to drift into soft moans and grunts, finally ending in laughter.

Phil stopped wrestling with his covering. Even in his fevered state he recognised those sounds from somewhere in his past.

'*Yes, it certainly is a girl but it doesn't sound like she's in trouble.*' Puzzlement turned into understanding until eventually he began to chuckle softly to himself. '*Oh my,*' he thought, '*I'm going to have fun telling Fati about this when I get back home. Oh my, oh my.*' He continued to chuckle as he fell back to sleep with a smile on his wrinkled old face.

Charlene ate some of the stored dried fruits and nuts then handed the packet across to Arthur. He had pronounced the danger almost over after the house was searched and automatic fire peppered the windows and walls. Some hit the garage and one went through the car above them but did no damage to the occupants hiding below.

Each safe house had food and water for three days. A torch, spare batteries, blankets and pillows. They were big enough to fit two, just. Arthur decided that they should head back that night.

He wasn't worried so much for Heidi's sake but more so for Charlene. What if she were to break down or they have to outrun a patrol? He saw how she withdrew into herself, just like she did when something triggered her trauma. Post traumatic stress disorder, *PTSD* she called it. '*It must have been bad.*' He thought to himself. She would rock and whimper, disappearing into some dark place in her mind. He once tried to comfort her but it set her off screaming, he was too afraid to try again.

"How are you feeling, Chas, are you cold or in pain?" He handed her the spare blanket to wrap around her shoulders but she pushed it away.

"I'm OK, I just keep having these horrible thoughts. Hearing the gunfire reminds me of when I met Heidi." She looked at him. "Arthur, I hate it here. We need to get away or do something, I think I'll go mad if I don't." She hung her head and placed her right hand over her face. Arthur noticed how her left hand couldn't even reach her face and it saddened him.

He gently touched her good shoulder. "Don't worry, Chas, Heidi has plans. When the weather clears up we're going to move north into the Flinders. Remember how we talked about it before. We should start planning with the others the next time we see them. I know Heidi will have some good ideas about how we can do it."

Arthur hesitated then climbed out of the hideout and up into the rafters of the garage to keep a lookout. He smoked nervously while he thought about all he had seen and the pain of his own losses. All of a sudden he began to cry. He wept quietly so he wouldn't disturb Charlene.

That evening they were ready to leave. Arthur had found a bicycle next door and serviced it with the tools in the garage, like he'd seen Phil do with their other bikes. He'd already reconnoitred their route back to Fatima's house.

On his final trip back he quickly touched base with his lover, gave her a brief of Charlene's condition, a hug and then he was gone. He raced back on his bicycle to the hideout to lead Charlene safely home.

There was a cold wind that night so he wrapped her in a blanket, held her good hand and walked her slowly back to their new home. They stopped every few minutes to listen for anyone following and to let Charlene to rest a little. Charlene had lost so much strength that even walking exhausted her. Arthur was also very aware that he definitely did not want to lead any terrorist back home to Heidi again. She would certainly murder him if he did it a second time.

Only once did Charlene stumble, when she kicked a tree root in the dark. Arthur was by her side in a flash and caught her before she fell. He was like a mother hen fussing over her so much so that she pushed him away. Like any gallant knight in shining armour he ignored her. He continued to hold her good arm as they walked slowly in the darkness.

As they approached their home Arthur stopped in the shadows and let out a soft whistle. It went up then down in pitch. A torch flashed briefly. He sighed with relief, Charlene began to cry. As they walked into the front yard they were met by a sobbing Heidi and Fatima. Fatima tried to hush the three friends as she guided them in through the back door. The fire was lit and the heat was suffocating but Charlene didn't notice. She fell into the lounge chair and was fast asleep in moments.

Tony's route had been more straight forward than the others and he took full advantage of it. He arrived home before everyone else, worried about Annie but more so about Lucy. She was his heart and soul and he tried everything in his power to keep her safe and happy. It didn't work, nothing in this miserable world did any more, he thought.

Tony recalled the time when they were young lovers and how much they enjoyed being with each other. Since the apocalypse they hadn't had a moment's intimacy. All fire had gone from their relationship. He missed the part of her that made him feel so alive and so special.

He didn't know what he could do to make up for all the misery the world had dished out to her. Trying sometimes just made him feel empty and useless. It was too hard to be happy even for Annie sometimes, but he never blamed anyone but the terrorists. He had dreams of killing terrorists, of running between houses, firing his rifle and watching them fall. The dreams were so real he would wake up and look at his hands for the assault rifle he was firing, but they were just impotent dreams.

Late the following morning after Charlene and Arthur arrived home the dwellers were sitting around talking. No one had heard or seen Stacy or Abraham since the explosion and Tony said that he had checked out their house the previous two nights, but there was no one there. Arthur said he would go with him next time.

"I need the exercise after sitting in that miserable hole for three days. It's not good for a young fella to be idle." He smiled at his little joke, he didn't notice that no one else smiled.

Heidi told the new arrivals that Phil was missing. Tony explained how they had both run from the station and dropped their gas bottles in the bushes, then headed off in different directions. He went left and Phil went right. Arthur mentioned he hadn't seen Phil either, none of them, Stacy, Abraham or Phil, since he gave the warning. They were all worried, the loss of their own kind was painful, and hit them all hard.

It was almost four days since the gas bottle incident and everyone was restless as they sat silently in the back garden. By this time not even Fatima moved to do anything, not even to clean up after breakfast. Deciding she needed to find their fellow dweller, Heidi collected some street maps and began working on a search grid of where Phil might possibly be.

"If Phil went to the right then that puts him about here when the gas bottle exploded," said Arthur, pointing to the map. "He couldn't have gone far, no more than fifty metres between the time they dropped their bottles in the bush and the explosion. I think it must have knocked him over and he's injured. He must be holed up somewhere in one of these houses in this sector. That only gives us a dozen or so houses to search. If he isn't inside then he may be hiding outside in a garage, or under a house." Arthur deliberately didn't mention the other possibilities.

It was almost fully dark when Heidi and Arthur gathered some blankets, water bottles, a first aid kit, torches and headed out with their maps. Charlene was too exhausted to offer her services. She knew she would just be a burden if she went with them. Phil was her favourite, she loved that kind old man but feared the worst.

Tony wanted to go with them but they told him to stay behind and look after his wife. Lucy had been feverish slipping in and out of consciousness all day. Fatima, the only one who knew anything about healing, tended her carefully, cooking a special brew of herbs and meat broths. Tony was worried, too afraid to leave her side in case she got worse, or she did something to herself.

"Good luck, be careful and please find my man," Fatima said. The kindly old woman hugged them both then closed the door softly behind them. She unconsciously stoked the fire up and simply sat watching the dancing flames. Her mind wandered over all the possibilities of what could have happened to her husband. She grieved quietly so as not to upset the others.

The two were dressed in black and Heidi had blackened their faces so only the whites of their eyes showed. They wore black gloves and their torches were black and taped so only a slit of light showed. Riding their BMX bikes it wasn't too long before they reached their destination. Heidi was quite sure she would find Phil, she had a good feeling about the trip.

"Arthur, stay outside and stand watch for me. I'm going to start with this house. It doesn't seem to be as badly shot up like the others. If you see anything suspicious, give me the low whistle warning." She went in through the broken front door.

"Phil, Phil?" she called softly. Heidi went from room to room but in the dim torch light saw no sign of occupation. Amazingly there was very little damage to the inside of the house. All the others they searched were severely damaged but not this one, funny, she thought.

She startled when she heard a sound, a soft buzzing sound. 'That's not zombies, wake up to yourself girl!' she steadied her nerves, 'that's snoring.' Heidi was afraid and about to get Arthur when she stopped in the hallway and listened again. 'That sounds like Phil's snoring.' She smiled to herself in relief and followed the sound. It led to the main bedroom.

She found Phil, fast asleep, under the bed with his feet sticking out from under it.

"Phil, Phil, wake up." He mumbled then opened his eyes. At first he appeared afraid but then he smiled as he recognised her in the slither of torch light.

"Oh Heidi, hello, I was dreaming. I was eating a meat pie with roast potatoes and gravy. Oh my, it was so nice." He tried to sit up but he had no strength to move.

"Phil," she smiled broadly with relief, "here, drink this." Heidi opened her bag and produced a bottle of water. She helped him drink then ran softly to the front door. "Arthur, I've found him!"

It took them three days to prepare Phil for his trip home. Fatima had come straight over as soon as she found out. She brought him some food to eat. It was something she'd made the day before, pigeon pie with potatoes and gravy.

Tony went with them on the night they brought him back. Lucy was now recovering under Fatima's superb care.

It took Tony, Arthur and Heidi all night to carry him home. They used his own home-made trolley when they could. He'd lost so much weight that he was as light as a feather, but his knee was so badly sprained that every movement was agony. They made a stretcher out of old jumpers and two wooden oars. It worked but swapping between trolley and stretcher, walking through back yards and over fences, made it one of the worst nights they'd experienced.

Phil was so grateful to be home that he announced he was going to learn to make wine from the excess fruit they brought back from their trips around the neighbourhood.

That put a smile on everyone's face because the terrorists had raided every liquor store in the city and alcohol of any kind was hard to find these days.

That night over dinner he had them all in stitches as he told them of his bedroom lovers.

"But dear, I didn't think you'd remember the sound of love-making at your age," said Fatima with a wink.

"My dear, I can still see every curve of your gorgeous eighteen year old body in my minds eye, and that's over fifty years ago." He smiled back at her as they shared a brief but special moment.

Chapter 11

Nulla - terrorist safe house

Nulla hid his bike in the shopping centre, one of those teenage girl clothing stores that seem to plague every mall. No one would bother searching it for anything useful, he thought. He drove the scavenger's Mitsubishi four wheel drive while Glenda drove their smelly Nissan, all the windows were open and they had rugs under their buttocks.

They drove slowly through streets littered with dead bodies, parked cars and pile ups. Many times they drove up onto the footpath or rerouted around blocked streets.

The vehicles slowed as they entered a leafy street with expensive houses, their lawns overgrown with grass and small bushes. They pulled up into the driveway of one and drove around the back to its enormous garage. Simon got out and opened the roller doors. It could easily hold half a dozen cars.

Nulla motioned for everyone to join him as he got out of the SUV. "Here we are, safe house number two."

"Is this another drug house, Nulla?" asked Luke. Luke felt comfortable around Nulla, they'd managed to develope an appreciation for each other. Both enjoyed silence and didn't need to chit chat too much.

"Yes, mate. Follow behind me, safety off, be prepared for anything. We don't know what crazy arses will be inside."

He arranged the three to take position around the back door while he called out for the occupants to come out. There was no movement or noise from inside the house.

Nulla opened the door, it wasn't locked. He walked through the house with Luke behind him.

"Safety's on!" he ordered loudly.

Inside they found two dead bodies sitting slumped in lounge chairs. One was still holding a crack pipe in his shriveled hand. Nulla introduced the dead men as Errol and Flynn.

"These two bastards are killers, we're lucky they ain't still alive because we would've had to put them to sleep. They're club enforcers, hit men. They'd kill you for your shoes and have been known to chop people up while they were still alive. I've met them and fortunately I've not had the pleasure of working with them."

"Nulla, how come you know so much about these drug people?" asked Glenda staring at the dead bodies on the lounge.

"Haven't the boys told you? I'm a patched member of this club. It's an underground club, no names, no identity, just killers. I was introduced by my father, he was one of them. I learned to kill and do bad things I really don't want to talk about. But these two, well, they were the worst of us all. These two, I wouldn't turn my back on." Nulla directed the boys to drag the stiff, mummified bodies outside and bury them.

Turning back to Glenda he continued. "Now you know my background. It wasn't pretty, it wasn't much fun either, but it's behind me and I'm now what you see before you. I'm staunch and I will never be anything but honest. That's what

I learned as a member, be staunch, honest and don't turn your back on anyone."

The rooms were empty of humanity but held enormous bags of marijuana buds. One room was set up to grow cannabis and they saw it had been skillfully hooked up to a large rain water tank from outside. Glenda announced that she was very pleased to have drinking water piped to her house at last.

By the time the bodies were removed and the mess cleaned up it was dark. They prepared to settle down to a cold dinner to discuss their day's work.

Simon had been rummaging around in one of the rooms and brought out another 38 'Saturday night special'. He brought it and a bag of loose bullets to where Nulla was sitting. Together they sorted through the pile. Nulla handed him the spare .38 for him to keep, along with it's soft leather shoulder holster, and promised to give him a lesson in using it gangland style. Simon turned to Luke and grinned like it was Christmas.

Over dinner Glenda said, "I can't believe you wanted to shoot those dogs, Simon."

"I like dogs too, Glenda, but those were mangy mutts and they were eating dead people. They could have attacked us. Besides, they were probably diseased. I thought it would be good practice for your AK47." Simon was cleaning his weapon and had it stripped down and arranged on the lounge room floor. In his hand was a spring he hadn't noticed before and had no idea where it went.

Glenda replied. "Just because we can, doesn't mean we should. We aren't murderers, Simon. We're supposed to set up a resistance, we can't do that by killing every living thing we see for target practice." Pausing, she held the pull through while Nulla threaded it down the barrel of her new AK47. She pulled at the cord while he held the barrel still.

"What if the dogs did attack us? We'd need to defend ourselves wouldn't we?" Simon continued the conversation.

"What if humans no longer dominate the world, what then? Is it OK if the animals kill us for sport?" she said. Nulla noticed a slight smile on her face.

Luke rubbed oil into the firing mechanism of his Steyr and asked of no one in particular using a radio announcer's voice. "Will we survive this apocalypse? Will humans die out and their pets become the dominant species? Will humans one day turn into mutants because of the poisoned water?" He sounded bored.

Simon and Glenda both called him a nutter. Simon said that humanity would survive no matter what. Nulla suggested that the effects of the poison may linger for decades.

At midnight they all turned in for bed. Each had been rostered for guard duty and they knew that not even God would help them if they fell asleep. No one wanted to become Nulla's personal toilet.

The next week was spent setting up the house and bringing stores in from the first safe house. They decided to transport their gear by four wheel drive and left the bikes behind. It was when they saw a patrol one night and another

141

the night after, that they stopped going out of the house. They decided to keep their vehicles in the garage and out of view.

The following morning Nulla told Simon to paint the lights out with black paint, leaving only a tiny strip on the headlights.

"You never know when we might have to leave in a hurry, a blazing set of headlights is a dead give away," he told his young trooper.

Each day things got worse as the build up of patrols made it almost impossible to get out of the house. Nulla sweated over his street maps and listened to the CB with the boys while trying to come up with a plan for their survival.

After a week stuck indoors he called them all together. "Righto troopers, it appears that there are four terrorist groups. From what I've worked out this mob just extended their territory into our part of the city. Each terrorist army has a separate and distinct area to control. We are in Army Charlie's area and they are a wild bunch with little control from the top. It seems that they do what they want. The CB chatter tells us there are very few civilians in this area. Those not dead are imprisoned as work crews, slaves basically. So there's just us and the terrorists."

Although they saw no patrols on their particular street the sounds of trucks and vehicles on the main roads nearby, kept them on edge.

"If we stay this close they might not bother to look in their own backyard. We need to be extra careful and set up a CB listening routine and night patrols to spy on them. At this stage I suggest we trial it," he mused out loud. "We just have to make sure we only move about by night and use our night vision gear," said a resigned Nulla.

They already knew to forage for food and cook at night and kept a skeleton guard during the day. But they felt trapped and they couldn't escape without leaving most of the gear behind. Their proximity to the enemy severely limited their freedom of movement.

"But that's OK, the SAS did most of their work at night and so will we. Besides, we have night vision," said Nulla.

Every second night Nulla took one of his three troopers out on patrol. They would spend most of their time in the local neighbourhood using their night vision goggles. They counted the patrols, noted routes, which vehicles they used and the number of occupants. They recorded if the enemy patrols were on foot or truck, four wheel drive, station wagon or sedans. Every small detail was recorded and evaluated.

If they didn't return by dawn or soon after then the plan was for the house to be abandoned. They set up safe houses around the suburb to escape to in an emergency. Nulla showed them how to set up and disarm booby traps. He drilled them in bomb making and sabotage for when he felt they were ready to go to the next level.

If they were caught on patrol, Nulla told them they should first try to outrun the terrorists.

"Avoid firing your weapons because they'll think we're civilians. If they know we have guns they'll do a house by house search and find us. Guns are our last resort."

He also said that if cornered they should kill as many terrorists as they could.

"I hate to say this troopers, but if you're captured they'll torture you. You will talk. No one holds out against torture unless they are dead. Forget Hollywood, that's just plain bullshit. No one expects you to hold out so don't try to be a hero." They looked at each other, their faces grim.

"That's why it's important to get out of here if we don't turn up by dawn. It doesn't necessarily mean we are captured or dead though. We could be hiding out and waiting for dark to escape."

Those first night patrols he used to train them in their light-enhanced night vision and infra-red goggles and scopes. It was harder than they thought and very disorienting. They used a park not far from their house. It was surrounded by trees and there they practiced walking, lying down, crawling, running and sighting their weapons. Returning home before dawn they would often fall asleep without eating. Nulla ran these patrols until using their night vision goggles became second nature to them all.

Mid summer approached and the nights became warmer. Glenda and Nulla had been stalking a foot patrol for several hours and were a long way from their house. It was now standard practice to extend their range well into enemy territory, this was the furthest they had gone.

On this particular night a second patrol came into view. The Army C terrorists they were following checked the new comers. Nulla heard a loud challenge then the terrorist's began yelling abuse at each other. He pulled Glenda into the bushes.

"It looks like our friends don't particularly like their neighbours. This doesn't look like a friendly chat."

The voices became a screaming match which then escalated into a strained face-off. Two patrols of equal strength, both armed and looking for a fight. Neither backed down. This was a territorial dispute and quickly devolving into a shoot out.

"Glenda, this is going to turn into a fire-fight any moment now. Follow me over the fence and we'll try to get away as fast as possible." Just as he said that a rifle fired in the hot evening air. Promptly a tremendous roar of automatic rifle fire broke out interspersed with screams of pain and curses.

Nulla and Glenda raced for the side gate and ran through. They got to the back fence and Nulla helped Glenda over. As she landed he heard the sound of breaking glass, Glenda cried out in pain.

"Argh! Nulla, I've hurt my leg. I've cut it on the glass," she whispered, agony and urgency in her voice.

Nulla climbed onto the fence and looked down with his night vision goggles. It shed an eerie, green glow showing a distorted view of a broken window with Glenda standing in the middle. A piece of glass had sliced into her leg, she groaned again. Nulla jumped down and helped her from the broken window pane.

The sound of gunfire ceased and was replaced by the screams of wounded and the roar of racing vehicles. The two could clearly hear the sounds of activity from the invisible terrorists. The two infiltrators were terrified that they would be discovered.

Nulla wasn't sure which side won, he didn't care. He held Glenda by the waist and walked her to the back door of the house. She stumbled at every step and he could hear her voice catching in her throat as she tried to breathe deeply to keep from crying.

Nulla opened the back door, it was unlocked and had clearly been ransacked. The kitchen was a mess, the cupboard contents emptied onto the floor but the bedrooms remained reasonably untouched. He carried her into one and helped remove her trousers. In the sliver of torch light he saw the cut to her lower leg, blood oozed out of the wound with each heartbeat.

"Righto, just stay still while I bandage this up." Nulla's hands shook as he opened her backpack and pulled out a trauma bandage wrapping it tightly over the wound. The pressure soon stopped what appeared to be arterial blood pumping out of her.

Nulla looked at the young lady in the pale light of his screened torch. He whispered to her that she was, officially, their first battle casualty. His humour was wasted, Glenda had passed out.

With no choice but to stay put, Nulla sat on the lounge smoking while he thought the situation through. He decided to leave Glenda while he went back to organise a rescue as soon as it was safe. The boys were probably in a panic having no doubt listened to the terrorists reports of the conflict on their CB radio. In which case they should know they were safe, or so he thought.

Simon and Luke had packed their gear ready for flight. In their rush they'd forgotten to listen to the latest terrorist reports. They heard the initial ones of a contact in the direction Nulla and Glenda had headed and presumed it was them. They missed the last one which described the border dispute. They exited the house and moved some of their most valuable gear to the closest safe house and left behind booby traps just as Nulla showed them. Luke also set secret signs so that if Nulla did make it back, he would know the whole place was booby trapped.

Nulla had very little in the way of first-aid beside the single bandage they each carried in their slim back packs. He found some aspirin but knew Glenda would need more than that for such a bad injury. The big fear was always inflammation and blood poisoning, it could kill her.

His mother was their tribal healer and he remembered how all the sick people of the tribe would go to her. Recalling how she used caster oil for everything from boils, cuts and belly ache to blocked bowels, he found a full bottle in the bathroom. Not sure how to use it he just poured it on the bandage and hoped it would do its magic, just as his mother had done.

Loud voices and whistles came from up the street, it was frightening to think they could easily catch him with his proverbial pants down now. As long as they didn't come near, he knew they were safe. The hours passed with a lot of vehicle traffic and more foot patrols. There came a growing roar of voices as the terrorists gathered at the battle scene. By now it was well after sunrise.

Nearly a thousand troops from Army C and D had converged on the intersection, the scene of the clash between the two terrorist armies. The territorial dispute had raced out of control and now the leaders from both sides met to establish their boundaries.

Nulla watched from the upstairs window as the leaders sat on stools right on the intersection. Through his binoculars he saw four bound terrorists brought to stand in front of the massed troops.

One of the leaders stood, waved his arms about and gesticulated wildly. Nulla guessed what might be coming next and continued to watch. The Army C leader called out a broad chested man who carried a sword that looked like King Arthur's broadsword, Excalibur.

The prisoners were kicked to the ground and their heads pushed forwards. The executioner stepped forward, and after everyone had bowed their heads in prayer, he proceeded to chop the first two heads off.

The third victim proved a bit more difficult than the first two. It took the strong man three swings before he managed to hack his head so that it too fell to the ground. The last victim refused to cooperate and Nulla watched as the leader ordered a soldier to grab the man and hold him still.

'This is going to get ugly,' thought Nulla.

The victim wouldn't squat down but the enforcer threw him roughly to the ground and pushed his head forward. The executioner stepped back and forth as he readied his sword but had to pull up several times to avoid hitting the enforcer.

The cavalryman zoomed in and watched as the leader gesticulated wildly, his hands flailing the air. In frustration the swordsman swung his sword with enormous force at the struggling victim. To Nulla's horror and amusement the enforcer's head and the victims arm both flopped to the ground. The enforcer's body twitched in his binoculars field of view and he fought not to pull his eyes away. The ex-gangland hit man didn't want to miss this.

The toughened cavalryman watched bemused as he saw the terrorist soldiers rise up in an uproar, waving their arms and weapons in the air. The Revelationist executioner appeared extremely agitated and began hacking at the forth victim who was now trying to stand up. He continued to swing his huge sword until the victim's head finally parted company from his shoulders and rolled towards the crowd. One man kicked it causing a mass of terrorists to leap forward kicking at the severed heads like it was a children's soccer match.

Struggling to keep from laughing, Nulla stayed long enough to watch the terrorist armies paint a line on the intersection to show the boundary, then they dispersed. He breathed a deep sigh knowing that they wouldn't be doing a house search.

He heard a noise from the room Glenda was asleep in and came down the stairs, calling out softly to her. She was awake and called his name in reply. He went into the room where she was sitting with a blanket over her slim figure. One leg was covered by the blanket while she sat examining the other. His breath caught when he saw her, and he felt a fire brand lance through his chest.

Glenda looked up at Nulla with relief and smiled wanly. "Where have you been? I was worried you'd left me alone." His heart melted when he saw the lost look in her eyes.

He coughed nervously. "I just witnessed the official 'drawing of the boundary' ceremony. They won't bother looking for us, they don't know they've spies right in their midst. It was a boundary conflict between the two armies, and it looks like things are back to normal. Except your leg." He pointed at her bandage, conscious that his finger wanted to reach out and touch her.

He jerked up his hand and spoke, "That might be an arterial bleed, so you're staying in that bed for a week before I even think about moving you."

Glenda pouted. "Everything's been going so well too, Nulla. I feel such a loser. Our longest patrol into enemy territory and I go and cut my leg." She looked up at him and grimaced, "At least I don't have to do guard duty for a week."

"Don't you bet on it." He smiled, his perfect teeth shining in the gloom of the darkened room. Glenda felt a little light-headed herself, so she closed her eyes before she blushed and gave her thoughts away.

Nulla spent some time looking for books and anything else to entertain his invalid patient. He then set up one of the beds in the upstairs loft so she could sleep there in greater safety. It took a few hours of careful, quiet maneuvering, but it was done before nightfall. He also found some food on a shelf high up in the pantry with tins of food and packets of dried fruits and nuts. There was even a block of chocolate and a bottle of red wine. How the terrorist's missed that he couldn't imagine.

That evening he set up booby traps at both entry doors. He warned Glenda to be careful if she had to leave the house. Kneeling beside her he told her that he was heading back to their base to plan her rescue. Glenda covered her face with her hands and cried, then begged him to be careful. His heart broke to see her like this but he had no choice.

Nulla bent forward and kissed her on the forehead but as he tried to move back she grasped his shirt and pulled his face to hers. She held him, and in that too-short moment he realised how he'd never experienced such a soft, sensual kiss like this before. Gasping in shock and confusion he pulled away, the taste of her tear-tipped lips locked into his mind.

Staggering back a few paces Nulla mumbled, "I'm, I'm sorry I, I... I better go. I promise I'll be back as soon as I can... I... I..." He fled down the stairs and out the back door. He'd stepped outside dodging the booby traps all in a state of total unconsciousness.

'*Oh shit, what am I going to do?*' Nulla said to himself. He stopped, rebuilt his 'mind palace' of calm, and pulled himself together. Dragging his night vision goggles into place he set his backpack and tightened the straps. His eyes hardened as he focused on getting back to his troopers safely.

There was no moon and it was pitch black. A few blocks before he arrived at their safe house, a patrol drove around a bend and the headlights lit him up. His face snapped towards the light, with cat-like reflexes he melted into the bushes as it drove past.

'*What am I thinking? Get your mind out of your pants, Nulla, and think survival!*' he said to himself. He was angry for thinking thoughts more suited to a stroll in the park on a summer's day. The truck stopped with a squelch of its brakes not ten metres past his position.

'*They must've seen me!*' he realised. The truck crashed its gears and started to back up.

"*Damn!*" he said softly. In a split second he was thinking of the best course of action: kill them all right here, right now, or evade capture. Killing them would bring the entire Army C onto both safe houses and Glenda would be captured for certain. Maybe they'll think they saw a possum or a stray dog? Yes, his best choice was to fade into the background. He turned and quickly scanned the front yard of the house he stood next to. *'Just good enough.'* he thought and scampered off into the bushes at the side of the house.

He stopped and listened, curious to know what the patrol would do. There was yelling coming from beside the truck, so he listened carefully.

"When I give an order I want you to damn well follow it! I told you to stop! You just don't ever listen do you!" The voice grew louder turning into an enraged roar.

A frightened female voice replied, "Sir, I stopped when you told me. I didn't see anything sir, but I did stop, sir."

The first voice continued, his shouts rising higher in pitch. "Bend down and touch your toes!" Then Nulla heard a slap followed by a squeal. It seemed to go on and on. The squeal turned into a sob and then a mix of sobs and screams.

The girl wailed for mercy, "I'm sorry Captain McCarthy. I'm so sorry. I promise I won't disobey you ever again, please stop."

Captain McCarthy's voice grew hoarse as he said, "You know what you need to do to make it up?" There was a pause, "You'd better be quick with it then."

Nulla crept away from the disturbing sounds and found his way back to the safe house. With his mind a mass of confused thoughts he almost stepped on one of the boys booby traps. He stopped immediately when he heard a rapid *'click click'*.

"Boss! Stop! Booby trap in front of you, don't move!" came the firm, whispered order.

Simon stepped from out of the bushes and walked over to Nulla. Also wearing his night vision goggles, he guided Nulla around the traps to the back door, and inside the safe house.

Luke hadn't been able to sleep that first night and he called to Simon in the bed next to him. They both had the same idea and went straight back to the safe house to wait it out. If the terrorists came for them then it was tough luck, they'd fight it out to the death if need be. It was important for them to be there for their friends when they got back, if they got back.

Having now been awake for forty eight hours Nulla collapsed into the lounge chair. He briefly explained the situation as the boys handed him a hot cup of tea. As he was talking he closed his eyes and fell asleep in the middle of his sentence. The cup slipped from his fingers and fell onto the carpet. It happened so suddenly that the boys worried something was wrong. They checked his body for wounds and when satisfied that he was just exhausted, they pulled a blanket over his shoulders and left him. They resumed their guard duty. There was no way they would let their hero down.

Chapter 12

Charlene - back to uni

The dwellers eventually dispersed back to their own homes once they realised that Stacy and Abraham had disappeared, most possibly in the gas explosion. Charlene felt useless, she had nothing to offer her beloved dweller friends, so decided to get back to her psychology studies. But she worried, '*how can I collect a bundle of text books and journals to continue my studies when we live so far from the university?*' she asked herself.

Charlene spoke to Heidi who was all for a visit to the university but knew the logistics of getting there were prohibitive. Rule number one was not to even think about using a vehicle. Terrorists still patrolled the streets. If captured the dwellers knew they would be tortured and would divulge the whereabouts of everybody they loved and cared for.

Tony was visiting for the day with Lucy and Annie. The boys suggested they use their motor bikes. Heidi argued that the problem was the same, noise and visibility. Patrols had dropped off but they were out and about every day and night. She reminded them there were road blocks and hidden listening posts still out on the streets. Heidi reiterated that 'risk' meant not just risk to themselves, but a risk to everyone.

That was the end of the argument, no one ever won an argument with Heidi.

Arthur said that he could ride there in his BMX bike. "Chas, what if I go and bring back some books for you. You know, criminal psychology and those other books you wanted from the library?"

"Arty, that's sweet of you, but I need very specific forensic psychology books and journals. I need to do some special in-depth research, to find out exactly what makes a terrorist tick. Freud said that if you know what motivates someone then you can predict what they'll do next. I need to spend a week or more there. It'll mean a sleepover to explore the library properly. Then I need to bring a lot of those books back here," was Charlene's polite response. "I know you mean well but you'll get lost inside the library. In fact, you might not even find the library once you get there."

"Hey, what about a double?" chimed in Lucy. "I know you can't ride with your crook shoulder, but Arty could double you on his bike."

"Hey yeah, or you could ride in the trolley Phil made." Arthur perked up and his eyes suddenly brightened. "A trail bike would still be my choice. I could get you there and back in a day."

"No! No motor bikes, Arthur! You know the rules. What if you get ambushed or there's a chase? Are you going to put Chas' life on the line for a joy ride?" Heidi wouldn't let up on issues of dweller security. She went quiet for a moment then spoke up forcefully.

"OK, listen-up because this is what we're going to do. We go as a group, the three of us; Arty, Chas and myself. We'll have to let Phil and Fati know, so they don't worry about us missing at the next market day." Heidi stopped talking and looked around at the faces.

Charlene started to believe that Heidi's idea might actually happen. "So we go? How will we get there? It's miles away and we'll need food and water..." Just as she felt positive she drifted back into a depression thinking of just how enormous a task it was.

"We use two BMX's. We'll adapt the trolley Phil made to carry food and water for you, Charlene. It can be done, besides, I'll make it work." Once Heidi made up her mind she always followed it up with action - it had become her trademark. Phil sometimes called her 'Action Heidi'.

A few evenings later, Heidi and Arthur met with the dwellers inside the supermarket. The particular location, inside or outside, changed regularly, and the security whistle Heidi insisted upon, had evolved into clicks mixed with whistles. She hadn't neglected her own studies either and read everything she could get her hands on about military tactics and SAS reconnaissance strategies.

Phil wanted to go with her since he knew the university like the back of his hand, but his wife immediately ruled against it. He was still convalescing and his knee remained swollen and bruised. There was no way she would let him travel across the city on a bike, sleeping in strange houses, and leaving her alone. So he promised to give Heidi a hand-drawn map of the university, and a list of books he wanted her to bring back. He showed her where his office was, and asked if she would bring back the photos on his desk.

They planned to leave in seven days. Arthur was chief scout and would reconnoitre their routes. Tony volunteered to go with Arthur and support him. Heidi had already begun planning the houses they would stay at on their way in, and a separate route back. If all went well it should go off without a hitch.

They were all excited and afraid at the same time. This was going to be like a holiday for the three of them. Charlene had worked hard at copying extra maps and plans from Phil's drawings. She knew the university well enough herself, but she didn't know all the entrances and exits like Phil did. It was important to know from which direction to approach the library in case the capmus was occupied. The last thing they wanted was to travel right across the city, only to find they couldn't get in because the terrorists had occupied part of the campus.

Arthur worked steadily with Phil over the next several days and nights, pulling down and then rebuilding the two BMX bikes. Phil had already built several trolleys that could be towed by hand and bicycle, but this was a special unit for towing Charlene. Phil took great pride in his work and the trolleys performed superbly in their trial runs.

"Why didn't we think of this before, Arty? I must be getting old," said the careworn old man. Arthur was too polite to agree and just smiled as he watched at the meticulous way Phil pulled his BMX wheel bearings out. He packed them in grease and then put them back in. Arthur had never learned a thing from his step-father, so this was all new to him.

Dweller life had become so predictable that anything new was like fresh air to Arthur now. He always asked if he could help and Phil was more than happy to show him how to use his collection of tools at every opportunity.

By Friday they were ready. Heidi had packed enough food that if they were holed up, for any reason, they could survive at least a week. She was meticulous in her planning right down to the clothes they would wear to, from, and inside the university.

They decided against bringing sleeping bags and the plan was to take what bedding they could find in the last house they slept in, right next to the university. If they found the place free of terrorists they would sleep in the library itself, right next to the books Charlene needed. If that was impractical they would create a safe house nearby.

Charlene was excited but she was also very afraid. Even though Arthur and Tony had reconnoitred the route she was filled with dread at the thought of being caught again. Her post traumatic stress flared and she couldn't sleep, she was restless and irritable. The strategies she developed to help her overcome the traumas in the past few months however, helped her remain fixed on her goal. She pushed through her fears and stuck with the plan.

Knowing that travel would be slow, towing the two loaded trolleys, the three adventurers headed off a few hours after sunset. Arthur's specially modified BMX now sported a trolley with a seat for Charlene and loaded with gear. They were all very skinny and Arthur had little difficulty with her extra weight. Heidi brought up the rear with the

BMX pulling another trolley loaded with food and water. It carried more weight than Arthur's and could double up as Charlene's trailer if anything happened to his.

That first night was uneventful. It was hot and humid in what was turning out to be an unusually wet summer in Adelaide. There had been so few patrol sightings that sometimes the dwellers wondered if the Revelationists had given up and gone home. But they knew better than to let their guard down.

That second evening they made good time, finally reaching the outskirts of the university campus by early morning. Arthur broke into the nearby safe house. It was the worst house in the street of beautifully presented homes. At least they would have been beautiful if their owners were still alive to lovingly tend their gardens.

To Heidi this was like going on a camping trip. She excelled in all aspects of survival these days and had the food warmed in a pan, and spoons in everyone's hands within minutes of Arthur lighting the fire. Closely observing Charlene, she saw how her friend suffered from sitting in the trailer for so long. She decided they wouldn't move into the university for another twenty four hours, giving them all time to recover. In the meantime she would send Arthur to reconnoitre inside the university itself.

Arthur pulled out the maps and he struggled through their plans again, but he had trouble remembering things. Heidi made a point of painstakingly going through everything with him until she was sure he understood.

"It's OK Arty, do it later, get some sleep, your eyes are about to fall out of your head. Sleep now, study later." They wrapped themselves in blankets and the three fell asleep, curled up together as their fire burned down to ash.

When Arthur arrived back from his recon trip that night he was very quiet. He looked at Charlene and waited for her to say something.

"And?" asked Charlene impatiently. "Come on, what did you find, tell me?"

"It's been burned. I guess the terrorists don't like books. There are piles of burned books and some of the buildings are burned too." He then looked up, his eyes shining as he pulled out a psychology journal from his jacket front. "But I did find this and others like it. A heap of these magazines all about psychology." His face beamed.

"Wow, thanks," breathed Charlene at last, "but they aren't called 'magazines', they're called 'journals'. Were there many?" she asked, her face beginning to brighten.

"Yes, thousands of them. Rows and rows of these journals and books too," Arthur said with a boyish smile.

Heidi spoke up, "Arthur, how much of the library was destroyed?"

"There's about six floors to the library, the psychology floor wasn't touched, just the bottom ones. Some of the flames must have gone up into the second floor, but the rest were filled with books and these maga..." he paused and corrected himself, "I mean 'journals'."

"That means we can get what we came for, Charlene," said Heidi. "I'll focus on finding Phil's office and collect his belongings. We sure are in luck this time. Woohoo!" It wasn't a scream nor was it a hoot, it was a softly mouthed 'woohoo'. The dwellers were all softly spoken now, often whispering their conversations. It was extremely rare to hear anyone speak at a normal conversational volume.

The next night they moved into the top floor of the university library and began building piles of books and journals. It was Arthur's job to move them into the safe house for transport home later. Heidi scouted out Phil's office and collected a bag of his books and photos. She even took a beautiful bronze Greek statue of 'Chaos and Erebus' that he had sitting on his desk. She noted in her wanderings around the university that most of the buildings remained untouched.

Charlene's mood lifted. She was in her element stacking piles of books on psychopaths, post traumatic stress disorder, terrorism, various forms of psychotherapy, forensic criminology and her favourite psychotherapists Rogers, Jung and Freud. She found journal after journal examining so many interesting things that she just couldn't decide what to keep and what to leave behind.

On the forth afternoon of their adventure a band of terrorists gathered around the duck pond opposite the library. They built an enormous camp fire and began to party. Out of curiosity Heidi and Arthur crept closer to watch. The smell of tobacco and cannabis permeated the stifling heat of the summer afternoon. There were a few hundred revelers drinking and dancing to the loud music coming from one of the trucks.

Around dusk one of the terrorists brought in six meek prisoners who proceeded to cook on the open fire and serve food to the party-goers. Every now and then one of the terrorists would take a prisoner into the back of the truck. As the party warmed up they saw some of the terrorists pair off, lay down on the grass, and make love in front of everybody. It soon turned into an orgy.

Heidi was thinking of her own experiences and turned soberly to Arthur, "I think we might be able to save at least one of those prisoners."

Arthur's eyes widened in fright. He sucked his breath in and gasped at his lover, "No you don't, no way!" He almost shouted. "Not while we have Charlene with us. What if the terrorists search the library? How can we hide Charlene, the bikes and trolleys and the prisoner? No we can't, and no we won't. You keep telling me to practice self control, well, now it's time you practiced some of your own." Arthur was firm and frightened. He knew that once Heidi got something into her head nothing could stop it happening.

"Yeah, I guess you're right." She turned away. "I can't watch this, let's go."

Resigning the prisoners to their fate they crawled backwards into the bushes. The two carefully made their way up to the top floor of the library where their camp was, beside their growing pile of books. Charlene could hear the noise from the party growing louder and was starting to shake violently.

There was a soft 'click click' in the stair well. Charlene snapped herself back to the moment. At first try she failed, but with some effort managed to make three clicks in reply. Heidi saw what was happening to her dear friend, she went over and took her by the hand. She led her out of the corner where she was curled and sat beside her on one of the library benches.

"You saw them too? I want to rescue those prisoners but I can't," said Heidi as she reached over and held Charlene tightly, burying her tearing face in her friend's soft bosom. Charlene shuddered with a mixture of ecstatic joy and emotional exhaustion.

"I know what it's like to be defenceless and afraid." Heidi said lifting her face and looking at her friend. She wiped the tears from her eyes and put her hand to Charlene's face. "I think we should start preparing to leave tonight and head off tomorrow evening. We have a long way to go, and Arthur," she looked at her lover's questioning frown, "you still have to get these books stacked and stored in the safe house. That's going to take forever if these terrorists hang around all night."

Heidi stood, and with heavy heart walked over to the room where they'd set up their living quarters, and began preparing dinner. She needed to keep busy so she wouldn't think of the plight of those poor prisoners.

"Charlene," she called softly. "Make sure you study and learn everything you can about these psychopaths, because one day we just might need that knowledge." With that she put the pierced tins of food into the fire.

Phil loved the bag of goodies Heidi brought back from the university, especially his Greek statue. Fatima insisted the three sleep-over while she made them a special dinner with cup cakes for dessert. She used fresh roasted hazelnuts from the trees that lined the neighbourhood, and eggs from the chickens they kept in a well hidden pen nearby.

While they ate they talked about the state of the university, the library and the prisoners they'd seen. It was a lively conversation and Fatima was the first to say that she would support a rescue attempt.

Heidi spent days working on a suitable argument. She needed to convince the dwellers they should go back to rescue at least one of the prisoners. Although she wanted to blow the terrorists to hell she knew that was stupid, it would just bring retribution down on everyone. But an escaped prisoner was nothing as long as they could make it look like an escape and not an attack. Now she had Phil and Fatima's support she needed to speak with Tony and Lucy. It was Tony that she really wanted on-side to come along with her and Arthur.

A few nights later they all met at the supermarket. Tony and Lucy shared their cigarettes with Arthur as they chatted quietly in the warm midnight air. Lucy struggled to keep Annie awake by talking about the book Heidi had given her. Annie was always more awake during the day than at night and that made the night gathering so awkward for Lucy. Tony carried the burden of going out alone and he sometimes teamed up with Arthur to prowl shopping centres and houses together. It was fortunate that the dwellers got along so well.

Lucy and Tony listened to Heidi's speech of how they might rescue the prisoners. Heidi noticed that Lucy soon became agitated. She asked what would happen if they were caught or killed in the attempt. The teenager explained that she was working on a plan and wouldn't go ahead unless everyone agreed on it.

Tony nodded, he was clearly interested. Lucy remained unconvinced and stone-walled every argument. In the end they agreed to talk about it during their next dinner-date at Phil and Fatima's house.

Charlene rarely went to these shopping centre meetings, the walking and night air took too much out of her. It usually took two, or even three days to recover. Eventually it was Heidi who told her she should stop going. Charlene felt she was letting everyone down. It wasn't until Arthur explained how they lived in fear something might happen to her on these trips, that she nodded in understanding, and agreed it best she stay behind.

It was depressing to be the odd one out, totally dependent on everyone and completely unproductive. That motivated her to work harder with her reading and study of what drove people to become terrorists. She also worked on her own issues and realised that Post Traumatic Stress Disorder was one heck of a nasty disorder. She read everything she could on how to recover. Some of her reading delved into meditation and working with mental imagery but she was often confused by their explanations. If only she could find someone who knew how to heal her mind. She could manage without an arm but controlling her mind was her biggest concern.

The next dinner party was quite a hoot. Tony had found some bottles of green ginger wine and it tasted incredibly horrid. Fatima soon solved the problem by mixing it with some home-made lemonade and it turned into a heavenly elixir. Everyone got slightly drunk. After little Annie fell asleep in front of the fire the conversation turned to discussing the possible success of a rescue mission.

Tony explained that he'd spoken at length to Lucy about going with Heidi and Arthur but she was still uncertain. They then discussed other possibilities and settled on taking extra food and water and storing it in the safe house near the university.

Charlene suggested that she, Lucy and Annie should move in with Phil and Fatima for the duration. The elderly couple were always delighted to have the young folk for company. They had all grown fond of each other over the past months and even warmed to the prickly Lucy.

It was Lucy who had the final say. She was the only one with a child and in the end they deferred to her. If Lucy said no, then it was off the agenda.

Lucy looked carefully at her daughter, then at her husband, and finally at Heidi. It was only then that she spoke. "If we're going to do this I have one condition. Heidi, we all love your drive and enthusiasm but you take too many risks for everyone. You're very run down, look at you, you can barely keep your eyes open and you've lost so much weight. I think you should sit this one out and leave it to the boys. Two is faster and safer than three." She tried to soften the words with her eyes.

Everyone had enormous faith in the dynamic teenager, 'Action Heidi', but Lucy's words made everyone sit back and reflect. They all now turned to look at the young lady, they waited for her to respond.

Heidi sat still for a moment then stood up abruptly, without looking at anyone she walked outside. When she came back a few minutes later they noticed tears had streaked her cheeks.

"I understand Lucy, that's a fair call and I have to agree. OK, let's do it then." But Heidi wasn't ready to release control, oh no. "I suggest we all move some of our belongings in with Phil and Fatima next week. Arthur and I can start bringing supplies across and once we have that done we should all bunk in together to start planning and training. All in favour of action as soon as we're ready, please raise your hands." They all raised their hands, even Lucy.

It was mid morning. The two dweller scouts had seen her on several occasions since they'd made their way to the university a few nights ago. They'd done their preparation well; reconnoitred the grounds and stocked their safe house with food and water. Now they were ready for stage two; establishing contact with one of the prisoners.

It was quite easy. The young woman usually collected a stack of firewood and took it to a truck on the other side of the campus. The boys had followed her twice before and knew every move she would make. None of the guards ever bothered to watch her and so the scouts felt it was safe to talk to her from the cover of the bushes. The guards were always listening to music, smoking, drinking or sleeping.

"Psst, psst!" called Tony to the girl. "Hey, walk over here so we can speak to you."

The girl saw them among the bushes. Looking over her shoulder to check the guards she slowly walked towards them. The emaciated girl pretended to drop her bundle of firewood. As she bent down to pick them up, only a few paces from Tony and Arthur, she spoke quickly.

"What do you want?" she said in a frightened whisper. "You'd better just get away from here or they'll catch you and torture you." The girl was covered in scabs and sores, as skinny as an ice addict and twice as dirty.

"Tell us when the terrorists are holding their next party here because that's when we can rescue you and your friends," whispered Tony, leaning closer to her.

"What?" she asked her eyes lifting incredulously. "Rescue us? Are you crazy? We'll just die. There's no food out there and besides they'd just hunt us down. We're better off staying here with them."

"But... we have a small group of survivors and we'll look after you." He couldn't believe what he'd just heard. Tony's voice reflected his disappointment when she didn't jump at the chance to escape. The two young men looked at each other wondering what was wrong with this girl.

"I don't think any of the others will want to escape either. We're cared for well enough as long as we do as we're told. You should go back to where you came from. Go away, it's dangerous here." She finished collecting her sticks and straightened up.

Tony called out to her as she walked away, "We'll be here tomorrow, same time, same place. If you change your mind, be here."

The boys looked at each other as they silently made their way back to the safe house. Once inside the scouts discussed what to do if the prisoners refused to leave with them. It had never entered anyone's mind that the prisoners would want to endure such horrid conditions.

Neither had noticed the guard walking towards the girl to stare beyond her at the bushes where the two had hidden.

Chapter 13

Nulla - love nest

He woke up late in the afternoon confused but in a heightened state of awareness. After a wash, some food and a chat with the boys, he settled down and prepared to be reunited with Glenda.

He invited them to make suggestions on how to bring her back to their safe house. The boys thought they should all go and camp there for the duration, but Nulla vetoed that. He was confident they could now cope by themselves, and he praised them for being so efficient.

Going outside into the bright sunlight he checked the booby traps. He told them they were set as professionally as any cavalry trooper would have done. The boys beamed with pride and he told them to leave some of the booby traps set permanently.

Given the terrorist patrol may have seen him last night he planned on an alternative route back to Glenda. He told the boys to just sit tight and he would bring her back on the fifth night. If he wasn't back then they should go and find him. Nulla gave a description and the address then showed the best route to take on their street map. He also instructed them to set their CB back up and make sure the batteries were fully charged from their solar charger.

They needed more up to date data on Army C movements and details of their conversations. The terrorists now controlled most of the city of Adelaide. He also instructed them to set up the long antennae again and try to re-establish contact with Charlie in Sydney. Charlie transmitted quite regularly on news from Sydney since the 'apocalypse' as the boys called it. They were instructed to practice their Morse code too.

Nulla placed great confidence in his boys knowing they'd be careful in their communications with 'Sydney Charlie'. They had been busy screening all HF and UHF channels for traffic before the terrorist incident and Nulla wanted them to resume monitoring. The boys set up a roster to do four hour shifts, twenty four hours a day, until he returned.

The powerfully built aboriginal warrior stepped out with a loaded pack of food, water and his weapons. The first quarter moon was yet to rise and he wanted to be deep into his trip before it did. He knew the moon rose two hours later every evening so he should get there before it was up. He also noticed that the weather was turning cool and he expected rain.

Luke escorted him part of the way and set up a mini safe house over the rest of that evening, about a kilometre into the journey. A safety measure that Nulla said wasn't necessary, but the boys insisted. Privately, Nulla was pleased they were using their initiative and pushed him when they believed they were right.

He waved to Luke as he stepped back into the pitch black night, his night vision goggles set squarely on his head, and his Steyr in his hands. Nulla's step had a spring to it and he started to hum an old love song from his childhood,

'*The Girl From Ipanema*'. Straight away he stopped and shut his mind back down.

He rebuilt his state of calm. '*Focus, you love sick fool,*' he told himself. '*The last time you did that you almost got yourself killed.*' Chuckling to himself he settled down on his journey and arrived well before dawn.

Checking the signs around the house he was satisfied that no terrorists had snooped about while he was gone. With a quickening heart he stepped into the kitchen and whistled the code for 'coming in'. Then he called out to Glenda just in case she was waiting with her AK47. Unloading his pack from his tired shoulders he put the food in the kitchen and the first aid kit in the downstairs lounge room.

Glenda limped to the top of the stairs and called softly down to him. "Nulla, come on up here and say 'hello'. Don't force me to go down there, don't make me stop the car."

His skin tingled at the sound of her voice. He felt more alive than he remembered in his whole life. "I'll be up there in a minute Glenda, once I've made some breakfast and set security. Go back to bed and be a good patient." He tried to be gruff but to his own ears his voice sounded like a love-struck teenager.

With the breakfast fry'up finally done he turned off the camp-cooker just as it began to rain. The clouds had built up through the night and the storm broke soon after sunrise. He wiped the splatter of oil from Glenda's plate of powdered eggs and mashed potato fritters. Then he poured UHT milk, which he'd found at the very back of the cupboard, into

Glenda's cup of tea. His feet tried to run the other way and he nearly tripped as he walked up the stairs as he carried the tray of food.

"Glenda?" he whispered her name softly.

She was wide awake and rubbing her eyes as she sat up waiting for her handsome rescuer. With a squeal of delight she saw her cup of milk tea. "Milk, real milk!"

Setting the tray down on her lap he watched her eat. "You must be starved," he said watching her shovel the food into her mouth with her fork.

"Wouldn't you be if you hadn't eaten real food in nearly three days? Those fruit bars aren't a meal by any stretch of the imagination," Glenda said through a mouthful of food. She slowed a little and with a twinkle in her eye said, "Come on, big boy, you eat too. You can't just sit and watch me eat, that's cruel. You must be just as starved as I am."

He picked up his spoon self-consciously and did as he was told.

After breakfast Nulla set about removing her old bandage and checked the wound. The castor oil seemed to have done its job. There was no inflammation or infection and the deep cut was beginning to heal nicely.

"Looks like mum's remedies really work," he mused. Gently he rubbed more oil around the wound, careful to avoid rubbing too vigorously, then he put a clean bandage on. It was a nasty injury and Nulla told her that they wouldn't know if the glass had missed vital tendons and ligaments until she could put some weight on it. He explained that he had no idea how long it would take before she was ready to make the trip back to their safe-house.

If it wasn't for the pain of her wound and the pressure bandage Glenda would be having the time of her life. Here she lay with a handsome hero of a man, sitting beside her, waiting on her like a devoted puppy. She'd only been with a few men in her life and they had been wealthy, intellectual types. A real he-man was something she never thought she would relish as she did right now.

Two long and lonely nights was enough for Glenda to think seriously about her life: where she had been and where she was heading. She didn't know if she would still be alive this time next year. Even though everyone considered her an independent type, she knew it was just a cover, she was all mush inside. Glenda desperately wanted someone to hold and protect her.

Those first few days were a horror, watching her boyfriend dying in agony sent her into a panic. Then an incredibly handsome man arrived and gave her a reason to live. Over the weeks together she realised he gave her hope, not just of survival, but hope of love. It was very obvious to her that Nulla was different. He never said a bad word to anyone, and was always bright and cheery. Nulla behaved like a gentleman, intelligent and considerate of her and those pesky teenagers. The way he carried her and tended her wound did it for her. An urgent desire for love entered her heart the night he had to leave and it now struck like Eros' arrow. She didn't want it to fall out, ever. She now realised that Nulla meant everything to her.

When Glenda finally acknowledged what she really felt inside, she began to worry. All the time he was gone, ridiculous thoughts raced through her mind, his body pierced by bullets or strung up on a rope. She saw him poisoned and shot and... it made those waiting hours a misery. But when she heard his whistle, everything felt right again.

After breakfast Nulla slept the morning away, she could now hear him moving downstairs. Glenda decided it time they talked. She was becoming agitated and needed to know if he wanted her as much as she wanted him.

"Nulla?" she called in a soft voice. "Nulla?" she repeated a few seconds later.

"Yes?" he replied, she could hear his footsteps running on the stairs. "Is everything OK? Do you need something?"

The rain began to fall heavily on the shed roof outside the window, the noise as soothing as a tropical waterfall. A clash of thunder followed and Glenda shivered. "Sit here, next to me, hold me, please." She stared up into his eyes and with the next thunderclap she reached out to him. Nulla bent down, gently easing himself beside her, unsure.

Glenda held him close pulling him down so that he leaned over her. They held each other as the storm grew wilder, then their lips met. She moaned softly and her fingers reached upwards to stroke his face. Her sensual fingers grasped the back of his head pulling him to her each time he went to move away.

The hardened warrior managed to free himself for a moment and asked, "Are you sure about this Glenda? I've fallen so hard for you and I don't want to ruin this." She just reached up and pulled him back down. Another thunderclap and the rain smashed furiously on the tin roof in a roaring torrent of sound.

"Just be quiet and make love to me you fool," she groaned into his ear.

They made love all afternoon while the storm raged outside. To Glenda it felt like a dream. The rain, the thunder and the love making all blended into one. There remained just one problem, her leg. It got in the way of everything. Every time she moved, her leg moved, and she would moan from the pain. Nulla, never quite sure if it was pleasure or pain, would stop and wait for her.

Their love-making stopped at almost every moan. Glenda would have to sit up and rearrange the position of her leg again and again. It was perhaps the longest lovemaking session since Adam discovered the pleasures of Eve.

"Love, it's getting late. I'm going to run a patrol around the house. You stay here and I'll whistle as usual. Keep your rifle beside you." Nulla got up and propped the pillows under Glenda's head so that she could hold her assault rifle easily. He leaned forward and kissed her, a long slow kiss. She pulled at him but he resisted. "Not now my love, I have soldiering to do. I'll be back in an hour."

It rained all day and well into the night. Nulla waited for full dark before pulling on his night vision goggles and camouflaged poncho. He didn't mind the rain, where he came from rain was a novelty and he never got bored with it. When his mates saw him watching the rain they would jibe him for being a desert bunny. But he loved being different, and he loved the rain.

He crept out the back door and around the side of the house. Then he made a sweep of the four houses either side and across the road. It was a good excuse to get outside and think, to get his mind back to reality and out of the dangerous fantasy of love.

His mind went to Glenda, there was no way he would let her out on another patrol now. Her leg wound would probably put her out of action for months anyway. If she were ever in peril he wouldn't be able to make rational decisions, and that could get them all killed.

It was a hard decision to make but once he made it, he felt better. He climbed into the house opposite and rolled a cigarette. Listening to the rain fall outside he entered his mind palace and let his mind dwell on the situation by itself.

'No more patrols for Glenda then, but what will she want to do?' he pondered. 'She could do the cooking and prepare each patrol's equipment and routes perhaps. Hmm, maybe she'd like to learn Morse code and manage the CB listening post?'

He wasn't all that convinced though and kept mulling over what he would say to her. 'She won't be happy, but she's now a liability and I wouldn't be able to live if *something happened to her.*' Stubbing out his cigarette under the lounge chair, he considered Glenda's safety. '*I have no choice and neither does she, I need to take her off the front line.*'

Nulla, satisfied with his decision, stood up - just as a four-wheel drive rolled past the window.

'*Damn! Terrorists!*' he said to himself. He ran out of the front door and closed it behind him. He watched as the vehicle continued down the street. It stopped only a half dozen houses past where they were holed up. A small group of men and women climbed out. They walked through the front gate and into the house. A gust of wind carried their voices and he thought he recognised one of them.

Looking through his night vision scope he zoomed in and saw that they were dressed in the usual terrorist uniform of black shirt, but some now wore a black bandanna with the same white writing. It seemed to be a thing that had taken off with them recently. He kept watch. When he saw they might be staying inside the house he raced back to their safe-house and in through the back door.

He gave the code of warning and called out, "Glenda, it's Nulla, I'm coming up, don't shoot me." He leaped the stairs two at a time.

Glenda was sitting up in bed but this time she held the AK47 in her lap. "What's up big boy, baddies?"

"Yes, a few houses down the street, same side as us. We might be in for some visitors. I think one of them is that same psycho captain I saw earlier. My guess is they're up to no good. This guy is a sadist, he likes to dish out pain. I don't think they're doing a house to house search though, not in this rain. It's probably more like a party or something." Nulla spoke fast, his breathing deep and his voice was tense.

Glenda noticed the raindrops on his face and put her hand out to touch them. He looked at her and a smile formed on his lips. "Haven't you had enough, madam? Goodness, our lives are on the line and all you can think of is lovemaking." In reply she chuckled deep in her throat. Nulla felt strangely aroused. "I'd better go outside and check on them, they won't be expecting any visitors in this rain."

"Nulla, are you sure that's safe? Shouldn't we just sit tight and wait it out?" Concern showed in her voice and he looked at her and smiled again.

He cupped her face in his dark hand. In the dim light it contrasted nicely he thought. "It's all right, I have a license to do this remember? My tribe bred fierce warriors for thousands of years. We feasted on terrorists before your people crawled out of their caves. I know what I'm doing, I graduated basic training too you know." He laughed lightly, he was enjoying himself again. "Glenda, my love, I'll be careful. If they see me I'll just kill them all and hide the evidence - gangster style."

The rain didn't let up so Nulla picked his time, in the middle of a heavy downpour, to slide like a shadow up to the side of the house. He didn't expect to meet any of them outside, but just in case, he held his knife at the ready.

Creeping along the side of the house, he saw light coming from one of the windows. Peering inside he saw them all stripped naked in front of a roaring fire. Two were engaged in sex while the others were drinking and smoking, relaxing on the lounge. Nulla couldn't tell which one was the psycho captain. He stayed there watching to make sure they were just doing the orgy thing.

Just as he decided to creep back to the safe house he noticed one of them stand up to grab a burning stick from the fire. The big man ordered the two seated on the lounge to grab the couple making love on the floor. Laughing he jabbed the one on top with the burning brand. The young man cried out in alarm then tried to stand up.

'That must be the captain, it sounds like him,' Nulla thought.

The captain kicked the young man in the side and jabbed him again. Nulla saw smoke rise from the man's flesh. The young man screamed and received another kick from the captain. He doubled over but the two holding him dragged him back to splay him immobile on the floor. The captain picked up another red hot stick and began to burn patterns in the man's back, smiling delightedly at the young man's screams and sobs.

Losing interest in making patterns the psychopath captain held the burning end near the man's rectum. The screams renewed afresh and Nulla decided that he'd seen enough and withdrew.

'Strewth, that bloke's a fucking maniac. I need to get Glenda back to the safe house, this location is now compromised. They could just as easily have chosen Glenda's safe house,' Nulla mused to himself as he worked his way quietly back to Glenda.

He decided to tell her everything at once, about his love and his concerns for her. Nulla told her he didn't want her exposed to lunatics like the captain and he wouldn't let her go on patrol any more.

"I can't think straight knowing you might be in danger, Glenda." He finished by telling her of what he'd just witnessed.

"We sure picked a bad place to have our honeymoon." she giggled. "I can't walk so we'll need transport of some sort. What about a bike or a wheel barrow. Lordy, a wheelbarrow, what am I thinking?" Glenda frowned and the lines on her forehead stood out. "Love, I don't care much for patrolling anyway. I only wanted to come along to be near you, silly." She looked up at him and smiled, her face lit up and Nulla thought of how lucky he was.

"I'm just as happy cooking as listening to the CB as doing anything else. If I can't walk on patrol then so be it, at least I'm better off than that poor terrorist just up the street. Give me a job, but first, get me out of here."

The rain stopped early the next morning and they made plans in between their lovemaking. Nulla visited the party house, the vehicle was gone and the house empty. He wondered what happened to the tortured terrorist. He didn't like the terrorists, they were the enemy, but he didn't like torture either. If he had been on patrol with the boys they would have stepped in and exterminated them all and hidden the vehicle. The current risk to his lover was far too great to have even considered doing that.

Over lunch they discussed how to get her back to the safe house with Luke and Simon's help. "Why don't you go and bring the boys back here. The next night we can head back on bikes or something. What do you think?"

"Night travel has been safe so far." Nulla put his hand to his face and rubbed at his eyes, the thought of another trip to the safe house and back again wasn't a pleasant one. "Righto, I'll get the boys to create two safe houses on two different routes, that way if we get pushed across by patrols we have a good chance of hiding in one of them." It hadn't rained all day and the sun shone bright and hot. The bright rays of sunshine brought hope of a better future. "I'll leave this evening, I don't like to do it, I really don't want to leave you again. I'm going to miss you, you know."

He left that night and surprised the boys when he arrived just before dawn. They made him some food and a hot cup of black tea, just as he liked it. Nulla didn't feel like talking but he wanted to explain his plan, asking the boys to think about it for him. Then he crawled off to bed.

While he slept Simon suggested they put together a couple of bikes. "Luke, what sort of bike is easy for a one-legged woman?"

"Hmm, a one-legged woman you say? What about a one wheeled wheelbarrow, like a trailer? Turn it back to front and tie it with rope, that might work," he replied.

"Yeah, it might, good idea Doctor Einstein." Simon started to draw on the note pad while Luke looked over his shoulder.

"Yes, that's it, I think we could manage it. But we better set up those two safe houses first and while we're at it we look for bikes, pumps, tools and wheelbarrows. It'll need to be light-weight though, a plastic one, not one of those heavy concrete wheelbarrows."

"What if a patrol comes around the corner while we're pulling Glenda in the wheelbarrow? We'll get caught like we're taking a dump in the middle of the road," said Simon.

"We just have to take that chance. Besides, isn't that our job, close quarter combat, to protect civilians?" replied Luke soberly.

They worked out the safest routes and suitable safe houses. Next they discussed transport and they eventually agreed on using Simon's drawing as the model. Nulla said he needed to get back to Glenda that night and they would be responsible for all the preparations and to make the trailer.

"No worries, boss," said Simon, "my dad was a welder and we made billy carts and all sorts of weird bikes, this'll be a piece of cake."

Looking at Simon in surprise Nulla thought, 'This fellow has the confidence of Gandhi and he might even pull it off.'

"Righto, let's get on to it. Today we plan, this evening you boys go out looking for materials. Stay away from the main road, but this hardware store here, should have wheelbarrows or trolleys of some sort. You'll probably find bikes in people's garages too. And no Hollywood stunts," he finished with his usual admonishment.

"Boss, we know where some bikes are, this house here." He indicated a nearby street on the map. "We've been eyeing them off for ages. Simon and I sometimes go over there and do tricks. We are teenagers you know." Luke shrugged and gave a disarming smile.

"OK, bring them back here, you can work in our garage, and make sure you practice the wheelbarrow thing with one of you inside, to iron out any problems. It has to be perfect at fast speeds. We don't want to get caught with our pants down," said Nulla.

"Is that like being caught doing a dump in the middle of the road?" asked Luke, turning an innocent face to Simon.

That night everyone had their jobs to do. Nulla went on his trek back to Glenda, fearful that something might have happened while he was gone. Simon and Luke brought back two BMX's and a mountain bike for Nulla. Then they planned their trip to the hardware store for the following evening. They would work at modifying the trailer during the days and then set up the two safe houses during the nights.

Nulla knew he'd given his young troops an enormous task but knew they wouldn't fail him. He trusted them implicitly now.

His plan of moving into the city to raise an army of civilians was a failure. None of them had seen neither hair nor hide of a civilian since they'd arrived.

As he stalked his way back to Glenda it began to rain again. It didn't stop him planning his next move, to get out of this God-forsaken city. He decided to find a safe place where he and Glenda could raise a family.

Just then a tremendous explosion broke his concentration, through the mist of light rain he saw a ball of flame leap into the night sky not too far away. He set his mental compass to accurately record the direction it came from.

Nulla's face brightened, '*There might be a resistance out there after all, we just haven't been able to find them. Maybe Captain Ridge's plan for a resistance will turn into a reality after all.*'

That morning Glenda and Nulla spoke of their plans to raise a family as far from the terrorists as possible. Over breakfast Nulla told her he wanted a few weeks to do a proper reconnoitre of the region where he saw the ball of flame. He felt sure that if he could find the resistance group they could all escape the city together. Nulla finished his tea, lay back in his lovers arms and collapsed into an exhausted sleep.

It only took a few days for the boys to manufacture the bike trailer and to set up the safe houses. Just after midnight Nulla was shaken awake by Glenda. "Darling, the boys are here, I just heard their whistle."

Nulla jumped out of bed, quickly pulled on some clothing and whistled his warning reply. They already knew about his booby traps but he wanted to remind them to be careful. With his Steyr at the ready he leaped down the stairs and waited in the dark. He sat at the bottom of the stairs with his weapon and night vision goggles.

"Hey, boss." The boys also wore their night vision goggles and they clasped hands as they met.

"I see you managed to avoid my booby traps. Righto, set up in there," Nulla patted them on the back and pointed to a spare room, he then went to make some tea and get them some food. "How long did it take you to get here?" he called over his shoulder.

"We left about three hours ago and rode like maniacs. We did the ambush thing every quarter hour," reported Simon. "We put the bikes in the shed like you said, all's clear outside. We did a patrol when we arrived and we saw zero enemy from the time we left safe-house base."

"Good work, boys," called Glenda from the top of the stairs. She was now dressed and bottom-crawled down to the lounge where they sat around a glowing candle. It was still dark in the early hours of the morning and she needed the hot black tea to wake herself up.

"I've almost given up worrying about real milk when we ran out," she said a little too cheerily for a pre-dawn cuppa. "If you boys ever find some UHT milk, I will love you forever."

Simon gave Luke a nudge and they giggled like school kids. Their giggling increased when they saw Nulla holding Glenda's hand in the dark.

"Today we sleep. I'll stay guard till dawn, then Luke you take over, Simon four hours later. We'll eat all we can before dark and clean this place up before we leave. We head out at midnight." Nulla stopped then said, "Did you boys hear an explosion a few nights ago just north of here? The night I left home base. About 2 am, there was an explosion and a huge fire ball."

Simon shook his head. "We could have been at the hardware store about that time working on the trailer. We decided to build it there because that's where all the equipment and tools were. We had fun too, collected heaps of stuff we brought back to the house."

"But we did hear a lot of CB chatter about the explosion when we got back," added Luke. "Apparently a whole patrol was killed and they said they'd shot up some civilians next to it. They talked about it for a few days but nothing much after that."

Simon then said, "By the way boss, we're sure you wouldn't mind but we found some remote control helicopters and we've been trying to fit an infra-red camera on them. We've been experimenting to see if we could use them at night as a new way to patrol. We raided a few stores near the warehouse and have lots of spare parts. It's a good project for us bored teenagers, it might work too."

Nulla looked at them. "Nice work Mr Wright, you pair amaze me with your ingenuity. Yeah, it might work. Righto, keep working on it just don't fly during the day and always have someone on watch. It's bed time for now. Simon, you're first watch at dawn. Good night, sleep tight." Nulla helped

Glenda back up the stairs. After a lingering kiss good night he went back downstairs telling the boys to stop giggling and to get some sleep.

He poked his head into their bedroom and called to them, "Don't force me to 'you know what'."

Pulling out his tobacco pouch he rolled a cigarette then sat in the lounge to finish his cup of tea. Smoking in silence for a while he steadied his thinking. *'So much to plan and prepare for,'* he thought then headed outside to do a tour of the grounds.

Chapter 14

Charlene - Arthur's fight

The next morning Tony and Arthur considered the possible scenarios of what might happen when they met with the prisoners. Arthur suggested they go early and spy out the ground but only one of them should make the contact. They both had the same concern; what if the girl told the guards? It was an uncomfortable thought but it had to be considered.

They were very conscious that they didn't have any weapons. It was agreed upon many months ago that using weapons would only draw down the wrath of the terrorists and cost them all their lives. It was better to exist side by side like this than be hunted down and exterminated. Fatima had argued that the moment they used guns the entire terrorist force would be directed against them. But right now the two felt completely naked without a weapon, not even a knife.

Tony wanted to make the contact but Arthur explained that if he was caught then Annie would lose her father. Tony considered for a moment then slowly nodded his head, that put a stop to the disagreement. Arthur was to make contact while Tony was to observe. They would place their BMX's at hands reach and they had three escape routes worked out with three possible safe houses to go to. If their plan went to hell then they were as prepared as they could be. 'Heidi would be proud,' thought Arthur.

It was mid morning as Arthur lay stealthily hiding in the bushes near the duck pond. Tony observed him fifty metres away from a little bush covered hillock. He used his high magnification binoculars and swept the area for signs of danger.

As Arthur settled himself among the bushes a canvas covered truck appeared on the grassy lawn in front of the administration block. There was a loud roar while the truck jerked for a few metres as though the driver had slipped in the clutch but couldn't find the right gear. It then picked up speed and made towards him bounding on the uneven surface.

'Holy shit!' thought Arthur, 'I'm in for it now!' He leaped to his feet and raced for his BMX oblivious to the terrorist's shouts. Arthur didn't care if they saw him, he had one thought in his mind – to get out of there. At the same time Tony saw the truck and did the same thing. He hoped that the two of them heading in different directions would disorient the terrorists and give Arthur a little more chance of escape.

The young girl was pushed from the truck and fell painfully on her knees. At the same time a squad of terrorists jumped out and ran towards the escaping BMX's. Three of the terrorists had the sense to raise their rifles, took aim at Arthur's back, and fired.

Arthur felt a bullet whip past his head and another hit the back wheel of his bike. He was just starting to pick up speed when it slewed to the side and spilled him to the ground. He tumbled to his feet, leaped up and began to run.

There was a building ahead and he thought he just might make it. He could feel his heart beating right up in his throat.

Dodging from side to side like he'd seen on TV, Arthur had only a metre to go before he put the building between himself and the rifle fire. Four more terrorists joined the three already firing and a burst of automatic fire knocked Arthur to the ground - he fell face-first into the dirt.

Tony heard the gunfire and knew that his friend was in serious trouble. The escape plan was to never to go back to rescue if the other is hit. The survivor must get back to the safe house as soon as they could with the bad news.

But Tony was in two minds. 'Should I go back and try to help my friend or should I warn the others?' He thought of his wife and daughter and that was enough to convince him of the wisdom of their original plan. He slid off his BMX and grabbed his emergency escape pack, he was on his way home within seconds. Tony knew he had a minuscule window of time to get away from the house before the terrorists started their road patrols.

Arthur was in considerable pain. When the bullet hit his leg he thought the truck had knocked him over. With tears of pain pouring from his eyes and limiting his vision he limped into the nearest building. Holding his hand to his leg he felt blood gushing through his splayed fingers. He realised he was bleeding furiously and he had to try and stop it. The thought of leaving a trail of blood for the terrorists to follow was at the front of his mind. Ripping the cotton jacket off his back he tied it tightly around his thigh. The bleeding slowed and he began to hobble as fast as he could along the corridor.

The terrorists hadn't bothered to chase him too actively. They saw where he entered and they went to both front and back entrances, and simply waited. Their captain dragged the girl by the hair along with him. She went meekly hoping to be rewarded but became increasingly anxious with each twist of her hair.

"Thought to get away did he, idiot! He's either in a room on this floor or one of the others, no rush men. Light up a joint and pass me one. Anyone got a drink?" Captain McCarthy was an old hand at hunting down and torturing 'house rats', he wanted to stretch this one out.

McCarthy hadn't had a prisoner tortured for weeks and was relishing the chase. To make it more enjoyable it was a house rat, they usually screamed and pleaded for mercy better than his own men. How he loved to play with them. When he heard the term, 'like a cat playing with a mouse' it described exactly how he enjoyed it. Teasing, promises then more teasing. Sometimes he made them do something stupid and he would promise to let them go free. But a moment later he'd come back and change his mind. McCarthy was becoming aroused at the thought, he looked at the girl at his feet considering whether he might use her before they cornered the house rat.

Just at that moment one of his men raced up with a marijuana joint and he inhaled deeply. He forgot about his urge and thought instead on what he would do with the prisoner.

"OK men, lock and load, lets make this slow and smooth. I don't want him hurt and I don't want it over with too quickly. If you see him don't approach too closely, come and get me. Anyone who disobeys will be my bitch for the week." His men knew what that meant and there was zero chance of anyone disobeying Captain McCarthy, the hero who captured the 1st Armoured Cavalry, zero chance.

By this time Arthur had looked into most of the first floor rooms and saw nowhere to hide or escape. He sobbed as he heard the laughter of the terrorists outside and knew there was very little time. His leg was dragging now and bleeding through his cotton jacket bandage. He had left a trail that even a blind man could follow. Arthur decided that if he were caught he would undo the rough bandage and let himself bleed to death.

The next door revealed a large industrial science laboratory and he decided that this was where he would make his stand, if he could call it a stand. The dwellers had always talked about either escaping or dying quickly and Arthur had already seen how the terrorists torture their prisoners. As he was looking into the back room of the lab he noticed a grill set in the floor just wide enough for a man to squeeze through.

The room stank of something bad but Arthur was too preoccupied to process the smell. He was skinny but strongly built from all the manual work he did. Lifting the grill he climbed inside but there was no bottom nor rungs to stand on. He let himself down further but still no bottom. Realising he had no choice he just let go and fell.

He landed in a pool of water, it was a large drainage pipe. It smelt really bad so he stuffed the corner of his T-shirt into his mouth and breathed through it. The smell was suffocating. His leg was burning but he had a glimmer of hope now and started to crawl along the tunnel. That horrible smell was getting worse and his eyes stung so badly that he could hardly see for the tears. It finally registered, it smelled just like a toilet.

'*That's methane,*' he remembered from his science lessons. Science was the only subject he enjoyed and he always paid attention when he bothered to attend. '*This must connect to the sewers,*' he thought to himself. '*And methane's highly flammable. Oh shit, what if they drop a grenade in here, the whole sewer will explode and me with it.*'

Just as he dropped into the larger pipe the terrorists entered the building. Some were stoned and most were laughing, pushing and shoving each other like teenagers. One accidentally fired a burst from his AK47 and bullets whined along the corridor.

"What damn idiot did that?" screamed Captain McCarthy. "Sergeant, put that man under arrest and send him back to the truck. He's my bitch for the week."

His sergeant grabbed the stoned, shocked soldier by the shoulders and shook him till his rifle fell to the floor. He told another to take him back to the truck and make sure he didn't run away. The teenager was now sobbing with fear. McCarthy was well known for the cruel treatment of his bitches. He enjoyed orgies and liked it both ways, especially the wild and painful ways. McCarthy had an enormous appetite for other people's suffering, it turned him on.

Arthur crawled as fast as his bleeding leg would allow. He knew that when they followed his blood trail they would find the open grill and throw grenades into the tunnel. Even if they threw one in the wrong direction the shrapnel would rip him apart and the concussion would shatter his inner organs. He didn't want to think about the fireball. It was imperative that he get to a pipe junction quick, really quick.

"Hey, Captain McCarthy, over here! I can see blood." called one of the terrorists, a pimply youth who bobbed his head in obeisance as he spoke.

"Well? Follow it you idiot, but go slowly and not too closely. If you see him call out and I'll come up." The captain pulled at his joint then tossed the butt on the floor. He sat down on one of the classroom stools. "Corporal Layla, give me your joint!" The captain fondled her breasts while she handed over her joint. He was becoming aroused again as he got closer to his victim.

Arthur thought the pipe would never end. His vision was starting to fade and his strength was leaving him. The smell was overpowering and he now struggled to breathe.

His leg was useless and it dragged behind him, he knew he needed help soon. He could only expect to bleed to death, suffocate or the terrorists would grenade him. Arthur felt his mind wandering and so deliberately stopped thinking. Instead he focused on putting his good leg forward and his weight on his hands. One pace forward, one pace forward...

"Captain, he's gone down a hole in the floor!" called the head-nodding terrorist. His Adam's Apple bobbed up and down as he swallowed, terrified he may have done something wrong.

"OK, I'm on my way but I bet he's just hiding, these tunnels go nowhere." McCarthy was excited, he rubbed his groin with his free hand, things were getting interesting.

He looked at Corporal Layla then the filthy girl at his feet but decided against it. Torturing and raping the trapped house rat would be much more fun than rutting these bush pigs, he thought. Army C, Captain McCarthy, stood up and sauntered slowly towards the sound of his troops.

He stood above the hole and looked in. "Pew! It sure stinks in here. Hey, you idiots! I can't see a blasted thing! I need light! Someone get me a lighter!" he ordered.

He felt a lighter thrust into his hand. Standing over the smelly hole he flicked the flint wheel to ignite it.

Light, Arthur finally saw light at the end of the pipe. His brain swam in the filthy air and he started to believe he would make it out of there alive. A glimmer of hope sparked inside his mind just as a spark ignited the highly flammable methane in the laboratory.

With an enormous WHOOOSH he was blown out of the end of the pipe and into a rushing torrent of water below. Months earlier the mains water pipe had broken and continued to rush into the unused sewer pipes. There was no fresh sewerage but enough methane to fuel a minor explosion. The erosion hole Arthur fell into was fresh water. The terrorists had maintained water pressure throughout most of the city to flush out the poisoned water. They were now using the city water supply.

It was cold and he was numb and sore all over. The flames had burned his hair and clothing. If he hadn't fallen into the water he might have been burned alive. He was barely alive as it was. Arthur floated for a moment then the cold hit him and he came back to the present. Floating on his back he came to an open concrete channel and eventually to a rusted ladder. He held on to catch his breath, and, feeling like death itself, he painfully pulled himself out.

As he emerged from the storm water channel he noticed that one of the university buildings was smoking and people on fire. He was too dazed and shocked to even think why that was a good thing, but he instinctively smiled.

"Fuck me," he groaned, "I knew they'd grenade me." Then he noticed his lack of clothing, the burns on his arms and then he felt his face. *'I'm pretty badly burned, eh.'*

Then he felt his numb leg and it wouldn't move. Memories flashed of the tunnel, the BMX crashing into the dirt, the pain as he was hit by rifle fire. It all came back to him and he realised that he really was in serious trouble.

Arthur began crawling towards the houses opposite. Any house would be better than being out in the open where the terrorists would easily find him. The front door was open to the first house he came to and he gratefully crawled in.

Unusual sounds broke into his mind as he drifted in and out of consciousness over the following hours. He woke some time later to find himself naked and lying on the floor of a strange house. Next to him were two dead bodies long mummified, their insides eaten by maggots. It smelled of death so he crawled towards where he expected the bedrooms would be. His body was starting to shake uncontrollably and his leg still bled a little.

He crawled into the nearest bedroom and through the rubbish on the floor. He saw a single bed butted against the wall. It was neatly made so he dragged himself in and fell asleep. His sleep was as quiet and still as the bodies in the other room.

It was two days before Arthur could move. The first thing he did was put on the clothes that were lying on the floor. They smelled of mold and it made him nauseous but he didn't really care. He looked at his skin and his leg, he was a mess with scabs everywhere. His burned back, scrotum and buttocks hurt like hell and his leg was a mass of bruising and dried blood.

Arthur fashioned a bandage from the sheets and wrapped his leg. The pain was staggering. His leg was so swollen that the skin was 'as tight as a mummified corpse' he thought to himself. Every movement tore open many of the hundreds of scabs and they would start bleeding again. The wounds opened and wept all over his clothes. He felt disgusting, itchy and dirty.

He found a tin of peaches in a cupboard and it tasted better than anything he'd ever eaten in his life. The juice moistened his mouth and he drank it greedily. There was a fish pond in the backyard and he drank the water from that.

The sugary meal gave him energy and lifted his spirits. He started to think positively, *'maybe I'll survive long enough to get back to Heidi?'*

Later, lying in his bed he thought, *'I need to get to the safe house and see if Tony's left a note or something. I need the supplies and I need to set up a signal for him.'*

His mind was starting to work analytically just as Heidi had taught him. Arthur was a willing student when Heidi was the teacher. Thinking of Heidi made him emotional but drove him to work out what he needed to do. It was two days since he fell into the tunnel and was blown out again and he hadn't seen or heard any terrorist activity. Perhaps the terrorists chasing him had all died and no one knew he'd survived the explosion.

He felt his leg wound and explored the entry hole in his thigh and its exit wound near his knee. The bullet had travelled right through his leg, no wonder it hurt, he thought. Feeling around for more wounds he didn't find any. He knew that blood poisoning from dirt, cloth or other material stuck inside his wound, would kill him. A clean wound was essential for survival.

He found some disinfectant and various creams in the bathroom cupboard. There was enough water to wash and keep his wound free of puss while he dressed it with fresh bandages. Despite the pain he tried to move his lame leg gently but gave up trying to do his own physiotherapy after he passed out. After that first proper cleaning his leg was so stiff and swollen that he feared he had more bullets in there, but by the end of the day the inflammation had reduced considerably.

His burns, though not as severe as he first feared, irritated more than anything. He itched all over as the scabs fell off and new skin covered his buttocks, legs, back and head.

That night he felt well enough to make his way to the safe house he and Tony had shared a week or more earlier. It was only a few blocks away. Tony's backpack was gone but everything else was there. Arthur went straight to the food and water cache and had a wonderful meal of tinned food. Given his situation he didn't know when he might be forced to hide again and knew that building his strength was a priority. He didn't like the idea of dying hungry or thirsty.

Arthur spent the rest of the night in front of his small fire. Processing his situation the way Heidi had taught him, he decided to stay put and give himself time to heal. It was a two day bike ride to get home and in his condition he would be vulnerable all the way. If he came across a patrol they would easily capture or kill him. He didn't relish the thought of being shot again.

'Besides,' he thought, 'how can I peddle a bike with just one leg? Those terrorists have crippled me just like they did to Charlene.'

He placed a small stone on top of a brick at the front and back steps. It was unobtrusive and anyone seeing it would walk right past. But to the trained observer it was a sign to say he was there. This was the signal Heidi and the two scouts had agreed upon in situations like this. While he waited Arthur carefully divided his food and water into daily allotments, he knew he might be there for quite a long time.

It rained on and off for the first half of summer and water filled a shallow children's swimming pool in the backyard next door. Not trusting the city water Arthur spent part of each day collecting water and putting it into the empty bottles he found. He also collected last years dried fruit lying on the ground and those still hanging on the trees in the neglected back yard. There was enough extra food and water for him to survive for a few weeks longer. He knew he needed a long time for his leg to be in any condition to ride home.

Venturing out to search the other houses for food was a no go. The best he could do was hobble and a hobble wouldn't save him if a patrol came around the corner. Going through backyards would mean climbing fences which would open his leg wound, so he didn't. Fortunately there was plenty of firewood to burn from the wood shed - the fire was good company when he was feeling miserable and alone.

His burns healed quickly. The fact he went head-first into deep, cold water, saved him from debilitating third degree burns.

'*I'll keep my boyish good looks,*' he cheerfully thought to himself as he checked himself in the bathroom mirror.

The best part of each day was spent reading. For a young man who truanted from school and avoided books like they were a disease, he soon become fascinated with the books he found. Reading everything he could find, he discovered an amazing world of fantasy he never knew existed. There were dozens of books on animals, dinosaurs and children's literature. He even found a fascinating collection of books on Australian history and fiction in the lounge room. Some days he just lay in bed to read, only getting up to go to the toilet or eat.

The hot summer days passed slowly, his wounds healed and his strength was returning. Still, no one had come to rescue him, and he began to worry.

Chapter 15

Charlene - Tony's torment

While Arthur was in hiding, the arrival of Tony put the dwellers in a spin.

Heidi asked him a million questions then made the sober decision to move house. Tony had only taken a single night and part of the morning to ride home. Phil suggested that perhaps Arthur had escaped to safety. He didn't want to verbalise the other possibility.

Phil also advocated that, just in case, they should immediately debunk to the safe house that only Heidi knew of. They started preparing that very morning. As soon as evening arrived they began dragging their trolleys loaded with food and belongings to their new home.

Tony was devastated, perhaps more so than any of them. He was never one to make friends easily yet he and Arthur had developed a strong and enduring friendship. They had grown especially close during their time on reconnaissance. There was also a destructive sense of betrayal. He'd betrayed his best friend by allowing him to walk into the ambush, it should have been him. He shouldn't have left Arty when he rode away, and when he heard the shots fired he should have gone back. Tony felt he should have waited to see if his friend had escaped and needed help... he should have, should have, should have...

Every night Tony lay awake going over every item in his mind. He saw, as clear as day, exactly how he should have done things so that his best friend would still be with them. He became hollow-eyed and morose. Lucy endured his long periods of silence. He wouldn't communicate with her, he'd just sit staring into space. She was worried and so was everyone else.

Charlene was worried too, she decided to step up to the mark and take him under her wing. Having lived with her own depression she thought she might be able to help him. Perhaps some of the things she'd learned in her books from the university would work. They began to sit together and talk softly in the evening by the fire. Tony spent a lot of time crying on her good shoulder.

Lucy was becoming a little concerned about the amount of time they spent together, and their shared intimacy. She feared they might get just a little too close. Charlene was a stunning young lady all of twenty years old, blond haired and single. Lucy was in her early thirties and the trauma had done nothing to improve her looks, she thought. Before things got out of hand she needed to talk to Charlene.

The following morning Lucy walked over to Charlene sitting alone, outside in the screened back patio. She sat beside her on the bench seat, her face unreadable. "Charlene, I need to ask you something... but I feel very uncomfortable talking about it."

"I think I know what you're going to say, I've watched you staring at me and Tony." Through her own trauma Charlene had become quite intuitive and knew that this conversation had to happen, eventually.

Charlene decided to take the initiative. "I like Tony, he's so gentle, but I'm just not that interested in men. I, I think I'm a lesbian, Lucy. I think I love Heidi, but I could never tell her."

She looked into Lucy's confused brown eyes and continued, "Please, can you keep that to yourself, just between us?" Charlene smiled and shifted her frozen left arm, it made her appear so vulnerable.

'*You are so beautiful,*' Lucy thought, '*but I had no idea you might be a lesbian.*'

"I didn't know, Chas, I'm so sorry for being jealous. You're so young and pretty... and I thought... your secret's safe with me." Lucy set her shoulders square and moved the conversation to safer ground. "So, how is Tony going, do you have any ideas on how I might help him?" The conversation now shifted to psychotherapy, Charlene's favourite subject.

"I think he has 'Survivors Guilt', it happens when someone survives a tragedy but everyone else is killed or wounded. I guess in some ways we all have it. I know I feel guilty for living, well so does Tony. He's also lost his best friend. He and Arty got on really well and now he's alone except for you and Annie. He carries an enormous amount of guilt for leaving Arthur behind. Tony needs a lot of love, hugs and time to heal. I don't know what else though." Charlene waited for Lucy's reaction.

Lucy sat there listening and taking it all in. "I think I understand. And you're right, we all feel guilty. But now that Tony's lost his best friend, how do I heal all that? So hugs, hmm," said Lucy, almost to herself.

"You can't do it all yourself, Lucy, he has to heal himself too. That's what the great psychotherapists did. We just provide the space for him to heal and that space is our friendship and understanding," Charlene said. "Another thing is that he has to go back to find Arthur. But he can't do that until we've all agreed. And we need to wait for Heidi to find herself too, she's as lost as Tony, only she won't show it. I'm worried about her."

Lucy stood up, in her mind a plan was forming. "I think I should go and talk to Heidi. Not about you, of course, but about finding out what's happened to Arthur. It seems that nobody's going to heal until this muddled mess is sorted." The two girls went in search of Heidi.

It was nearly two weeks since Tony returned home alone and everyone was becoming depressed, irritable and restless. The thought of a two day trip back to the university was overwhelming, so they kept holding off discussing it. They were grieving too, and mindful that Tony and Heidi needed to come back from the dark place they were in.

The three girls sat around the fireplace that evening after everyone else had fallen asleep. They quietly chatted about food supplies, water and how everyone was feeling. Finally the conversation turned towards what they really wanted to talk about, finding Arthur.

Charlene blushed and automatically covered her face when Heidi asked her if she would sit closer, and keep her back warm. It was past midnight and chilly in the large house. Now that she'd told Lucy her secret she was extremely self-conscious. She shifted closer and reveled in the warmth radiating from Heidi's body.

"We need to go and check. I've had this dream nearly every night that he's in a safe house waiting for us. He keeps telling me not to worry. It's weird and driving me crazy. Am I crazy do you think?" Heidi asked her two friends.

"Not at all, Heidi, Tony said he never saw him shot, he'd just heard the gunfire and then an explosion. If he was wounded that would explain why he hasn't shown up. He's probably in a safe house somewhere just like your dream showed you," was Lucy's delicate reply.

Lucy knew that this was a sensitive moment, Heidi hadn't said anything before about looking for Arthur. She'd normally clam up when people tried to talk about it. Something had shifted and now Action Heidi seemed to be back with them.

"I think we should try to find him the night after next, that gives us time to prepare. I'll go alone if no one else wants to come with me, but I hope Tony will." Heidi looked at Lucy, her eyes moist and tears ran down her cheeks. "I want him back." She began to sob.

Charlene's heart was flipping back and forth between wanting Heidi single and wanting her happy. She said, "Heidi, I'd go with you but I can't ride a BMX. I'm sorry I'm so useless, just when you need me." She meant it.

In a daze Charlene's finger tips gently touched Heidi's cheek and traced the tears down to her red lips. When she noticed what she was doing she quickly pulled them away and blushed.

Lucy saw it and quickly spoke up, "I'll speak to Tony, I have a feeling he's ready. What's your feeling about it, Charlene, you've spent more time with him talking about this than any of us?" Lucy turned her face to Charlene as she spoke. The firelight played around her gaunt face and prominent cheek bones. Charlene thought Lucy was fabulous just then, and gave a heartfelt smile to her friend for rescuing her.

She reflected for a moment and replied, "Yes, I think he is. The past few times we spoke he didn't go over the same ground over and over like he usually does. He was more positive and mentioned that he wanted to go back. He didn't say when but he is starting to think about it. That's got to be a good sign, doesn't it?"

The girls stopped talking, the silence dragged on and finally Lucy said she was turning in. She grabbed her sleeping bag from the corner of the room and climbed inside. Lucy snuggled up close to her daughter and Fatima on the mattresses in front of the fireplace.

The only two left awake were Charlene and Heidi. Heidi put an arm around Charlene's shoulders mindful not to squeeze too firmly.

"You know what, you've been so wonderful to me since you saved me. I could never have asked for a better friend. You came into my life at my lowest point and stood by me, supporting every silly little idea I've had. Not once have you said 'no' or 'don't' or 'did you consider', not once. Please

Charlene, don't ever leave me." Heidi kissed her gently on the lips then went off to find her own sleeping bag.

Charlene sat still, silently relishing Heidi's kiss, her warmth lingered on her shoulder. She stayed seated enjoying the warmth of that special moment, even fantasising that she was Heidi's lover. Charlene cherished every moment like this, storing these memories safely for when she might need them.

The next day Heidi, Lucy and Charlene called a meeting. Heidi brought up their plan of the night before and the dwellers each had their say. No one said they shouldn't go but there was a lot of discussion about how to go about it.

One of the topics was how much water to take. Did the water in the pipes still carry poison? Would there be enough fresh rain water lying in ponds and water tanks? Was it safe to drink? Charlene reminded them to take their iodine and sodium chlorite tablets to purify the rain water of bacteria and parasites.

Phil said he would prepare the spare bikes and make sure they were running just right. He'd even made carry bags for them out of the leather he'd cut from a neighbour's expensive lounge chairs.

It was Heidi who approached the difficult point of who would go with her, and there was only one, Tony, and everyone knew it.

"Tony, you haven't said anything yet. I need to know what you think because I really need you to come with me.

There's only you and me and I'll go alone if I have to, but I want you to be my partner on this. I need you."

He looked at everyone in the group as they sat under the spreading shade of the apricot tree in the back yard. "I know I need to go but I'm frightened of what I'll find. If I see Arthur..." he stopped talking and choked back a sob. "If we don't find Arty alive I don't know how I'll cope." He sat back and wiped his face with the back of his hand. "Yes, I am going, it's my responsibility and he's the best friend I've ever had." He finally said what he'd wanted to say.

"If I can say something you might all think weird, I've been dreaming about Arthur since Tony got back. I keep seeing him in a safe house wrapped in bandages. It breaks my heart every time and I just couldn't bring myself to accept it. I've felt paralysed with fear all this time but now I'm ready, we go tomorrow night." She stood up and walked inside. She busied herself making tea and coffee for everybody then came back out.

After she handed out refreshments Phil said he could get the bikes ready for tonight if she wanted. Fatima smiled and added that she had the food packed and Tony said he was ready to go now. Heidi stopped and looked at them. What wonderful people they were, she thought, and burst into tears.

"Tonight it is then," she sobbed and hugged everyone.

"Mum, what's daddy and Heidi crying for?" Annie asked from half way up the apricot tree. "Is everything all right?"

"Hush, darling, daddy and Heidi are going to find Arthur and bring him back. That's all," soothed Lucy.

"Oh, OK. Daddy! Will you bring me back some Phantom comics please? I've read them all twice and it's getting boring." Annie climbed higher. "And tell Arthur to bring back some more books too. I want to finish the Famous Five series. Tell him to look a bit harder this time because he's always forgetting."

That evening the dwellers prepared to say their goodbyes not knowing whether they would even return. Phil promised to keep a lookout at the crossroads safe house. He said he would prepare the halfway house for their return and stay there by himself for the next two weeks. There were tears and best wishes and the two set off on their BMX's complete with new leather carry bags and loaded back packs.

This was Tony's forth trip, two had been recon and one was the real thing. He was lost in thought as he guided Heidi along the secret route that led, for the most part, through forested pathways and parkland.

They made good time and holed up for the night at the midway safe house where Phil would be staying. When they left the next evening Heidi made a signal for Phil. It was the curtain folded across the window as though the wind had blown it. It told everyone who knew the code that all was safe inside and that they had been undisturbed by patrols.

It was almost dawn when they arrived at the final destination, the safe house Tony and Arthur had stayed in. It was the one they expected Arthur to use if he was wounded.

Both Heidi and Tony were nervous. Tony's stomach was so knotted that he almost threw up. They pushed their bikes quietly under bushes a street away and came in on foot. They made sure they were twenty metres apart, Tony insisted he take the lead. He said that it was he that left Arthur behind, and he should be the one to find out what had happened to him. Heidi understood and let him go first.

Tony saw the stone and the brick as soon as he stepped into the front yard. It was a full moon and no sign of patrols or anything else to cause concern. He went back to the pathway and signaled to Heidi that all was fine. She ran up silently on the balls of her feet.

"Tweet tweet tweet." Tony let out three low whistles and waited. He did it again and they both trembled in anticipation.

"Let's go inside," said Heidi, barely able to stop herself from leaping forward and running in through the door.

"I'll lead, follow me." Tony took her by the hand and led her to the back door. They were as silent as the night itself, no one could fault their stalking skills that night.

Tony opened the screen door and whistled again. He did it one more time before he opened the back door. It was pitch black, all the curtains and blinds were drawn and no moonlight entered the house. He crept up the hallway to the bedrooms with his taped torch and peeked in. He signaled

Heidi to wait while he went into the lounge room where they had shared their meals.

There he found Arthur, curled up on the floor sound asleep.

Arthur jerked awake in terror when he saw two blackened figures calling his name. He leaped into the air and came down with a crash as the blankets caught around his legs. He let out a yelp of pain.

"Arthur!" cried Heidi and ran to him, holding him tightly. Her camouflaged face paint wiped off on the soft, fluffy stubble of his chin. Arthur struggled then calmed down once he woke to the fact this was his partner and the other was Tony. He was overwhelmed and joined Heidi and Tony in crying, laughing and hugging.

They spent the next hour talking and catching up on the events of the past weeks. They looked at Arthur's back and leg and he was pleased to hear that it looked to be healing cleanly. The skin on his back had some red among the growing patches of pale new skin. Eventually the party quieted and they wrapped their blankets around themselves. Heidi held Arthur in her grasp and wouldn't let him go, not even in sleep.

Tony shook them awake just after midday. "Danger!" he whispered. "A foot patrol's coming down the path, it looks like they're doing a search, we might be in big trouble." He was panting. He'd been outside on the camouflaged shed roof as lookout when he spied the patrol.

"Grab a backpack each, put it on, put on your boots Arty. We might have to fight this one out. There is no way they are going to take us." With that Tony put on his own backpack then grabbed a heavy wooden tomato stake in his hand. He stood by the doorway out of sight.

"Heidi, we don't have much time, get Arthur into the kitchen. Hopefully they'll split off into each house one by one, we should be able to take this first terrorist. Then we run for it over the back fence."

Tony was in control now. Heidi understood that he knew the area better than she did and remained silent, following his instructions without question. Tony was acting like an urban warrior, she thought admiringly.

The terrorist had his AK47 rifle on his shoulder and was obviously bored. He had an mp3 playing in his ears and was chewing gum. He kicked the front door in and entered. He didn't even bother holding his rifle at the ready he just looked into the lounge room and was about to leave again when he stopped and gasped.

"Well I'll be damned!" he said out loud when he saw the bandages and clothing strewn around the floor. He trembled as he noticed the smoking fire against the brick wall and other signs of occupation. "Hey! You rats living here, come out where I can see you. I won't hurt you." He spoke firmly as he began to swing his rifle off his shoulder.

Tony struck swiftly and brought his wooden stake down on the rifleman's head with a single killing stroke. The terrorist dropped like he'd been hit by Thor's mighty hammer.

"We are in deep shit folks," said Tony and called the others to him. "I'm taking this AK47, it should give us a bit of a chance against them if we get cornered."

Tony stripped the body of everything he could and put the two spare ammunition magazines into his trouser pockets. "We'd better head out the back, now. Follow me."

Chapter 16

Charlene - Tony's last stand

They crept out of the house and towards the back fence following Tony. He locked his hands together and helped Heidi over, then Arthur. There were yells and calls now coming from inside the house as the terrorists found the body of their mate. Their victim's partner, Corporal Warren, had stopped to relieve himself in the bushes before entering.

Warren called for his squad to gather around him. He was excited and relished the opportunity for a rat-hunt. It had been months since they'd caught any 'house rats'. He was so excited that he felt the need to pee again.

"Get your butts here, we have house rats and they've killed Crazy Rick." The squad of eight gathered together in the front yard of the house and the squad leader set his plans. "We form two squads. Steve, you take Harrison, Lana and Tenny, clear this house then go through the back yard and over the back fence, that's the most likely direction they've taken. I'll run around the block with the rest and see if they cross the road. Then we go from house to house. You enter, we cover, then switch about. Remember your house clearing routines. We're going to have some fun!"

Corporal Warren continued hurriedly, he wanted to make sure his troop did it properly because it was his ass on the line if they lost the rats.

"If you see them, engage immediately, don't wait for us to come up. They'll probably try to escape once you open fire. They have Crazy Rick's assault rifle so expect return fire. It's unlikely they'll try an ambush. If they do we'll surround them. Whichever team takes them down wins a bottle of the captain's whiskey." His eyes glinted as he took his three soldiers and exited through the front door.

Tony wanted to make the safe house three streets further towards the river so he raced his group across the street and into the yard beyond. They heard rifle fire and bullets whined off the brick fence beside them.

"Get yourselves to the safe house, the one where we hid the bikes. Go, go now. I'll stay and give you time," said Tony soberly.

"No! Tony, no!" whispered Heidi forcefully but she saw he was firm. They were compromised and the rules were to separate and run. Arthur needed her to support him, so she grabbed his arm as they ran to the back fence and over it.

They heard more gunfire, then a ripping burst from immediately behind them, that was Tony, she thought. Heidi kept her head and despite her tears she focused on leading her wounded man to safety.

Tony saw four figures running across the street and let rip a burst of automatic rifle fire. He'd been in the army cadets in high school and remembered firing an aged, World War Two, Lee Enfield .303 rifle, but this was the real thing.

He felt fantastic, thoroughly enjoying the feel and vibration when he fired the AK47 back at those who had taken so much of life's joy from him.

He dived into the front yard and took position behind the brick retaining wall. Bullets flew over his head. When he looked up he saw four enemy running towards him so he aimed and fired another short burst. One went down screaming, hit in the chest, the others ran behind cover.

'Gee whiz, this thing is magic!' He smiled and fired another burst at the house and saw pieces of concrete and brick flying into the air.

The second terrorist team had raced around the block a few seconds behind the first when the fighting started. They were now right in the middle of the street. Tony was about to fire a third burst at the brick house when he saw them.

'I don't believe it, another mob and right in my kill zone!' he said to himself.

The fire from his captured AK47 hit the second team mid flight and it looked like he hit every one of them. They were only ten metres from Tony and he couldn't miss. His weapon clicked empty so he reloaded with the magazine in his pocket. He was very aware that he only had one spare magazine left.

He leaped across a side fence and into the front yard two houses down. He turned as he heard a burst of automatic fire zipping around him. Looking back he saw a figure squirming on the street, and although wounded none of the terrorists stopped to help him.

'Damn, I only got one.' Tony swore to himself and fired again but this time through the bushes.

There was a loud scream and he knew he'd hit someone. Next came a stream of abuse and he laughed, he was enjoying himself for the first time in… heck, he had to think. The only word he could come up with right then was, *'ages'*.

He saw three enemy trying to get around the house so he fired at them. Bullets whined off the concrete walls. One then ran across the yard on the other side of the road, he fired but missed, hitting the bushes to send small branches and leaves flying. His second magazine was done and as he put in the last clip a dread filled him. He violently pushed it aside to uncover the elation he had earlier.

'I'm finally getting my own back at these bastards,' he thought and smiled.

It was becoming a little uncomfortable for the terrorists too so they pulled back and rested on their heels behind cover. Corporal Warren sent one of his squad back to the intersection to find reinforcements and bring them to him. They waited, but meanwhile Tony extracted himself and entered one of the houses. He dearly wished he had more ammunition and his goal now was to ambush someone and take theirs.

He went up the stairs of the two story house which overlooked the exact position where the squad were resting. Tony saw one of them hand out his cigarettes and planned how he could take them out – and their ammunition.

'Bugger it, I'll just open fire and kill the lot of them, race down and take what I want. I'll make this a rolling brawl if that's what they want.'

The window was broken and he simply leaned his weapon against the frame, sighted and then he pulled the trigger. To his absolute amazement his bullets hit their mark and knocked three of the enemy over and the rest scattered. A wailing cry broke out from one of the wounded, it made the hair on his head stand up.

'*Time to run and get that ammo before they regroup. They won't expect it,*' he said to himself, enjoying the thrill like it was an adventure.

It was only a matter of seconds before he reached the three dead and dying terrorists. He looked around the corner to see if the others were about and heard them talking and arguing loudly.

"No! You will damn-well do what I say! It's only one bloody civilian, you pathetic jerks. Now get your arses back there and push forward!" came the corporal's harsh voice.

Tony knew he only had seconds to spare. He sped to the bodies and pulled off two ammunition belts of AK47 ammunition. The one still crying struggled, trying to stop him and grabbed at his ankle. Tony absently kicked him in the head.

Grabbing the ammunition belts he felt a strange rush of pleasure through his body. It was almost sexual and his feet barely touched the ground as he raced back to his previous position.

Once back inside he had to stop, calm down and think strategically. '*Darn it, come on think! It's not about shooting it's about hit and run. Pull yourself together!*' He almost spoke out loud he was so frustrated. '*Think!*'

Looking around he knew he had to draw the enemy away from Arty and Heidi, he had to keep them occupied for as long as he could. The best way was to find somewhere that was easily defended and had an escape route. That was it, he thought, get back outside and find a brick wall and a pathway to the back of a house and into the next street, always heading away from the safe-house his friends were heading for.

To his right, further down the street, he could see the perfect assault position. Jumping over the side fence he dived behind the wall, just as the terrorists were reinforced and opened fire. Bullets sprayed around him hitting the bricks and the trees above. Leaves and branches fell and the automatic fire intensified, forcing him to lie down in desperation.

'Damn it, I think I'm screwed now.' He cast about looking for an exit and decided to crawl backwards to the side of the house. The gunfire didn't stop or reduce in intensity, it kept coming. What he didn't see was the terrorist squad running up the street towards him under covering fire of their reinforcements. By the time they could fire into his position, Tony had disappeared.

By now Tony had lost his feeling of joy. He was frightened and perspiration dripped off his forehead and into his eyes. He flicked his head to dislodge the drops from his vision, then wiped his arm across his face. He'd doubled up to come in behind the terrorists providing covering fire, he now crept to the back of the house where he had collected the ammunition. His heart thumped heavily inside his chest, he knew he might soon die.

As he crept past the three bodies he saw more terrorists with their backs turned looking at something.

'Darn perfect,' he thought, 'this is just damn perfect!' He opened fire with two short bursts from his assault rifle. The terrorists fell in a heap, they were so close there was no way he could have missed. The fire brought two others into range as they ran back to see what had happened.

"You bloody idiots," he whispered to himself and cut those two down as well. His enthusiasm was cut short when another squad opened fire from behind him. The enemy fire was from long range and although it didn't hit him, bullets spattered the house he was standing next to, frightening him. He raced at top speed back to where he had initiated the contact doing a complete circuit of the battlefield.

Tony now squatted beside two bloodied bodies, reloaded and waited for the terrorist reinforcements to move into range.

And they did, carefully creeping around the edge of the house where they had last seen him standing. Tony opened fire and took out another two but it also gave his position away to the squad further down the road. Now he was trapped, pinned between the two squads.

He reloaded his weapon quickly, feeling the hot barrel and mused that he had missed his calling. This was fun, he should have joined the infantry. The enemy now realised that this single house-rat had made mince-meat of their platoon, and they were feeling it, having lost over half their troops.

There was movement in the bushes beside Tony and he put a burst of fire into it. There were screams and the slap of footsteps on concrete as he heard people running away.

A burst of fire now ripped back at him from those same bushes.

'That's stupid of me not moving away', he thought, just as a bullet hit him in the neck. He smacked to the ground from its force and his weapon was knocked from his numbed fingers.

Tony put his hand to his neck and felt the blood spurting into his palm. In slow motion he reached out for the AK47 and chambered a round, ready. Just as he sat up he noticed two terrorists step onto the grassy yard right in front of him. He fired a full magazine into them, cutting them both down just as they looked up.

"Take that, you pricks," he gurgled painfully as his weapon clicked empty.

Tony's head spun, he felt dizzy and he spat out a mouthful of blood. The concussive shock of the bullet had burst a blood vessel in his throat, he started to choke on the blood pooling in his mouth. He managed to stand up swaying badly just as three terrorists stepped into his blurred field of vision.

"You bastards." Tony struggled even to whisper, he groaned as he tried to raise his assault rifle.

His perspective then shifted and everything blurred into slow motion. Tony felt calm, there was no more pain as he watched the terrorist's bullets ripping into his chest from somewhere outside his body. With fascination he saw his eyes turn upwards and his body shudder as it fell backwards slamming into the ground.

The noise of the gunfire went on and on. The screams and yells made it sound like a battle of two mighty armies. The firing built to a crescendo then suddenly stopped.

An excited voice called out, "Cease fire! Cease fire! We got him! He's as dead as a maggot! Come and have a look, guys!"

Heidi broke into an uncontrollable sobbing while Arthur stood in shock, his body started to shake and tears welled up into his eyes.

The thought of going home without Tony was too much to bear as they staggered to the safe house. They knew they had to keep moving, but they were so distraught that they felt powerless to move. Finally Arthur pushed Heidi up and told her they needed to save themselves. Now that the dwellers had used weapons against them there was bound to be a house to house search. They needed to get away as fast and as far as possible.

Arthur tried but he found it impossible to ride the bike. They had to leave them under the bushes and hope they wouldn't be found. If they were, then the terrorists would know there was more than one rat and continue searching till they found them. As it was the evidence in the house showed one dweller. But would they bother to check Tony's body for wounds to see if the bandages were his? Probably not, but they couldn't chance it.

As they staggered through the park, overgrown with wattle and bracken fern, they heard the roar of heavy trucks.

The two tried to move faster but Arthur's leg and fitness weren't up to it. Eventually they came to the river, swollen after the rains of the past weeks. Heidi looked down at the water then at Arthur. The sounds of screaming vehicles was getting closer. They searched the water for a suitable tree or branch, a log, anything. Arthur pointed out a thatch of bushes, logs and rubbish all stuck together, floating towards them.

"Get into the water, Arthur, that's our only chance." Heidi pushed him and went straight in after him. The sound of trucks pulling up filled her ears as she dragged herself and then Arthur under the mess of branches and leaves.

"Captain McCarthy," called one of his NCO's, "one of my men saw something moving over there towards the river. Should I take my troop and investigate, sir?" asked the newly promoted Sergeant Warren.

Prudently he had sent another of his troop to sound the alarm and alert his captain. This meant another opportunity for McCarthy's chance of promotion. The more violence the more chance of moving up towards his goal, the top position as head of Army C. He'd lost twelve from his company, proof of the ferocity of the enemy he had to face.

With an impulsive flick of his hand he promoted his corporal on the spot for killing their first house-rat in months, and for raising his popularity with the soldiers. McCarthy was already revered as a hero for taking out the Armoured Cavalry in Adelaide; then for leading the fight against an imagined enemy commando in the science laboratory at the university. Now this was another opportunity, McCarthy was in a great mood.

"Nah, they're in those houses, man, take the platoon and start your house to house search protocols. Don't forget, whoever kills the next rat gets my other bottle of scotch," wheezed the captain. His face was a mass of burn welts and he had no hair on his head. Some of his fingers had fused together.

'You look like a damn sea monster,' thought Sergeant Warren, trying not to stare at his captain's molten face.

"Yes, sir!" he snapped into a perfect salute. He ran off roaring at his platoon to form and sorted them into squads to search the houses along the river bank.

Captain McCarthy coughed into his silk handkerchief. He saw blood spots there but ignored them. This had happened ever since the explosion. He'd just spent several weeks in the terrorist hospital, along with many of his platoon. They took every spare bed and were worshiped as heroes by the rest of the terrorist army, no one spoke of the lie.

McCarthy told his superiors of a vicious running battle with a platoon of enemy commandos, of how they'd been caught in the explosion which exterminated their enemy.

He'd hoped for a promotion to major but the general of Army C refused to promote a man with a melted penis. The three star general had quoted a verse from the Bible: *'No one who is emasculated or has his male organ cut off shall enter the assembly of the Lord.'* That was that, McCarthy was told he would never be promoted again.

Captain McCarthy had plans for his superiors though. *'It won't be long before I'll be running Army Charlie. I'll lead a coup and take it from you. Laugh while you can general, laugh while you can.'* He formed an image of the general and a small dog, in his mind's eye. Then he watched in fascination as the image devolved into the kind of torture he would like to inflict on his beloved leader. He became excited thinking about it and called huskily for his driver.

Unbeknown to the swarming terrorists, a pile of floating trash and bushes passed by, and two pairs of frightened eyes stared up at the captain.

Arthur and Heidi spent days sitting around debriefing with Phil in the half way house. They were both exhausted and severely traumatised, afraid to tell Lucy the bad news. The pair felt guilty that they had lived at the cost of their dear friend's life. Phil finally convinced them to go home and break the sad news to everyone.

"If you want me to, I'll tell Lucy. I'll call a meeting and break the news, but the moment they see just the two of you they'll all know. In fact by your absence right now they'll probably fear you're all dead. Let's not make things any worse than they are. Just get it over with. I'll be there to support you. Tony is a hero and you both did no wrong, remember that."

That night Heidi rode one of the bikes they'd put in the safe house while Phil and Arthur walked as best they could. It was slow but Heidi kept watch over the two invalids checking every street crossing well before the two got there. She kept riding back to hover by their side like a guardian angel.

As they approached their sprawling new home Heidi felt dread clutching at her heart. She had a moment of panic as she put her travelling gear into the shed next to Arthur's. With Phil in the lead they gave their arrival signal and walked in through the back door.

It wasn't easy, but Phil, true to his word, said what had to be said. He mentioned that Tony had sacrificed his own life for Arthur and Heidi, for all of them. Although they had no idea how many terrorists he'd killed, they were certain, given the amount of gunfire and screams, he had killed quite a few to save his friend's lives.

Lucy was a mess but tried to be brave. She had Annie to care for and tried to busy her grief away. She smothered Annie in love and wouldn't let her out of her sight. Charlene felt it badly, in some ways she believed it was her fault for agreeing that Tony should go with Heidi. There was a battle inside her head that went on and on, it made her feel miserable and useless. Every time she tried to talk to Lucy or Heidi they would make excuses and leave her sitting by herself. This made her feel even worse.

Arthur wanted to talk though, and when she wasn't sitting with Phil or Fatima, Charlene found herself talking with him.

They were all affected by the loss of Tony. Not only was he a good friend, father and husband he was also an invaluable worker. It now placed the burden of the heavy work on Arthur and the girls. Arthur was still very malnourished and as weak as a kitten, convalescing, just like Phil.

A few evenings later Heidi went out on her own. She was mindful of patrols in case the terrorists were searching in their quarter. They'd run out of soap and toothpaste and this was just a simple house raid. One of the nearby houses must have belonged to a hoarder because bathroom supplies of all kinds littered the house. Shelves, cupboards and even the floors were covered in boxes of shampoo, soap, toothpaste, toothbrushes and anything to do with cleanliness. The dwellers always went there for their toiletries.

It was just after midnight when Heidi headed back home to their new house. The dwellers no longer had separate houses. They now cherished companionship which outweighed their need for privacy and personal space.

Ever mindful of being followed, Heidi kept to the shadows. Even when the moon was behind a cloud she would huddle into the bushes and behind fences. Stealth had become a way of life and her reading taught her useful techniques that she incorporated into her nightly trips.

When she was only three houses away from home she stopped and glanced backwards. Her accelerated sixth sense worked overtime on these outings, this time she was sure she was being followed. The feeling was so strong it was tapping her on the shoulder. The last thing Heidi wanted was a stranger turning their world upside down. After what happened with Arthur and Tony, she wouldn't let it happen again.

She closed the back door softly and slipped into the firelight with her pack of supplies. When she spoke everyone stopped what they were doing to stare open mouthed at her.

"I'm not sure, but it's possible I was followed. It could be a dweller from another area looking for food, or it could be a Crusader. Arthur, grab the baseball bat, we need to prepare for a house invasion." Heidi tried to remain calm but her voice betrayed her fears.

Phil and Lucy were talking with Annie while Fatima was in the kitchen with Charlene. It was their usual pre-dawn cook-up and breakfast. They dropped what they were doing and stalled, they stood in shock, not knowing what to do. The tension escalated to fever pitch in a split second.

There was a rustle in the bushes beside the house and Charlene screamed. It tried to grow from silence into a high pitched shriek. The dwellers knew to keep quiet, it was how they survived, and Charlene struggled with all her might to silence herself. Pitched into a blind panic she grabbed her jumper and stuffed it into her mouth to stifle the sound. Her other hand became a clutching claw, opening and closing with each silent scream.

Lucy grabbed Annie and ran with her to their bedroom and hid her in the cupboard. "You stay there and no matter what you hear, don't come out. Got that? Don't come out!" Annie began crying and bit into her knuckles so she wouldn't make a sound.

Heidi found a stick she thought would knock a rifle from someone's hands. Phil ushered Fatima towards Annie in the cupboard.

The dwellers shivered at the squeak of the opening screen door. The fear was palpable, triggering an already unstable Lucy to completely crack. Her face screwed into a hideous mask, she had the presence of mind to grab a cushion and screamed into it, over and over. The veins on her temples popped as she wrestled with her close companions of grief, torment and fear. No one moved to stop her, they were preoccupied with their own struggle for self-control.

The back screen squeaked again and Arthur shook as he held the bat above his head by the door. He swayed back and forth wiping his sweaty hands on his shirt front several times. His facial muscles worked as he struggled with an inner battle. The rank smell of fear permeated the room.

The sound of bushes swishing against the side of the house came to their ears again. Heidi motioned for Arthur to stay at the back door. She ran into the kitchen and grabbed a carving knife then tip-toed to the front door with the knife raised. They stayed still and silent for what seemed hours. Arthur finally collapsed to the floor, exhausted. Heidi was pitched into a state of utter turmoil, she was torn between staying on guard or going to her partner.

Frozen, not knowing what to do, she whispered to herself, 'God, just give us a frigging break! I am sick of running!' Her head dropped to her chest as the tension drove hot tears to drip onto the floor. She stood like that for a full minute, then looked up.

Action Heidi jammed the knife under the front door to prevent it being opened and walked into the back room. Leaving Arthur unconscious on the floor she took up his baseball bat. She glanced at Charlene, curled into a fetal position on the floor; and Lucy, holding the pillow to her face on the lounge.

Hefting the bat above her shoulder, Action Heidi turned to Phil, her only comrade still standing and said, "We fight to the death, Phil. We aren't running any more."

Chapter 17

Nulla - Glenda's Battle

It was a stinking hot night, after the rains the mosquitoes buzzed and annoyed everyone. Luke moaned and said he hoped the terrorists were suffering too. The bikes were hooked up and their night vision goggles perched on their foreheads, their Steyrs loaded and ready.

Glenda couldn't make herself comfortable. Her trailer perched on a single wheel and she held on white-knuckled to keep it stable. Simon reached into his jacket and pulled out his .38 pistol.

"Glenda, take this and put your assault rifle down the side otherwise you might make the wheelbarrow tip over. The safety's simple. because there is none, just squeeze the trigger and it'll fire. Don't squeeze unless you want to shoot someone."

It was always in his possession now, well cared for and a work of beauty, his precious treasure. For Simon to loan his 'special' was a big deal, and Glenda was fully aware of his sacrifice. He showed her how to hold it, then spun the chamber to show its bullets.

"Thanks Simon, that's going to make a huge difference. Now I've a chance of getting home without falling out of this contraption. I'm sure Luke wants to see me tip out so he can laugh at me," she said, half in jest.

They had stripped their gear down to a minimum for speed and safety. If they ran into trouble they stood a better chance of fighting their way out. Nulla inspected each trooper and tucked the AK47 down snugly beside Glenda along with a belt of ammunition.

He checked everyone's night vision goggles and weapons. Luke insisted he take responsibility for towing Glenda, Simon said he would ride up front as lead scout.

"Boss, let me take Glenda, I'm faster than you and if we hit trouble I'll make sure she's safe. You concentrate on providing fire-power with Simon," said Luke gruffly.

They were all feeling nervous. Although they'd heard no chatter on their CB later than about ten pm, running into a night patrol was still possible. The trip went through enemy territory, and even with their night vision advantage, they all feared a contact could easily take them out.

Things started out well, Luke made sure to ride carefully for fear of tipping Glenda out on to the footpath. Trialing a wheelbarrow contraption with a teenage boy with superb coordination was fine, but with a wounded young lady, with an uncertain sense of balance, it was completely different.

The evening felt a little too warm and bugs lit up in their night vision screens annoying them. They silently rode the side streets with their bikes hugged up against the bushes as much as possible. As they entered their home-base street they began to relax a little.

Simon was out front, he stopped to wait for everyone to catch up before crossing the street. He looked to the left, nothing. But as he swung his gaze to the right he was struck by the sight of a patrol of twelve terrorists merely metres away. He threw down his bike and prepared his Steyr for the fire-fight, slipping it to semi-automatic.

Luke was so focused on keeping the bike upright he didn't notice a thing. His limited peripheral night vision goggles caused him to ride right in among the enemy patrol.

There came a shout and a scuffle as he knocked two terrorists over with his bike. A third grappled with him and they fell in a death-locked struggle. Luke was strong but his assailant stronger. With his hands around the teenager's throat the heavily built terrorist began to strangle the life from him.

Nulla was a little slow to respond but when he heard the crash and grunted shouts he skidded his mountain bike to the ground. Swinging his Steyr to his shoulder he clicked his safety off and engaged full automatic.

It was Glenda who fired first though. As she slid from the barrow to the ground she had the .38 in her hand and pointed at the enemy. It kicked once, twice, three times and three terrorists went down. She then saw Luke on the ground locked in a death struggle with a terrorist twice his size. The brute had his hands around Luke's throat completely shutting off his airway. Luke's legs kicked uselessly as he slowly gasped his life away.

Her forth and fifth bullets hit the terrorist in the back and he slammed forward his hands flying away from her brave guardian's neck. Luke lay gasping for breath in a state of shock, completely overwhelmed by the unexpected violence of the assault.

A split second after Glenda's first shot Simon began firing as he stood over his bike in the dark. The flames from his Steyr blinded him with his night vision goggles, so he flicked his head to make them fall down onto his chest. He took out most of the enemy in those important next few seconds. His rapid short bursts combined with Nulla's single burst of full automatic fire cut the entire patrol to the ground.

A single terrorist made the mistake of standing up, trying to get his AK47 to his shoulder. Glenda fired her last round and he spun to fall on top of his comrades.

It was all over almost before it had begun, the group stood in shock for several seconds. Nulla shook his head and spun into action. He quickly scanned the scene through his night vision goggles.

"Righto, boys, help Glenda into the black Mitsubishi and load it up with supplies as fast as you can. We've about two minutes before the terrorists realise where the firing came from and they investigate. We've no choice but to move to safe house number three. We are leaving this location. I'll stay back and drag these bodies into the yard, that should confuse them when they drive past. Go!" Luke and Simon spun into action and raced Glenda to the safe house just down the street.

As he raced his bike towards the safe house an image of Mr Thornton's weathered face flashed in Simon's mind and he heard his reedy voice, "*A 38 is deadly at close range and might save your lives one day.*" He shivered and wondered if the old pirate was still alive, he sincerely hoped he was.

Nulla grabbed the first body by the ankles and dragged it into the nearest yard. As he bent to grab the next pair of legs it kicked at him. The boot caught him just under the chin and he went over backwards. His rifle and night vision goggles flew into the air and he was momentarily blinded. Without his Steyr, Nulla felt fear for a split second.

Reaching instinctively down to his shin he pulled his knife from its leg pouch and drove his shoulder into the black weaving shape in front of him. Locking his leg behind his assailant's knee they spun and fell but it was he who was pinned to the ground.

Shaking with shock and fear he managed to free his right hand and stabbed upwards. He heard his enemy grunt as the knife plunged under its ribs. As he wrestled himself from under the body he felt a pair of large, firm breasts rub against him.

His mind went spinning, '*A girl? I've killed a young girl? God curse all Revelationists!*' he silently whispered in horror.

A blazing rage exploded inside and he silently cursed the terrorists for all the evil they had done to him and this beautiful world.

In a rising panic he felt about on the lawn for his weapon and goggles. He found his Steyr but left the bodies and his goggles where they lay. Time had run out to do any more.

Luke and Simon opened the garage door and helped Glenda into the front cabin of the patrol. She started the engine as soon as she got her legs into position then slid over to the passenger seat.

Luke emerged from the house with his arms full of ammunition and dumped them in the back. Simon followed with the CB radio, batteries and cables. They raced back and forth filling the back of the Mitsubishi Pajero.

Nulla screamed into the garage on his mountain bike and leaped in next to Glenda. As he drove forward Simon closed the garage doors leaving the bikes inside. Hopefully the terrorists wouldn't think to search the houses - but he knew that was just plain stupid of him to think they wouldn't make a thorough house to house search.

"Five seconds! Get your arses into gear we are going, NOW!" He revved the engine his face a mess of scratches and a bruise formed under his swollen chin. Both boys leaped into the back passenger seats.

Just as Nulla drove level with the front fence Simon screamed, "STOP!"

Leaping from the side door the teenager skidded into the house and bounced out again in seconds. In his hands he held something.

"What the devil was that about?" shouted Nulla in a state of extreme agitation.

Simon held up a bottle of tomato sauce and another of curry powder. "Supplies, I can't eat without my curry and ketchup!" he beamed at everyone. "Sorry, but I forgot to arm the booby traps, boss. Now they'll get a blast when they visit."

Nulla could only shake his head as he stamped on the accelerator, speeding out of the driveway and up the street.

With their head and tail lights painted out Nulla headed away from the scene of carnage.

"Luke, stand up through the sunroof. Shoot anything that moves!"

To Glenda he said, "Put your night vision goggles onto my head, quickly. I've lost mine and I can't see a damn thing."

"Simon, get both windows down and be ready to engage any targets to the sides." Nulla settled down to the task of driving through the restrictive greenish glow of his night vision screen.

A few seconds later they saw two sets of headlights approaching from a side street. Simon opened up with his Steyr. '*Brrrip, brrrip brrrrip*' it went and their ears popped. The smell of cordite filled the cabin.

Next, Luke opened up, the headlights made a perfect target. Discarded shells flew about the vehicle interior and Glenda caught one down the back of her shirt.

"Eeeouch!" she squealed.

The first car spun out of control while the one behind hit its brakes. It disappeared as their Pajero screeched around a corner and onto the main road.

Nulla accelerated knowing thousands of terrorists from all over the city would soon be searching for them. With the route clear in his mind's eye, he began to slow his breathing as he rebuilt his mind-palace. His racing thoughts slowed and he was now able to follow his inner map.

Another set of headlights headed towards them from a side street and swung behind them. In the dark it looked like a Ford utility and a spray of bullets hit the side of their Pajero. Luke fired several bursts but the weaving and bouncing of both cars sent his bullets everywhere but at his target. Simon moved across the back seat behind Luke's legs and opened fire.

For several seconds the sounds of automatic rifle fire filled the Pajero and Glenda thought she would scream.

Luke called out jubilantly, "They've crashed into a pole and... they... are... down! Woot!"

Another vehicle roared towards them as they crossed an intersection.

'Brrip click!'

"Loading!" called Luke as he ducked down. Simon leaped up to replace him in the sunroof and opened fire on the terrorist vehicle.

Bursts of 'brrrrip, brrrrip, brrrrip' assaulted their ears. Incoming bullets hit their Pajero and Luke howled, "Ouch!"

The firing continued 'brrrip, brrrip, brrrrip' then Simon ducked down and with a wheezing breathy voice called, "Loading!"

Up jumped Luke into the open sunroof while Simon reloaded then leaned most of his body out of the side window. He fired a long burst. The enemy vehicle swayed from side to side trying to avoid the incoming bullets but failed. Simon's last burst hit the driver and the car flipped as it bounced off the curb then slammed into a parked car.

"It's down!" he called out loudly and pulled himself back into the cabin and reloaded, all in the same fluid movement.

"We sure stirred up a hornets nest. We might need to scamper on foot. Be prepared to hole up in a house if we stop. Boys, have your ammunition handy, we'll need all of it. Glenda, if we pull over, stick to me and I'll carry you, got it?" Nulla turned his head to glance at her. He noticed her pale, stricken face, eyes wide with fear. "If Army C call any of the other armies to help, then we're in the shit. But I think they'll want all the fun for themselves. We just might escape clean."

Swinging wildly down back streets, driving like a maniac, Nulla smiled, knowing he would have been imprisoned for this months earlier. Stopping suddenly in a side street he pulled out his road map and turned on his torch. He studied the map for what seemed like forever. Simon pulled at Luke's trousers and whispered for him to swap positions.

"Luke you've got blood on your face, did you get hit?" Simon said, his voice loud in the quiet cabin.

Luke's eyes jerked back and forth watching the road as he spoke. "Riding shotgun with Nulla is fun isn't it? What? My face? Huh? Oh yeah, you kneed me in the nose when I was loading." He wiped his nose leaving a thin smear of blood on the back of his hand.

"Righto, boys, nearly there. Who's up top? Simon? Watch for movement and keep me posted. I think we're out of trouble. We're only a few streets away from our new safe house." Nulla soon turned into a driveway and drove all the way into the back yard. The engine died and he let out a deep sigh.

"Boys, secure our perimeter. Report back here in two minutes." He rested his head against the steering wheel for a moment and closed his eyes. Shaking with tension he sat up and leaned across to kiss Glenda on the lips. "Welcome to our new safe house, darling."

Each evening Nulla went out on reconnaissance trips with one of the boys. They found the exploded gas depot and searched for clues but discovered no other signs but a stripped supermarket nearby. He guessed that whoever fired the gas tank must live reasonably close. They wanted to make contact as soon as possible so they could get away from this unrelenting city. Convinced that there was no resistance and no chance of fighting the terrorists, Nulla just wanted to make contact and go country.

It was around midday when Nulla crawled out of bed and found his .38 pistol that Simon had given him. He walked over to Glenda who was brushing her mane of black hair in the mirror of their palatial bathroom.

"I was thinking, since I don't really need this, and because you're as handy with it as Annie Oakley... well, here." He handed her a beautifully worked doeskin shoulder holster he'd found on one of his trips. Into it's soft leather he had painstakingly inked a love heart and Cupid's arrow. The 38 'special' sat neatly in it's holster.

"Why love, that's the most beautiful engagement present I have ever received." She beamed up at him drawing his face down to hers.

An hour or so later Nulla called everyone together. "Righto, we're going to separate and run individual patrols to cover more ground." Placing the street map on the table he explained the grid pattern he'd drawn up. Their search narrowed down to a few small areas and the boys began to memorise it using the visualisation techniques Nulla had taught them.

"Are you sure it's safe, Nulla? I mean, to split up? I'm worried about the boys," said Glenda as she limped into the kitchen and poured everyone a cup of steaming black tea. Simon and Luke did a double take when they saw her wearing her new shoulder holster with its pistol over her pink top.

"Glenda, that's beautiful. I wish mine was as neat as that. Where'd you get it?" asked Simon. Glenda winked at him. The two boys turned to each other and giggled.

Nulla deliberately cleared his throat, ignoring them. "Glenda, these boys are experienced soldiers and I trust them like my brothers." Luke and Simon stopped laughing and looked at him in surprise.

"Don't underestimate the experience and skill of a teenager." Nulla went on. "After all, didn't a wise person once say, '*If you want to employ someone who knows everything, employ a teenager*'?"

Nulla broke into laughter. Glenda saw the look of puzzlement on the boy's faces and started giggling herself.

"That's not even funny," said Luke, who, for the first time, noticed that these two special people were really laughing. He hadn't seen Nulla or Glenda laugh properly before. "Seriously, that's not funny." Even though the joke went completely over his head he began to laugh too.

"You lot are either mad, or I just missed something," said Simon scratching his head. He smiled politely then went back to studying the map.

Just before dawn Nulla returned and woke Glenda. "I saw one, I saw one of the civilians, it looked like a teenage girl. We made the right decision, Glenda, we did it!" He grabbed her and hugged her till she gasped for air.

"OK, OK, steady up my handsome man. Go put a brew on and we'll talk." She was about to let him go then grabbed him by the shirt and pulled him to her. "This," she kissed him sensuously on the mouth, "is for being such a damn good soldier. You did your regiment proud today." She smiled and let him go.

"Boss?" she called affectionately just as he stood up, "remember the folks in the shopping mall where you found me? I'd like us to see if they're OK too. They might be the only people left alive in Adelaide besides us and that girl you saw."

Nulla stood for a moment then nodded. Walking into the kitchen he began thinking, '*I wonder if those poor people are still alive, maybe this is all that's left to resist the terrorists.*' He put the kettle on their blackened camp cooker then woke the boys.

As they sat around the table they chatted about the news. Nulla had gone out alone leaving the teenagers to have a night off. He liked to do that once in a while, it was good for morale. He described how he'd seen a figure right at the furthest grid on his map.

"I don't know who she is but she is smart and quick," he said. "I followed her and left a note. I stuck it in the back screen door where they should see it in the morning. I bet she'll be relieved when she reads it. I wrote that we would meet them there this evening, at midnight. I signed it; *'Sergeant Nulla, Australian Armoured Corps, Adelaide.'*"

Chapter 18

Sundown - Birdsville Track patrol

Chan and John now regularly patrolled with Cambra, Wiram and some of the other commandos depending on who was free at the time. They had set up camp on the road to Marree, over one hundred kilometres south of Birdsville.

Sundown left everything to Wiram who co-ordinated the long distance guerrilla attacks. They mined the roads, blew up trucks and ambushed patrols. They harassed their enemy at every opportunity and provided information on terrorist movement.

Sundown's plan was to keep the enemy reeling, always trying to guess where the next punch would come from. The terrorists hadn't made another assault on the Birdsville command since their defeat some months ago. Heavy autumn rains had made movement out of Birdsville impossible but the roads were now open and the commando were back with their mobile hit-and-run patrols.

While Sundown's Commando were waiting for the flood waters to abate around Birdsville, the terrorists had moved an entire battalion of nearly one thousand Alpha Army soldiers north into Marree. Major Lunney had lost his command and his beloved Deaths Heads were disbanded to be replaced by Major Daniels' Stosstruppen, Storm Troopers. They were preparing to push through Birdsville and connect with their comrades in Longreach and Mount Isa, in Queensland, and with Darwin, in the Northern Territory.

Their only obstacles were Sundown's Commando at Birdsville and the Australian Third Army in Alice Springs.

Assassin wanted to come on this patrol. He decided he'd spent way too much time running communications and making love to the commando's CB radio. He longed for the peace and quiet of the bush for a change. That and the excitement of upsetting terrorists. As soon as the roads were passable they hit the Revelationists at their new command post in Marree.

Chan proved to be a sniper of repute and John was a weapons expert much like Halo. The two ex-Deaths Head commando prisoners were nearly ready to be accepted into the community, but Sundown wanted to give them more time before bringing them back to Birdsville for their final judgment. He knew that a confrontation with his community wasn't going to be pleasant so the longer the two boys stayed out there, the better. The more terrorists they killed, the greater their chances of acceptance, it was as simple as that.

"Man o' man," complained Chan pulling on his boots as he waited for his breakfast. "It's damn hot and it's nearly winter. This place is just crazy, it's worse than when we did our basic training in the Flinders Ranges before the apocalypse."

"You did training in the Flinders?" asked Cambra, his ears pricked up.

"Yeah, John and I spent a lot of time on properties out there. One of the family's rented their farms to the Revelationist church each summer, when no one was around, too bloody hot. We did weapons training, explosives, skirmishing, patrolling, ambushing, you name it we did it," replied Chan as he tied up his bootlaces.

"What's their name? I might know them. I've spent a lot of time out that way prospecting with my father," said Cambra.

"They're owned by a family named Wilson. Old man Wilson and his son's own a lot of property out that way. We stayed at a different property each summer. Every Deaths Head Commando member had to pay up front. It cost us a lot of money to attend and it was compulsory otherwise you were kicked out of the Deaths Heads. We were the elite of their Alpha Army you know, the best of the best." Chan reminisced then continued, "One of the Wilson's cattle stations is right inside Wilpena Pound, Jack Wilson owns it. He's got some tough cattlemen with him, merciless arseholes they were, worse than some of our own officers. We had a few run-in's with them. You know them?" replied Chan looking at Cambra curiously.

"Yeah, I do, they own a lot of cattle properties throughout South Australia. They have a lot of money and a reputation for being tough and uncompromising. I wouldn't trust any of them as far as I could kick them." Cambra looked towards the CB in the truck but thought against radioing this new information through. He called out to Assassin and told him to let Sundown know the news when he was next on the CB.

"I wonder what mischief our boys and girls are up to now? I sure miss my missus," mused a sunburned McFly only half listening to the conversation. "These seven day patrols are too long I reckon." He was busy weaving parrot feathers onto a fish hook with thin nylon fishing line, his eyes never leaving his task. "Tomorrow we head back to base camp and we're going to have a day off and I'm going fishing. The Cooper Creek's still up and there's bound to be fish in there. We're gonna have fish for dinner tomorrow night guys."

"Bullshit, McFly," came Assassin Creed's voice from beside his trail bike. "I bet you a lobster cocktail you won't catch a damn thing." This was his first patrol since the mines battle, and, despite the joy of freedom he actually felt lost without his girlfriend and CB partner, Gail, next to him.

"Bullshit yourself, Creed, you're going to have to find a lobster by tomorrow night to pay your debt, buddy." The banter continued till Cambra wandered over to check on the state of Assassin's trail bike.

"Got that cable fixed, mate?" he asked pulling at it.

"Nearly done, bro. So what's doing today? We should be heading back to base camp soon shouldn't we. That hit we did on Marree the other night should hold them up a bit too." Assassin sat on his heels and pulled on the cable too, his repair held. Satisfied he stood up and reached for his mug of tea. The sun had risen above the horizon and a cool wind appeared as if by magic.

"I don't know, mate, they seem to be up to something," answered Cambra. "Our intelligence reports tell us absolutely zero chatter about what they're up to these days. They know we're listening in so now we're back in the dark. They've got extra vehicles on the road and building up stores and troops in Marree, must be battalion strength there now. The other night was sheer luck, we won't have such easy targets next time." He called over to John, the ex Revelationist Crusader. "What's those brothers of yours in Army Alpha up to eh, John?"

"Ain't no brothers of mine, Cambra," he answered. "They aim to push up to Alice Springs then Darwin. And don't forget they have outposts at Longreach and Mt Isa. They'll want to connect with them and control all traffic and cargo in the centre. I have a feeling General Himmler wants to take over each army group one by one." John stopped for a moment to push some food around the frying pans that he'd lined up on the camp-fire.

Cambra continued, "Is that really his name, Himmler? That's one of Hitler's generals. Himmler, Deaths Heads, Stosstruppen, sounds like the whole damn German army."

"Yep, General Himmler is obsessed with the Nazi's. They're all psycho, Cambra, they all want to dominate each other. You should have seen them when we had those conferences a few years ago, talk about turf wars. They're just outright power hungry bastards." John stoked the fire as he pulled the frying pans off. "Breakfast is ready fella's! Get it while its hot!"

"Bloody tinned'd figgin' food, and if it ain't bloody tinned'd then it's damned bloody dried," McFly said doing his Billie imitation. "Them damned bastard tins'll bloody kill ya's if yer not careful boys." He mumbled as he scooped the warmed vegs and beef stew mixed with powdered eggs into his starved mouth. "I'm so hungry I could eat a horse then chase down its jockey for dessert. I can't wait till Roo gets back, I sure miss his kangaroo steaks. I'm going to get Wirrie to take me out shooting when we get back. If we can't find any kangaroos or brumbys we'll shoot a cow I reckon."

"I thought you were going to catch some fish, McFly?" It was Chan's turn to tease him.

"Crikey! You bastard's love poking fun at me and my fishing! Just because we're in a bloody desert doesn't mean there aren't any fish here... somewhere." He started to laugh as he began packing his fishing gear away ready for their last day of patrolling.

By evening they were back at their base camp and Cambra sent Chan and Assassin to place the land mines on the road and set up the usual ambush not far from their well hidden camp. John and McFly would relieve them at midnight and were now in their caravan preparing for sleep. Cambra spent the early part of the evening checking weapons and gear ready for their swap over with Alpha Team the next day.

Just as Cambra was topping up the water in the four-wheel drive radiator there came the sound of a gunshot then two more in quick succession. Three shots, that meant enemy approaching - emergency!

He sprang for his weapons and called to McFly and John, but they were already out of their caravans strapping on their webbing. John carried their precious Javelin anti-tank missile launcher, he had his AK47 strap over his shoulder. McFly carried extra missiles for the Javelin along with his rifle, together they raced for their ambush positions.

"What have we got, Creed?" asked Cambra when he saw Assassin looking through their precious night-vision binoculars.

"Four vehicles, no lights, probably using IR or light-enhanced vision to drive. Slow speed, cautious. They don't look like Crusaders though. Have a look yourself." He handed the binoculars to Cambra.

"It doesn't look like any of the vehicles we saw at Marree last night, Cambra. I've not seen them in our army before either," came Chan's comment as he handed his scoped Blaser sniper rifle for John to look through.

"Looks like Bushmasters. Might be regular army, might be from Alice Springs. This is weird." Cambra handed the glasses to McFly who was readying the Javelin with John.

McFly stood up and looked carefully as well. "Looks like the cavalry, armoured cavalry. Shit, we're screwed if it isn't ours." He handed the binoculars back and finished setting up the anti-tank missile launcher, they just might be needing it he decided.

"Not ours, Cambra," said John quietly, "but they do look like Bushmasters. That front one is heavily armoured, if they attack we'll get slaughtered. Looks like 7.62 mm machine gun mounted and the one behind is armed with 25 mm cannons... oh wow, it's an ASLAV. We're either screwed or we're saved," mumbled John as he handed the sniper rifle back to his best friend, Chan.

The four looked at Cambra expectantly. No one hesitated in their preparations for the coming fight, but they knew a fight against armoured cavalry would cost them dearly. Against four heavily armoured vehicles they could all be killed. Even their Javelin wouldn't save them. Sure, it would take out the first vehicle but with a cool down time of thirty plus seconds on a cold day that would give their enemy enough time to locate and pummel their position with the 25 mm cannon and 7.62 mm machine guns. It would be a slaughter.

"Shit," Cambra whispered, "why me?" As patrol commander, Cambra had proven his tactical skill in many hit and run attacks on the enemy, but today, he realised he was being handed a real test.

"OK, fellas, I'm going out with the bike and flash the headlights at them. Maybe they are ours, if they fire then fuck them over for me and tell my family I love them. Then get on your bikes and try to escape. Assassin, get on the CB and inform Sundown, now. If we're captured, Chan, you and John stay low-key and no one mention they're Deaths Heads. Remember your escape, evade and capture protocols. Has everyone got that?" The boys looked at each other then nodded as Cambra ran off to bring his bike up on to the road.

Moments later the four vehicles stopped a hundred metres away and the commando patrol watched as two soldiers emerged from the armoured vehicles. They walked towards Cambra and his bike.

Assassin returned from his report. "Sundown said we retreat or give ourselves up, we're not to fight against armoured cavalry. Those Bushmasters can reach a hundred kph, faster than our bikes. I think we might be in deep shit fella's so let's pray they're ours. He'll be on his way with a heavy patrol as soon as he can."

"Damn it!" Sundown's voice exploded into the mic, then he calmed down. "Righto, got you, Assassin. I'm preparing a patrol now. If friendly ask them to wait for me, if not, give yourselves up. I mean that, no Clint Eastwood heroics, just hand them your weapons. We'll come and rescue you as soon as we can. Remember your protocols for capture. I'll stay open channel all the way there, get back to us as soon as you can. Good luck, out."

Pedro was still in the first-aid room with Lorraine getting his stumps dressed. He seemed to spend more time there than anywhere else. *'Poor beggar, he hasn't been the same since we lost Shamus. I better have a quick chat with him before we head out'*, Sundown promised himself.

Sundown turned and stared at Pellino who was in shock too, then he cursed again. "Shit! Pellino, can you please call everybody to the lounge, we need to start moving them to safety."

He stood up and leaned against the wall. Just when he thought they were ready to send a patrol to Alice Springs and contact the army base for support, or move to the Flinders Ranges, this had to happen. He pulled at his nose and rubbed his face in his hands.

'I am so tired of this,' he said to himself as he passed more orders to Andy who had just rushed in.

A minute later he heard, "Honey, come on down," it was his wife, "we're preparing dinner so everyone can eat while Wiram prepares the patrol. Don't worry, darl, Wiram has things under control and Harry's organising the vehicles right now." Pinkie walked over and stroked his hair as she pulled him to her. "Just when we start getting our love-life back on track another disaster like this has to happen," she said, her lips on his forehead.

Pinkie stopped when she heard Fat Boy calling from the dining room, "Come and get it!"

She ran down the hallway leading Sundown by the hand and held the door open as the oldies were wheeled in by Lulu and Danni. Fat Boy called over a pot of stew he was carefully lowering on to the table. "... and Billie, I didn't have time to add rum to your tea. Sorry old mate, you'll have to miss out this time."

Billie smiled and held up the hip flask Pedro had given him months ago, "'Be prepared' is me motto, Fat Fella, never without a drop of the ol' mount'n dew," he chuckled, his toothless grin always made Fat Boy smile.

"Fat Boy, you coming out with us? We'll be needing a cook." Halo chuckled and slapped his mate on the back as he groped at the food on the heavily laden table.

"Nope, I've never been separated from me bike or me food, ever. Anyone who stands between me and them generally gets flattened." He shifted his bulk so that Blondie could sit beside him.

Fat Boy looked around and noticed there was no Pedro and his voice roared across the dining room, "Where's me skinny twin brother?"

Everyone stopped and looked around. Lulu yelled in answer, "He's around the back having a smoke for dinner. I'll go get him for ya." She scurried off.

"No sweat, I'll go get the bastard. He's not ducking out of a Fat Boy feed. I cook, everyone eats!" and he lifted his bulk out of his chair and swaggered out after Lulu.

The two wheeled Pedro into the dining room. He appeared to have shrunk in size and his smile hid his sadness. "What's ya doing with me, can't an old fella have a smoke by himself away from this damn noisy crowd?" he pretended to protest.

"Now, Mini-me," said Fat Boy, in as delicate a voice as he could, "I thought I told you I was cooking tonight? And how many times have I told you to come and get me if you feel crook and can't eat anything? I'll get some stewed prunes, they'll clean you out and shift that morose mood of yours."

Pedro sat there and scooped some food onto his spoon and ate a few mouthfuls, just to please his giant friend.

"Hey, Blondie, how'd you go doing the CB training with Gail and Beamy?" asked Bill, who had just joined them at the table.

"I suggested they fix the antennae and tune the set properly. We need more distance and that might improve the reception." Blondie was a bottle blond and since her arrival her natural brunette colour had taken over. She always looked stunning no matter what colour her hair.

"Smarty pants, don't you go showing those two up now or I'll get Cambra to sort you out," smiled Bill as he reached for a plate of stewed kangaroo and camel with a mix of bush spices.

"Ah, Bill, promises promises. You know he already has two gorgeous girls at his beck and call, he certainly doesn't need me to fuss over as well." Blondie had fended off unwanted advances all her life and idle banter was one thing she excelled at, when she felt like it.

"Halo, hows the weapons training going with the girls?" Sundown had walked over to the group, his mind a million miles away thinking of every possible thing that could go wrong.

"They're fine, Sundown, really. They can shoot the pea out of a pod at a hundred paces," replied Halo opening his mouth wide as he shoveled more food in as though competing in an eating contest with Assassin.

"OK, good, they'll go with you and the civilians. You're going to be in command of 'Team Safe-House', and make sure you arm Danni, Lulu and Bill. You'll protect our civilians at all costs." Sundown looked up and saw Bill staring at him. "Bill, I don't want you exposed to action right now, sorry. I need you to get that plane sorted because I have a special job for you. I'll be keeping Donna, though. She's going to be my batgirl - you know, Batman, the one who runs errands. I want her close to me so she'll be safe." Bill nodded understandingly, then he chuckled.

Shadow sat down and said, "Sundown, you mean Donna's going to be 'Robin to your Batman'."

"Blimey, how the hell can I compete with all these brainiacs around me. I just want her to run my errands and be safe." Sundown wasn't sure if Shadow was having a go at him or not.

"Safe? Next to you?" Bill swallowed another mouthful of camel meat. "You're a bloody berserker!"

"Damn it, Bill! I'm trying to do my best you know. I don't need this shit." Sundown sat down and rubbed at his face again. It felt too hot inside the hotel's dining room and he was sweating.

"Harden up, princess," said Fat Boy sitting opposite him, "we'll get through this. According to Halo you always do." He roared with laughter and slapped his hand down on the table. Sundown coughed nervously and looked around, everyone was watching.

"I'm sorry, I'm just worried. We've not heard a thing since Assassin called." He nodded 'thank you' as Pinkie put a plate of food in front of him and handed him a spoon.

"Come on eat up, you and Wiram have a patrol to attend to don't you?" She stroked his head and began eating.

"Tricia? Where's Tricia?" Sundown dropped his spoon midway to his mouth.

"Umm, she's on her way to sort out the trucks and vehicles for transport to our safe place," said Halo, a blush forming on his face.

"You mean she's still in your bed keeping it warm," roared Fat Boy. He just loved the sound of his own voice booming above everyone else's, especially when it was stirring someone up, like it did now.

"Fat Boy, steady on now," said Blondie dryly, "you know you could upset someone with your humour."

"Shut up, Fat Boy!" said Halo. "She left my room an hour ago anyway. Besides Tricia really is outside preparing for the move. So jam that up your hairy butt and eat it!" He smiled and slapped Fat Boy on the back. The hollow sound echoed around the dining room.

Sundown was only a minute into his meal when Pellino came running into the dining room. Seeing Sundown he walked quickly to his side and bent down to speak into his ear.

Breathlessly he said, "Boss, Assassin called, they're ours! It's the bloody Australian Army!"

Chapter 19

Sundown - Alice Springs Command

The two officers greeted Cambra formally then inquired as to his unit and strength. Cambra politely asked them the same questions, it was a stalemate.

"How do I know who you are? How can you prove to me that you're on the side of the Australian people and not the Revelationists?" Cambra stood with an AK47 slung over his shoulder and a look of controlled resolve on his face. Even in the dark he could be imposing.

"We could ask the same thing of you, mate," said the one who introduced himself as Major Thompson. "Now stop stuffing us around and answer our questions or we might have to consider you our enemy. We would then have to shoot you and your four mates over there." He jerked his chin in the direction of the ambush.

Cambra looked at the major, his brain working overtime, '*how did he know that?*' Then he realised they were no doubt using IR and light-enhanced optics as Assassin had suggested.

"OK, I'll go first then shall I? We're a forward patrol of Sundown's Commando. We've been playing hit and run with the Deaths Heads, Stosstruppen, and any other Nazified Revelationists now based in Marree. We've had three major battles with them over the past 10 months - and we've won them all." He stopped and smiled smugly.

"We know all about you lot, nice work too. In that case," the major stretched out his hand, "I would like to congratulate your commando and welcome you to our Alice Springs Command, Australian Third Army."

Cambra decided he would invite them to spend the night at their camp site.

The major turned to his second in command, "Captain Lewis, inform the men we'll be bivouacking tonight with the famous 'Sundown's Commando'." Turning back to Cambra he replied, "Thank you, we are honoured."

McFly walked around the ASLAV with Chan, "I bet Halo would give his eye teeth to be here with us. If only he could see what he's missing, the first contact with our own army, at last."

Cambra and the major walked along the road together and talked quietly of events since the apocalypse.

"We've been fighting almost non-stop against their army. They've pushed us but each time we've held and pushed them back," explained Cambra. "We seem to be one step ahead of them. Our commander, Sundown, he's incredible, a real leader of men, he thinks and plans ahead. He also has a dedicated team behind him. We only have one ex-military left in action. Wiram's been our corner-stone, organising patrols and making sure we have everything we need. We have Pedro, he's a great old bloke, but sadly, he's had a bad time since our strategist, Shamus, was killed. But now you're here we can ease back a little, eh. That would be nice for a change."

"Ahhmm," the major cleared his throat politely. "I'm terribly sorry, Cambra, but we aren't here to relieve you, nor are we here to protect your community. We're a recon patrol only. Our orders are to avoid all contact with the enemy unless fired upon. My goal right now is to contact Sundown and talk with him. We wish to invite him to come back with us, to see what we can sort out regarding a permanent standing patrol at Birdsville or Marree."

"No sweat, major, just susing you out, that's all," Cambra smiled innocently. "Come on back to the fire, we've got a few bottles of spirits left, that should keep the cold out."

The major's eyes lit up. "Spirits? My health to you good sir! We ran out of decent alcohol six months ago. All we've had is vile, gut-rot some of the locals brew up, absolute rubbish. Lead on, Gunga Din."

The group shared their food and then began some heavy drinking until the patrol's alcohol was gone.

"Sorry fella's, but one more bottle then that's it," announced McFly with a slight wobble. Careful not to spill any he poured a finger of spirits into each man's mug then slurred, "Now where's my guitar, I have a need to sing." So they sang bush ballads and a few pop songs, chatted some and finished by telling stories of their fighting exploits.

Cambra told his story of the fight at the mines, the spinifex fire bombs and the one hundred kilometre walk with Wiram, twice. McFly then told them of the dreadful battle of Marree. As he spoke no one uttered a sound, no one moved. He stopped near the end and began to cry.

McFly was drunk, like everyone else, but telling that story evoked what he felt when he heard Sundown going berserk. He still heard the screams of the women and their strangled groans as they were bashed; he felt the helplessness of trying to get down the stairs through the hail of enemy machine gun fire to rescue his friends; he saw the image of Halo sitting semi-conscious rocking and moaning; Pinkie holding onto Sundown looking up at him like she was looking at a monster; Sundown standing in a daze; the laundry with its mess of guts and body parts; the smell of death; he lived it all over again in the telling. It still haunted him, often waking himself in the middle of the night with his own screaming.

Sergeant Doff, one of the experienced cavalry NCO's stood up and put his arm around the young man and sat him down. He spoke quietly until McFly settled down. Then he handed McFly his last nip of scotch. The fly fisherman downed it in one gulp.

"Thanks mate. Fark, I'm so sorry about all that," he said to everyone around the camp-fire.

He blew his nose and wiped his eyes. "I never want to go through that shit again." Then he bent over and vomited. "Darn, that's the last of your grog too, sorry, mate," he sputtered and fell back into the sergeant's arms, he was out cold.

Assassin then told them some of the tales he'd heard from Halo, the commando's self appointed historian and story teller. "Halo even got the girls to sew up a flag with our battle honours on it. We now have three pitched battles: The Mines, Marree and Birdsville. The Mines was a major battle where we lost our strategist, Shamus. It was followed by three running battles and ambushes. I missed nearly all of it though. I got a bullet in the arm and then was knocked out."

He rolled up his sleeve to show his scar and the soldiers gathered around to 'hum' and 'haw' their approval in the firelight.

"And then a bloody poisonous spider bit me. It pisses me off no end. I should have been there to help my mates." He went silent for a moment then brightened.

"But that flag, you should see it. A yellow rising sun, or actually it's supposed to be the setting sun to represent 'Sundown'. It's got rays coming out of it, those girls did a great job. Then there's the red of the blood we spill of our enemy and the red sands of the desert. And then the black of the... I don't really know if there is black in it..." his voice trailed off, lost.

Cambra spoke up, "You dopey bugger, Creed. It's yellow for the desert sun and Sundown's rays; red for the sands and our enemy's blood above and... shit! You're right, there is black in it too, black is below the sun." Cambra smiled, announcing proudly: "My girls are aboriginal and they have a way of making a statement. My goodness, they've used the background of the Aboriginal flag, how clever of them." He laughed as he turned to the mesmerised crowd. "Do you know what they did when I rescued them? I mean, when our commando rescued them at the mines?" And that was the start of another story of Shamus, the mines, the fire-fight, Beamy's grenade launcher and the Bofors. The story took a lot of retelling before the soldiers were satisfied.

When the troopers asked Chan and John about their battles they both said they had never seen a proper fight, except what they had done on patrol blowing up four terrorist trucks in Marree the previous night.

"Tell us again about your commander, Sundown, have you seen him in action? What's he like?" asked a young soldier eagerly.

Cambra looked at Assassin and took up the story. "Well, he's a baker, a bread scientist actually. Sometimes he'll bake us some beautiful breads and pastries too. But mostly he says he's too busy. But give him a gun and a knife then you better look out. The only one who's seen him in action, twice, is Halo, our weapons expert. Halo said that Sundown is so fast no one can stop his knife arm. He cut up a squad of four at the mines in about five seconds. Then there were the eight at Marree. None of us was there except McFly who you've just heard. He didn't see the berserker in action but he heard it and look what it did to him." He looked over at McFly asleep in front of the fire. Everyone turned and looked at the sleeping man, wondering in their own mind if they too would break, given such an experience.

"He sounds like a tough bloke, but how does he do it so fast?" came the same youthful voice from the soldiers huddled around the camp-fire.

Cambra brought his hand up to his face and rubbed the bristles on his chin. "Halo says that when they came into the room they saw the terrorists holding the girls prisoner. One of them, their leader, was about to carve up our mate, Beamy, lying on the table wounded. Another one had

Sundown's wife by the throat and that set him off. Halo and Sundown took out the first few with their automatics but then Halo was king hit and went down and Sundown's weapon hit empty, so he drew his knife. The squad leader then challenged Sundown to a knife fight but Sundown pinned him through the wrist bones with his own commando knife. He held him there screaming while he kicked the others so they couldn't get up. That's when he pulled his knife out and stabbed their leader in the heart, and within two seconds he'd taken out the rest. The last terrorist he bashed to death with his bare fists. I'm just glad I wasn't there, it would have been horrible. The three girls saw it all and they can't even talk about it."

The men were quiet as the camp-fire flames leaped high into the moonlit sky. Out of the dark came that same teenage voice, "What sort of knife is it?"

Cambra lifted his eyebrows in what might have been annoyance before starting up again. "It's a World War Two, British commando, thin-bladed knife, specially made for stabbing. Sundown won it from Shamus, the night before the mines battle. They were playing cards and old Shamus put up his commando knife against Sundown's compass. That compass is a beauty. It has an altimeter and all sorts of gadgets, like a Swiss-army knife. Sundown won and Shamus handed over his knife. Poor Shamus never needed either the knife or the compass because he died the next day. He was the first of our commando to die. Touch wood, he's also the only one. We all miss our strategio, he was a special bloke." Cambra stopped talking and stared into the fire, no one interrupted his musings, not even the youth with all the questions.

Someone threw a load of wood onto the fire. Assassin then told the rapt soldiers of the exploits of the other members. He told of Halo and McFly's fight at Birdsville when they leaped into the line of fire together to knock out a group of terrorists with their pistols. He laughed at himself when he described the drunken brawl outside the Marree Hotel when Shadow took out the riggers almost entirely by herself.

Assassin Creed saved his best story of Roo's sniping exploits at the Mines, when he saved the entire commando. Cambra then asked the soldiers of the contacts they'd had.

The captain explained, "Lads, we've been running patrols up to Darwin, down to the SA border and across to Queensland. We've had minor skirmishes against a few small enemy patrols but that's it. Our armour is far superior to anything they have, even their anti-tank weapons have yet to knock out a single one of our Bushmaster's or ASLAV's. They haven't really wanted to tackle us. They don't seem to want Alice Springs or the centre, they just want to control access to it. You lads have had far more interest from them than we have. We've spent most of our time organising the civilian population, trying to save what we can from starvation and thirst. That's been our triumph I guess."

The major cut in, his face red and beaming. All this talk of heroic battles made his blood rush to his head. "They did have armoured cavalry in the south around Adelaide but soon ran out of ammunition. Made their armour useless, the

268

idiots. We still have some cavalry, Abrams and APC's near Broken Hill too but we're keeping them under wraps for the time being. It's just not the right time to make a move." The major stopped talking and looked around. "Gawd! Did I just say that?" His tone became serious. "Right boys, that was confidential. Do not breathe a word of that to anyone or you will be court-martialled, and in these times that means execution. Got it?" He looked around and everyone nodded - except John and Chan who had gone to bed early on Cambra's orders.

When morning arrived the captain had his troops stay on patrol and allowed the hero's to sleep off their hangover. It wasn't until mid afternoon that Cambra and McFly could make an appearance and even then only John and Chan were in any condition to drive back to Birdsville to introduce their new found friends.

Chapter 20

Sundown - the demon plans

They met Wiram just before they came within sight of Birdsville. Sundown had been talking to them both, the major and Cambra, on the CB. Both parties stopped while John and Chan joined Pellino and one of the Bushmaster's to head back to the ambush site. Pellino had taken up the slack and was often called upon to lead a patrol these days, he loved it.

He, Bill and Sundown liked to go along sometimes so they could brush up on their patrolling skills and learn more of the fighting craft from the two ex-Revelationist boys. The two prisoners had turned out to be an excellent find for the commando. They often patrolled with Pellino who knew every trick in the book having worked most of his life in prisons.

"Why don't the youngsters get a break, Cambra?" asked the captain, "are they doing extra training or something?"

Cambra saw he was only mildly curious and replied as he brushed the flies from his mouth. "The new boys are in training, it keeps them busy and we need their young blood up front. If we get hit us older blokes just can't do what we used to do. They're good lads and need to earn their place in our commando, like everyone else."

"Yeah, I know what you mean. Week on, week off is pretty tough on the old body but hey, they did it in the last war." That was all that was said, but Cambra remained wary and uncomfortable.

They gathered in the main lounge of the Birdsville Hotel. Danni and Lulu proudly displayed their flag and the soldiers relaxed with some of Andy's home brew. It was a mixture of potato, carrot and fruit peelings, plus all kinds of starchy scraps from the kitchen boiled into a mess then he added his secret bush herbs and a special yeast mix.

"Quite simple actually," said Andy to the crowd of soldiers eager to learn his secret. "Just a mixture of bush flavours, that's the herbs; sugar, and that comes from the starchy vegetables and fruits; and then the yeast. Now the yeast is hard to come by. I keep a special strain in a bottle by my bed." He winked at everyone and there were nods of approval from the cavalry's hard-faced brewers. They quietly enjoying the fruity, full-flavoured beer as they sat and relaxed together.

"Bullshit!" called a reedy voice, "you just throw the shit together and leave it to rot. I've seen ya." Billie was sitting in the corner with Polly and Grannie, playing cards. "There's nothing secret about it, I've made home brew meself."

"You forget I've tasted your home-brew, Billie, and it tastes like shit. You have to admit mine is five star. Come on old fella, give in for once," Andy said with a chuckle.

"Yeah, s'pose so, it tastes like the real stuff. But it's still bullshit wot yer saying!" He went back to his game while Lulu sashayed herself over to the group offering them something to snack on before dinner.

While Shadow, Blondie and the two aboriginal girls fussed over the oldies and prepared the hotel for visitors, Fat Boy, Pinkie, Wilma, Mel and Jeda had been flat-out in the kitchen cooking for the new arrivals. They served up the Birdsville favourite - yeasted donuts with wild herb tea and fresh-roasted bush coffee.

The tea and coffee now came from dried bush herbs and seeds while the dough was a mixture of rice flour, wattle-seed flour and tapioca with some sweet potato and something like gelatin that Billie and the teenagers found out in the bush. The bread was a simple flat bread of the same ingredients minus the sweet potato and the special gelatinous ingredient.

Sundown sometimes came down to the kitchen with Fat Boy and together they'd try out new recipes on the community. Flat bread was a simple winner - but yeasted donuts won the day every time Fat Boy and the girls put them on the menu.

Their meal was mostly home grown. Mel, Jeda, Jenny and Wilma had established a colossal vegetable garden complete with chicken pens and fish tanks. Once the commando's patrols along the Birdsville Track made it safe they made several visits back to the Mungerannie Motel and brought back all of Mel's seedlings. They even brought back their goldfish to breed for the table.

Mel organised the rigger boys to put in a large pit and redirected the sewerage to be screened and pumped to feed and water the gardens. Bill and Cambra found solar panels in a property on one of their foraging trips, they wired them up to run the pumps. They had everything from lettuce to peas to tomatoes and even sweet potatoes and watermelons. It wasn't quite developed enough to feed an army but it was well on its way.

There was always the opportunity to hunt the cattle and wild animals in the desert scrub. Although some days they lived on dried meat on most occasions they had fresh beef, donkey, camel, horse, kangaroo and sometimes emu on the menu. The boys enjoyed hunting and rarely missed bringing something back.

"Thanks, mam. Donuts, wow, this is delicious, what's it made from?" asked a wide-eyed soldier while busily ogling Lulu.

"Don't ask. We're running low on everything except meat, but our cooks are magicians in disguise. That's damn nice, eh? I could eat a plateful all by meself." She smiled sweetly and made sure she wiggled her hips as she walked back out to the kitchen. Lulu giggled to herself as Danni headed out with more food. The soldiers watched, mesmerised, as another gorgeous teenager entered with tea and some fresh roasted bush-coffee.

"What a treat," one of the men said loudly. "Beautiful food and beautiful girls. I hope we get to stay a few days, I think we need this pampering more often."

Danni chuckled sweetly behind her hand. "Get out of it, you lot have all the territory to meet people and get spoiled, you don't need to come all the way across the Simpson Desert to see new faces."

Harry and Jenny's twelve year old son, Lenny, normally too shy to say 'boo', came in with Beamy. Together they carried a tray of Fat Boy's fresh food. Beamy was out of his arm sling and had deliberately coerced Lenny to help him carry the tray. He knew Lenny wanted to meet the soldiers and desperately wanted to look inside the Bushmasters and the ASLAV. Lenny, like his father, loved cars and hanging around the commando had fed his love of anything military.

"You think the boy could have a look inside your vehicles, hey, fellas?" Beamy asked one of the NCO's. "He's breaking his neck to get inside one."

"Sure, what's yer name, mate?" The beefy man asked Lenny. "Mine's Sergeant Doff, you know, the sound a tank makes when it backfires." He laughed at his joke. The sergeant called out to two of his off-siders and brought them over. Together they loaded up on food and drink and took Lenny, his little brother Liam and Beamy outside to sit in the Bushmasters. They listened to the HF and chatted about their favourite past-time, driving through the bush. The two youngsters were hushed and their eyes opened so wide with wonder that the soldiers couldn't help but smile.

"You poor bastards have been stuck fighting these Revelationists all by yourselves, huh?" Sergeant Doff asked Beamy. "Cambra and Assassin told us a few stories about it last night. That Sundown sure sounds like someone we could follow. Our piss-poor leaders turn tail and run at the sight of anything with a bloody muzzle. We're so chuffed to be here mate, we feel like hero's just having you sit in our truck." He ruffled Lenny's hair as the two boys crawled across him to sit in the drivers seat. "I can't wait to tell our mates back in the Alice that we've finally met the famous Sundown's Commando. You guys sure have an incredible reputation."

Beamy filed this information away as they continued to chat and eat. He was impressed with these men as well, professional but disillusioned. They just wanted to see action, real action.

"Well, if you hang around with us much longer, Doff, you'll see plenty of action. We've got a hit and run patrol out twenty-four-seven harassing the terrorists around Marree, you've met them. The Revelationists are terrified of us. You should have seen us at the mines action. Holy shit, we sure give it to them, but we paid a high price." Beamy instinctively rubbed at his chest wounds. "If you get a chance, talk to Halo, he's the only one who's seen Sundown's demon in action twice. It scares the living shit out of me each time I hear him tell his stories."

As an after-thought he said, "Hey Doff, why haven't you been in touch with us on the HF? We've been chatting with Sydney Charlie and others around the country but nothing military, what's up?" asked Beamy.

"We know Sydney Charlie quite well, good bloke. It's nothing to do with you, it's just the rules from our high command. We've been told not to communicate with non-military outfits, especially yours, for security reasons. We can hear you, and that's how we know so much about you. We listen and record the Revelationist's chatter as well, that way we can cross reference and validate the stories we hear. The terrorists are terrified of meeting you lot in action, but their higher command keep pushing them. We're waiting for the command chain to break down and the terrorists to start pushing back against their leaders. That's when we know it's time to hit them." Doff drank the rest of his tea and took a cup of coffee in his huge paws.

"And Sundown's Commando has been doing all the hard work of forcing the Revelationists to come unstuck. If you lot keep up the pressure then we'll see the whole established organisation start to crumble in this region." He finished his coffee, burped loudly causing the two boys to giggle. Doff then poured himself another cup while digging into the cakes. "And what's more, you're the only organised force in the entire country with repeated wins against the terrorists. Every other force has either dispersed because of starvation, or poor leadership. That's why we came out here, to get your mob on side - we need you more than you need us."

Beamy nodded, but inside he was thinking, 'Holy crap! I need to talk to Andy or Sundown about this.'

After stocking up on refreshments, Sundown left the milling mob of soldiers and civilians and took his team into the meeting room. He introduced his committee to the major and captain.

"This is Andy, my two IC, he runs everything." They shook hands and Andy sat down at the main table.

"Wiram is ex-military and in charge of patrols, security, ordnance and discipline. He's our Sergeant Major." Wiram nodded politely but Sundown could see the animosity smoldering behind his eyes.

"Halo is our Weapons Master in charge of weapons and training." Halo nodded and sat down with Wiram.

Pedro was sitting hunched over in his wheel chair. It had become part of his anatomy now that he couldn't walk in his tin legs any more. Lorraine had spent a lot of time with the old warrior trying to cheer him up while working to fix his infected stumps. It was a losing battle, his flesh was slowly rotting away and he was always in pain. His mood had shifted from cantankerous to despair and everyone noticed, Sundown in particular.

"This relic here is Pedro, our sniper and strategist. Without him I would be a dead man and so would the rest of us." Sundown smiled and Pedro nodded to the visitors then leaned back in his chair to ease the pain in his legs.

"I'm sorry mateys if I can't sit out this meeting. If I have to leave early it's because me legs is stinging and I'm feeling darn off. I'll stay as long as I can but don't go thinking I'm being rude if I just ups and leave." Pedro's voice was soft and he was clearly uncomfortable. It hurt the commando to see their hero like this.

"That's fine, soldier, if there's anything we can do then please don't hesitate to ask," said the major, acknowledging Pedro's contribution to the commando's successes.

"And this is Tricia, my right hand lady, she runs the girl side of things." Tricia pursed her lips and stared at Sundown. "Umm, well, she's head nurse and runs our first-aid and everything to do with hygiene and health. She's also my sounding board along with Andy here. When we need to make decisions I rely on Tricia a lot."

Tricia smiled politely, sat down and the meeting began.

"I'd like to first convey the Australian Government's congratulations on the work you are doing here. I know this is a team effort and not the work of one man. The community you have here is one of the very few that have survived against the odds. We've come across many communities since the apocalypse and none have gone beyond a threadbare existence. Your community is flourishing and you've also fought set battles against a trained and numerically superior foe. That takes courage as well as organisation. Please accept our congratulations." The major then got straight to why his squadron had crossed the Simpson Desert.

"Sundown, Third Army in Alice Springs have asked that you become part of our organisation. We want you to join us. You have stopped the enemy from progressing beyond Marree as well as blocked their contact with Longreach and Mount Isa. They can't join up without going through you or by a very determined trip through the desert. In short, we want to supply you with weapons and personnel to stay here and hold this piece of ground, to stop all enemy movement on this road." The major sat back in his chair watching everyone carefully.

Wiram was the first to speak and Sundown was grateful, he didn't quite know what to say. "I can only speak for myself but I don't think we need to join your mob and come under military jurisdiction to run a guerrilla force. We can just as easily act as a special, independent commando unit. I'll be walking out of here if we join your army. I've done my stretch and I won't be going back there."

Pedro nodded then spoke, "I agree with you, Wirrie, we have something special here and no one's going to put me back in uniform. I say supply us, sure, throw us some heavy weapons to hold any armour they sends our way. Provide a detachment of thirty or forty men, two APC's and your ASLAV and we'll work with you. But don't try to control us, we did well enough without you lot."

The captain had been observing their tone and body language, he spoke next. "Fella's, we expected you to say no. We haven't just walked in here to take over, but we think you should consider our offer. We can easily set up a standing patrol here by ourselves, but you already have one and a reputation of toughness and success. Your mob are battle hardened and we want you to join us to consolidate the eventual move to take back our country." He stopped when he saw the hostility in their eyes.

"No one wants to join the army, mate," this was Halo, the warrior who worshiped all things military. "No disrespect, captain." Turning slightly he nodded across to the major. "Or to you, Major. But we are doing fine as we are right now. Just send us that standing patrol, some armour, set up your observation and ambush points and we'll work together. I don't see anything wrong with that."

The major shifted uncomfortably then his face hardened. "We expected this, an independent commando is fine, we can live with that, but when we move to take back our country you'll need to come under military command.

We don't want people running about causing more problems for our government than we already have. We have plans to take back our country from the terrorists and it'll be as one force, one command and one rule. If you can't accept that then we will be walking out of here and you won't be seeing us again. No support, no armour and no reinforcements, or any kind of backup, when you need it."

The major's voice softened and he turned to look at Sundown. "I suggest you come back with us to Third Army command in Alice Springs and negotiate with our general. As it is you are a rebel organisation, without authorisation to use weapons or engage in action of any kind. Your commando is another terrorist threat the Australian Army have the authority to execute at any time. Under Military Law we don't need the government's permission to walk in here and wipe you out." The major thrust his chin out at Sundown and continued. "I don't need to remind you Sundown, that you have created a marvelous commando here. Your community are self supportive and they worship you. As I said before, we have not found a single community with the structure and harmony we've found here. I would hate to have to destroy it. But I will if we consider you a threat to the Australian Government and its people."

Wiram and Halo stood up their faces red and their hands clenched into fists. Pedro's lips were flecked with spittle as he mouthed soundless curses. Tricia quickly stood up and spoke clearly in her best British, private-school voice.

"Thank you, Major Thompson. If you and your captain would care to come outside and have some refreshments we would like to talk in private, without you, to discuss this matter. It's best we take a break and I'll get the girls to serve dinner." She walked around the table and ushered the two officers out of the room.

"Fuck off!" cried Halo once they had left the room. "There's no way we're going to let them destroy what we've created here. Who do these pricks think they are!" He was furious.

"That, my friends, is the military in action. Now you can see what I had to go through. I'll go walkabout before I join that mob again." Wiram stood his hands clenching and unclenching.

"OK, settle down everyone." Sundown's voice was soft and he remained seated. "Let's get some food into us and have a chat. There's a few things I want to discuss with you before we meet with them again."

Andy looked at Pedro then at Sundown. "Sundown, you're probably thinking what I'm thinking. But yes, let's get some food into us first."

Tricia had returned with Mel and Jeda and a tray of food, they ate while they talked. Sundown asked each in turn for their views and held the conversation tight and to the point.

"Folks, this is our community and their safety depends on our decision today. Just remember we represent our family here and the future of the children and oldies. OK, Pedro, I can see you're stewing up there. I know you're in pain but if you don't mind hanging around for a little longer I need you here with me tonight."

"Harrumph," said Pedro, he hadn't eaten anything all day. The staph infection was now in his blood and slowly killing him, he had no stomach for food. "I say stuff 'em! But that arrogant prig is just doing his job, I know, but what he says is bullshit. But, it's also absolutely bloody true. They can declare us terrorists if we don't fight under the government's authority. We don't need their weapons or their men, we actually don't need them at all, we know that. But when push comes to shove and they take up the big fight to drive those Revelationists out of the country, and they'll win you know, we need to be on their side."

"I think we should push for a position as an independent commando, one that rules itself and not under direct control of the army," said Halo and Wiram nodded his assent.

"Tricia? What do you think?" asked Andy.

"I need more time. We have a community here and if they're under threat I'll not live with myself. I say we ask them to give us some time to think it over. Then we send a delegation to Alice Springs and meet formally with their head of army," she said.

"Andy? What are these thoughts of yours?" Sundown had yet to add to the conversation preferring to wait until everyone else had spoken.

"Well, I'm not up on military law but the major is right. As Pedro said, the army, as an extension of the Government of Australia, have the right to declare our commando a rebel organisation. The Australian Government are still our ruling body until we know otherwise. We need to think carefully about what we want to do next. I was thinking we have two plans of action." He stopped to make sure he had everyone's attention. "Firstly, we can disband and go our separate ways, some to the Flinders Ranges, some to the Alice, some can go bush or set up in a homestead somewhere. Or we could accept their invitation to join up and come under their umbrella as an independent commando, but that means we will have to fight under their orders. But I have a feeling there is a Plan C as well."

They all looked at him, no one smiled until Pedro began chuckling. "You're a funny bastard, Andy, you knows what we'll do don't you. You've already seen the outcome of this meeting. But OK, let's throw this out some more. What if we tells them to piss off? We could head off to Flinders as a community and set up there, but then we'll be fighting more terrorists and more often. We'll attract more attention and the army will drop in again with the same offer. Then what?"

"We've heard nothing from Roo and Bongo. They've been gone three weeks and still nothing, we don't even know if they're alive," said Halo. "We don't know if the Flinders is safe. I agree with Pedro, if we go there we'll just be fighting closer to the terrorists home base. We need to negotiate our best deal, maybe as a parallel company, one independent and one military? Maybe, like the last world war we can enroll as volunteers for the duration. Strewth, I don't know Sundown. What if this mythical Third Army, turns out to be a bunch of morons with a psychopath leader like the terrorists, but with army uniforms and armour?"

Sundown looked at Halo and nodded, it was time to show his hand to his trusted committee. "Those are my thoughts too, Halo. These soldiers could just be con-men in uniform, though they do act like regulars." He looked at Wiram who nodded at the last point. "OK, thought so, so if they are regulars then they'll do whatever they are ordered to do, even if their leader, this general of the Third Army, is a psychopath." Looking at each one he continued. "I know that we seem to be in a tough position, but this is what we'll do." As one the group leaned forward as though Sundown were whispering.

"Andy, I need Fat Boy to go back to Longreach and get those aeroplane parts for Bill. I need Roo and Bongo back with a report on the state of the Flinders Ranges, and I need to know exactly what sort of man runs this Third Army." He looked at everyone, they were staring at him intently, waiting for his decision.

"I assure you I won't sell us out. We have always considered our people first, that's not going to change, not now, not ever. We make the best decision for our people, our family, even if that means we join them. Does anyone think otherwise? Please, speak up now." No one moved and he continued to wait for their nods of agreement. Slowly, one by one they agreed. He looked across at the two warriors who finally gave an affirmative nod.

"More than anything, I need to buy time. If I think we can continue independently, we will. It all rides on what sort of leader this army general is. If I'm not satisfied that he is one of us..." he paused and smiled.

Andy filled the silence, "You're planning to take command of Third Army aren't you."

Sundown looked at his admin officer and nodded. "I'll let my berserker out. Is everyone on the same page with me? If I need to take command of Third Army, I plan to." Sundown looked around at his committee and smiled. His demon twin sat quietly inside his being watching, hoping.

Andy and Pedro both chuckled quietly as Tricia got up and left the room. Wiram and Halo stood in shock.

"Boyo's, you really didn't think our Sundown would lead us into damnation now did you?" said Pedro gleefully. "Why, he's already led us there!" He roared as he wheeled his chair out into the passage way calling for Wiram and Halo to join him, a new lease of life in his limbs.

It was five minutes later that Tricia came back with the major and captain in tow and sat them down. There were only the five of them, Wiram and Halo had left with Pedro to resume their conversations over a beer and to talk with Bill and Fat Boy.

Tricia flashed her eyes repeatedly trying to get Sundown's attention but he didn't notice. Instead he quickly reopened the meeting.

"I do apologise for being rude," began the major, "we came here to offer support and knew you wouldn't be pleased. But the alternative is not pleasant. Sorry but we do need to know your intentions." The major sipped at his bush tea, enjoying its pleasant taste.

"We haven't reached a conclusion yet, but we do wish to participate in the push to remove these terrorists. We're prepared to do whatever is needed to get the job done. I'll go to the Alice and meet your Third Army leader and speak with him personally. You understand that as head of this community I need to know that my people will be looked after properly. After all, I'm hearing this for the first time and I need to know whether you can back up your words once we get to Alice." Sundown smiled politely.

"Fair enough," replied Major Thompson. "We leave tomorrow morning, you can take your second in command. We don't have much room but an extra one won't put too much strain on our comfort."

"Tomorrow? That's less time than I need. I want to speak with everyone in my community, and I'm firm on that. I need three days at least to sit and talk to everyone, and my committee need to sort out exactly how we wish to manage this transition." Sundown again smiled. "I don't see anything wrong with your proposal. In fact, I can see we could compliment each other very well."

Sundown saw the lined faces of the officers relax and knew he was back in control. "Give me a week and then I'll drive myself across the Madigan Line. It's going to be tough going after that rain but I'll do it and we'll meet up in Alice by the end of the month. If your army head doesn't like it then I need you to convince him. I have a successful community here and that's worth a few weeks wait. He's waited this long surely he can wait a little longer."

The major had his chin cupped in his hand, thinking. "We'll leave the ASLAV behind with a squad to man it. They'll help you patrol and provide some backbone to your small arms." He relaxed his arm and sat back up. "I'm glad you understand the seriousness of our situation, Sundown. Our resources are limited and our numbers small. Your commando may be the straw that finally breaks the back of the terrorists in our region."

The captain cut in, "Sir, the Madigan Line might take them at least three weeks to cross." He turned to Sundown, "why not use the French Line across the Simpson Desert, like we did?"

"Simple, you're heavy vehicles have no doubt chopped the track to pieces. It'll be unusable. That plus the recent rainfall has no doubt ruined it for even our best four-wheel drives. If we go any further south we'll run into the Marree terrorists, they've got posts just below the French Line. I'm not going to put my people at more risk than is necessary. Three weeks, it'll be hard, extremely hard, the Madigan Line is a tough haul and I'll need two vehicles and a squad of my own people, but it's safer. If you leave your ASLAV here I can afford to pull extra men off the front line. Besides, I might take my wife and have a second honeymoon on the trip across." Sundown's face brightened at that thought. When he saw the officer's reactions he knew the meeting was his.

Captain Lewis turned to the major, "Well, I guess that's OK, the terrorists didn't come near us nor would they given our armour. There's over a thousand sand dunes to cross on the French Line, we had a tough enough time with it coming in here as it was. They'll never do it after we've gone through a second time, he's right. The general didn't expect us to have Sundown till the end of winter anyway so we'll still be in front by a month."

"All right, we have your word on this?" Major Thompson extended his hand across the table to Sundown and they shook.

"You certainly do. I have a feeling we'll have a positive discussion and a satisfactory outcome. Sundown's Commando will go down in history as one of the pivotal commando's in turning around this whole damn apocalypse." Sundown then invited everyone back to the main lounge and joined the crowd.

Andy jumped in before they stood up to leave. He'd been thinking of what they needed and now was as good a time as any. "Major, before we finish, there are supplies we urgently need. Namely medical supplies and ammunition for specialist weapons like our sniper rifles, grenades and the Javelin. Some body armour would help too. We'd like more vegetables and fruits. Is there any chance of pushing this through?"

The major nodded slightly. "When Sundown gets to the Alice he can requisition anything he wants. We might not have much though, we're flat out maintaining our own troops and civilians, tinned goods for the troops is limited. But I'll see what I can do."

"Major, one more thing if you please," said Andy. "Our radio team need to be able to communicate with you. Can your boys teach our team your code? It'll save a hell of a lot of wasted time."

The major smiled, his thin lips pursed as he spoke, "Certainly, but you do realise that as a rogue commando I don't have the authority to divulge our communications codes until you have been inducted into our military. Any communications will need to go through our communications officer posted here with you." '*Bingo*!' he thought and his smile broadened. He'd finally scored a point against these tough commandos.

Andy grinned back at him. "Yeah, I knew you'd say that, but it was worth a try."

As they left the room Tricia grabbed Sundown by the arm and pulled him off into the kitchen. "Sundown, I just spoke to Beamy. He has some important information and you need to hear it. It's good, damn good."

Chapter 21

Nulla and Charlene

When dawn broke, Charlene woke to see the back door open and she could hear Heidi crying softly outside. She carefully untangled herself from a blanket that had been thrown over her and went straight to her dear friend. In Heidi's hand was a note.

"Heidi, what is it? Where'd you get that? What does it say?"

"It was left behind last night, it's from the Australian Army. Someone from the army left it here and we thought it was terrorists. I'm such a fool." She burst out laughing and crying at the same time. Charlene sat beside her in the early morning sunlight, barely warm enough even though she was wearing a jumper. She put her good arm around her friend and hugged her.

"But what does it say! Read it to me!" she cried, she needed to know.

"It says we're saved, they're coming to rescue us." Heidi then handed the note across to Charlene who read its short verse avidly.

"They'll be here tonight, I can't wait. What a relief!" She hugged Heidi again and kissed her on the head.

"What on earth is going on out here?" It was Phil, he'd barely slept all night. His eyes were bloodshot, his face sagged and his scant hair stood at all angles. He looked tired and aged.

Heidi stood up and hugged him, her tears smeared across his cheeks. "Phil, it's the army, they were the ones who visited us last night, look!"

Phil took the note and read it several times. "I can't believe it, why didn't they bloody-well come knocking instead of scaring the hell out of us?"

"I guess they didn't want us to shoot them as intruders. Seems pretty smart in some ways. They sure frightened us didn't they." Heidi was still crying and turned as Annie came outside to see what all the fuss was about.

"Go tell Auntie Fati and your mum to come outside, we have a special surprise for them," she whispered to the little girl.

"A surprise? Yeah! Mum! MUM!" Annie ran off into the house waking everyone.

The group sat outside in the autumn sunlight drinking Fatima's fresh-roasted coffee. They chatting excitedly about what they were going to do when the army arrived. Fatima worried what she should cook for them while Arthur worried if they would accept him into their ranks, he so wanted revenge against the terrorists. Charlene was excited but she was also quiet, too quiet for Heidi.

"Charlene, what are you thinking? A penny for your thoughts?" asked Heidi.

"Well... I was just thinking about last night and how frightened we were. We lost it, except you, Phil and Arthur. I made a mess of myself. I should have been the one to challenge those soldiers at the back door. I should have called out and stood up for my friends. When will I ever get over this freaking fear I have." She slumped into her chair her eyes starting to well with tears.

"Blimey, Chas, it should have been me. I should have had the courage to go outside and challenge them, not you." Arthur had taken Tony's role in championing Charlene when she spoke up.

"Knock it off you lot, I'm the oldest and it should have been me." Now Phil put in his bit as he stood up and flexed his muscles. The aged man was so thin it made Annie giggle. When Phil smiled the tension was broken.

"I'm sorry everyone, I just keep remembering I was once a whole person who would take on the world." Charlene stopped for a moment and glanced around for Annie. "But now things are different and I'm going to make my life what it was before this apocalypse. Annie, do you still have those Power Ranger toys?" Annie nodded, "Would you bring them out for me please?" asked Charlene.

When Annie came back she carried a shopping bag full of action toys. "Is this what you wanted?" she asked Charlene, her face filled with expectation.

"Yes, now pick one that's a real hero, just for me, for me to keep. I need an action hero of my own," said Charlene.

Annie tipped the toys onto the table and the adults watched as she named and stood the toys in a row while she considered Charlene's request. "Ah, this one, Kimberly, the Pink Ranger! That's you, Charlene." Annie smiled and handed it to her friend. "You can have this one, I've got spares anyway." She turned to the adults, "Anyone else want one?"

"That's OK, Annie," said Lucy coldly. "Charlene's the only one who needs a Power Ranger, the rest of us can do without." She helped her daughter pack the toys away. Arthur and Heidi looked at Charlene and winked. This wasn't lost on Fatima or Phil either.

When Lucy and Annie had gone inside Fatima spoke up. "It's been a hell of a night, let's not read too much into what Lucy said."

"You're right, Fati. Lucy's had a tough time losing Tony and then last night topped it off. We need to be mindful of our own limits too," responded Phil, seriously. "But in the meantime I'm going to feed the chickens and gather some eggs. Coming with me, Charlene?"

"Me and Kimberly!" she said as she jumped out of her chair eager to escape the tension only Lucy could bring to disrupt the dweller's harmony.

Glenda wasn't happy at being asked to stay behind but she knew how important this meeting was for Nulla. The group had decided that it should be Simon who escorted Nulla to the meeting with the dwellers. Luke would stay behind with Glenda and listen on their CB for enemy activity.

"We've only got an hour's bike ride, Simon, so get a move on," yelled Nulla from his bedroom.

"I'm sorting out my weapons, I've lost my 38 and can't find it. Glenda!" he called from his bedroom, "where did I put my 38 after we arrived here?"

Glenda was in the lounge room sewing buttons onto her sweater, Luke was at the radio. "Simon, it's on the bench where I left it. Next to the biscuit tin."

She didn't even look up when she heard Simon's grunt as he found it. "Thanks, did you clean it?"

"Yes, I used the pull-through and oiled it. Came in handy, didn't it?" Now she looked up and saw Simon's face break into a huge smile.

"Yeah, sure did, she's a little beauty isn't she." He wandered off spinning the chamber planning to oil and re-arm it ready for their trip. "You just never know when you might need a small hand-gun like this baby."

Nulla left Simon to cover him as he approached the back door. They had broken a hole in the fence in readiness for a fast retreat if they needed it. Simon wore camouflage paint and both wore their night-vision goggles. Nulla could see the lit candle at the back door and a big sign that said 'WELCOME'.

He knocked on the door and announced clearly, "Armoured Cavalry, Sergeant Nulla, please open the door and show yourselves."

Charlene opened the door and went straight to the soldier. She extended her good hand and began crying. Nulla saw her arm in its sling, he took her hand and said softy, "We're here to help you. Please, is it safe for my trooper covering us, to come inside with me?"

"Yes, yes, it's safe here. Please come inside, we've got a banquet for you. We're so happy to see you." She broke down just as Heidi and Phil walked out to meet their rescuers.

Nulla explained the situation as he saw it. Despite the let-down at such a tiny number of rescuers, the dwellers were enthused by Nulla's composure, confidence and his positive manner. All but one that is.

"So there's just you, two other fighters and your girlfriend?" asked Lucy acidly as her face contorted into a frown.

"Yes, you could put it that way, madam, but we've outfought the entire terrorist army all year, and that's all it took. I'm sure you will agree we can handle ourselves." Nulla didn't take shit from anyone, and this lady hadn't shown one ounce of respect since his arrival.

"I wouldn't put my trust in a handful of civilians or soldiers like your lot. It's not even the damn army, why should I?" continued Lucy her face tight with suppressed emotion.

Heidi looked awkwardly at Phil, who nodded and spoke. "Lucy, that's enough. If you want to stay here, you're welcome. Fati and I are too old to go waltzing around the country-side anyway. But at least give the others a chance, and Annie."

"We put so much hope in that letter you left behind.' Lucy completely ignored Phil. "What a damn let-down, especially after the torture of last night thinking you were the terrorists stomping around outside the house. You scared the daylights out of us. Aren't you even sorry? You come here with this, this child, expecting us to greet you as the all conquering hero come to rescue us. What a damn let-down you are!"

The dwellers looked down at the table top. Heidi had begun serving the meal but suddenly no one felt like eating. It was so uncomfortable she fled back to the kitchen. Fatima walked in just as Lucy finished speaking. Not having heard any of the conversation she picked up straight away that something was wrong.

"Oh, isn't anyone hungry? I've made a lovely entrée of deviled eggs, hot and spicy like everyone likes them..." Her voice petered out to silence. She quickly exited to the kitchen wondering what was happening. Charlene got up taking Annie with her to the kitchen with the excuse of helping. The girls were deserting.

"Looks like it's just us boys and you, Lucy. You've managed to ruin everyone's dinner, thank you. I hope you're satisfied now?" Phil was fuming but controlled himself. He had never really felt comfortable with Lucy, in fact, no one really did, but tonight she excelled herself.

"I don't care, Phil, I've lost everything. I wish I had died when I was sick and if I had known I was going to lose my good husband, I would have killed myself then." She started to cry, big sobs wracked her body. Her shoulders shook and an enormous roar escaped her lips. It was frightening to listen to. Simon stood up almost knocking his chair over and retreated to the corner lounge chair not knowing what to do. Nulla just stood and walked around the table to Lucy.

"Lucy," he said firmly but softly, "we're here to do our best for you. I don't give a rat's arse if you don't approve or if you don't want us to help, but we're here anyway. When you stop your slobbering and whining we can talk like adults. And that 'child' I brought with me has killed his share of terrorists. He's a warrior and I wouldn't trade him for a dozen elite soldiers."

Nulla leaned forward and took Lucy in his arms drawing her deep into his powerful chest. She struggled but he wouldn't let go. Lucy began screaming and tried to hit him but he held firm.

Eventually she stopped struggling and wept. Hardhearted Lucy now held Nulla seeking to bury herself in his safe, secure manliness. She cried and the tears helped wash her pain and suffering away.

Phil, Arthur and Simon watched in amazement, none of them expected the evening to turn out like this. At first they thought Nulla was going to slap her, especially after what he said to her. When he held her and wrestled with her they didn't know if they should get up and stop him. But now they were grateful they didn't. Lucy sobbed quietly in his arms as meek as a kitten. Simon looked shyly at Arthur who caught his eye and gave a weak smile. It was a 'holy shit did you see that?' smile.

Heidi looked in on them from the entrance to the kitchen and noted everything. "Is it OK to bring the food in now? It's going to get cold and taste horrible."

The meal turned out to be a success after all. Fati fussed over everyone, especially the two newcomers. Lucy was subdued but kept leaning her head on Nulla's shoulder, only to bury her face in his chest and cry some more. Nulla held her tightly in his arms each time.

"Folks," he announced at the end of the main course, "we have a chance to get away from the city. To make a life of our own, in the country somewhere. We aren't too sure yet where but I know I will be doing my duty as appointed, to build a resistance and fight these terrorists until they are no more." He paused. "Anyone who wants to join myself, Simon here, Luke and my partner Glenda, are welcome."

Charlene spoke first. "Nulla, how are we going to do it? How can we cross the country without being caught? That's my concern, being caught again. Look at me." She lifted her frozen left arm and tried to straighten it, without success. "That's what they did to me, and I don't want another experience like that, none of us do."

"We're in touch with a group in Birdsville. If all goes well we'll hook up with them, join forces." Nulla continued, "We listen to every conversation these terrorists say on their CB network, and that's a secret so don't tell anyone. If we take the back roads we'll have an open run once we get out of the city, then all the way to the Flinders Ranges. It can be done with planning and night driving. We got here, we survived here, and we'll soon be leaving here."

"Can you teach us to shoot?" asked Arthur speaking for the first time. He looked at Nulla and Simon's rifle in the corner of the room and their military gear, he shivered with excitement.

"Simon?" Nulla passed this to his man-at-arms.

"Yes, Arthur, we can do that. You'll love the Steyr too, it's awesome," Simon said with a grin.

"OK, count me in." These were his last words that night too.

"Me too. I want to learn to shoot as well," said Charlene. Everyone looked at her in surprise, even Lucy and Annie.

"How are you going to shoot a rifle, Charlene? You've only got one arm," said Annie. Lucy squirmed uncomfortably trying to hush her daughter up.

Charlene wasn't going to let anyone dampen her enthusiasm, not even little Annie. "I'll learn, honey, I'll learn somehow. I've felt so damn useless all this time and now I want some revenge. Thanks Nulla and Simon for coming to visit us, I now have hope that we'll survive this mess. Now, can you teach me too, Simon?" She looked directly at the teenage warrior who shifted awkwardly in his seat under the gaze of this pretty, blond-haired beauty.

"Yeah, sure, I can teach you to shoot. I've taught girls before. I mean, I taught Glenda, and she saved our bacon with just a pistol. Sure, I can teach you how to shoot." He smiled at her knowing he was doing the right thing.

"My boys will teach everyone how to shoot, in fact, we all need to know how to defend ourselves." By this time Fati was preparing to serve dessert, a delicious sago pudding with a mixture of Indian spices and a baked cake base with a jam layer.

"I'm sorry, but did you just say you're going to teach us how to shoot? You mean with rifles and stuff?" Heidi asked as she spooned the last piece of curried carp into her mouth.

Nulla looked up from his empty plate, "Yes, Heidi, everyone needs to know how to protect themselves and each other. If you come with me you learn how to kill. I hope that's not a problem?"

Heidi sat quietly mouthing a few words but nothing came out. Arthur looked on, he'd never seen Heidi speechless before.

"I, I guess it's all right," she finally said. "We've never really had to use weapons before. In fact, we were afraid to because it'd draw the terrorists to us. But if you can get us out of here then I want to learn to shoot too."

"Lucy? Do you want to learn to defend yourself too?" Nulla asked looking directly into her eyes. He wanted to give her the opportunity to have her say, before she withdrew into herself.

"I want to learn how to kill them. Any thing, any way, any weapon, I don't care. I'm with Charlene, I want revenge for what those cowards did to us, all of us." Lucy returned his stare. "Nulla, yes, I want to learn to shoot too."

Fatima and Phil weren't sure what they wanted to do. The more they listened to Nulla the more they wanted to go with him. But they were now quite settled in their twilight years with their chickens, vegetable gardens, fruit trees and books. What more could they want in life?

At the end of their dessert Nulla stood up and announced, "I've got to get home to my missus." He motioned for Simon to follow. "She'll be wondering where I am. I'll be back tomorrow with Luke and then we'll talk some more."

Charlene appeared to have suddenly become the dwellers spokesperson. "Nulla, thank you for coming here. We look forward to seeing you and Luke tomorrow night. Simon, don't forget your promise and please find some spare weapons for us soon." Simon nodded. "When we wake up later we're going to talk among ourselves. We should have some answers and some questions for you when you come back."

The two warriors nodded and turned towards the door. Just then Lucy rushed across the floor and threw herself into Nulla's surprised arms. "Thank you," she said simply. She kissed him on the lips then stepped back.

"And Nulla," Fatima called just before they left. "The night after I want the four of you to come and stay with us for a few days, maybe move in with us. Then we can plan exactly what to do. If we agree to go we'll need solid planning. Besides, we've got spare bedrooms and clean sheets and I'm sure Glenda will enjoy the female company." Phil and the others nodded.

The small group of house dwellers experienced various levels of excitement as the two army representatives walked into the early morning darkness.

Chapter 22

Nulla and Charlene - leaving the city

They moved in over the next few nights and things settled down to a routine of training and planning. The group agreed that they should take two four-wheel drives only, more would slow them down and most likely cause them problems. They found two large Toyota Cruisers which Phil and Arthur worked on together giving them a thorough service and then outfitting them for the trip.

In the meantime Simon and Luke taught the girls and Arthur how to handle the AK47 and the Steyr. They didn't do any live firing but they pulled them apart and drilled the process of managing a misfire, magazine changes, cleaning, oiling, running with a weapon, aiming and night vision firing.

Within two weeks the company had spent every day drilling with weapons by day and by night. Even Annie enjoyed the exercises and was proving to be just as proficient as the others. Simon took command of the training using the same methods Nulla used with he and Luke.

Fatima spent a lot of time cooking and preparing meals, she also organised Heidi and Charlene to begin packing and storing their dried food and cooking gear into plastic containers. Nulla and Phil showed Simon, Luke and Arthur how to pack the vehicles in the most efficient way.

Phil enjoyed the company of the boys more than he thought he would. He was amazed at how quickly the two teenagers engaged with himself and Arthur, and how well they picked up the mechanics of servicing the vehicles.

Glenda felt a little lost until Fati took her under her wing and gave her odd jobs to do. Glenda wasn't a cook, she was more a communicator, but she soon learned house management and food preparation as quickly as the girls had done when they had moved in together.

The boys spent a lot of time together working on the vehicles and their weapons. Nulla finally agreed to allow the three boys to ride motor bikes while everyone else went in the Toyota's. Their reasoning was that it made more room for everyone else, they could fit more food and equipment in and they could ride shotgun in front and behind in case of an ambush. It certainly made sense but as in all things Heidi felt she should have been consulted first.

It took three weeks of working days and nights, constant patrols, training and many extra trips to the supermarket and hardware stores.

The night before they were to leave Heidi walked into Phil's workshop to check on things.

"Phil, do we have silenced mufflers for these damn noisy cars and bikes? The terrorists will hear us for miles," she asked with her hands on her hips.

Phil looked at her, then at Arthur, then at the bikes. "Well, Heidi, I never thought of that." He stopped what he was doing and called to Arthur, "Arty, looks like we have extra work to do tonight, can you go and get the boys please?"

"Hmm, just as well I was here to remind you isn't it," she said and walked back out a bright smile playing across her face.

Arthur and the boys rode their push-bikes to and from the motorcycle shops bringing mufflers and baffles and all sorts of odds and ends for Phil to work with. It took three extra days before he was satisfied the bikes rode as silently as he could make them without losing power or speed. The two vehicles were fine. He did try to modify their mufflers as well but gave up. Throwing his tools into their bags he declared they were ready.

"Nulla?" Arthur said as they inspected the equipment, tied extra ropes to the roof racks and repacked the trailer. "Nulla, can we go out tonight, just us bikers, and trial run our bikes? We need some practice before we leave."

Nulla saw the hopeful look in his eyes but shook his head. "Sorry, mate, that's a no go. We don't have time. I need you boys here to help pack our gear. Besides, it just might bring the Revelationists right to our doorstep. This is exactly the time we need to be under cover and as quiet as mice."

The look Arthur, Simon and Luke gave Nulla made him laugh out loud. "Haven't I been training you fella's to think for yourselves. Luke, why did I say 'no'."

"Because you're mean and stopped having fun when you were three years old and now you don't want anyone else to have any fun," sulked Luke.

"Right, spot on, I am a mean bastard who'll keep you alive. Now go and grab the food bags Fati and the girls have packed ready for stacking. Simon, did you store the water on board where I told you?" He continued giving orders and keeping the boys busy so they wouldn't annoy him any more.

Phil watched the exchange with Nulla and Luke. Once the boys were gone he walked over. "Nulla, how do you think the boys will go once we head off? Do you think they'll stick to the plan and not ride off all over the place? Just curious."

Nulla's grin said it all. "My boys know that if they play up on me, they'll lose their rifles. It's simple arithmetic Phil, find their weak point and jab it once in a while, they soon learn." He went over to Phil's tool kit to help the old man sort out the essentials to take with them.

That afternoon Nulla called the boys over. "I've been thinking, fella's. Simon, remember that shopping centre we stopped at, where we found Glenda? Those people we said we'd come back to visit?"

Simon nodded.

"Do you think you could ride your bikes there tonight and check the place over. See if anyone left any messages in the bin. If there are survivors then contact them and report back here. Do you reckon you can do that by yourselves?"

The boys were already nodding excitedly. Luke spoke up, "You betchya boss! We'll start planning right now! Come on guys, we have some planning to do. We leave at midnight!"

Nulla spent half the night on the CB radio talking to Sydney Charlie and the Birdsville commando. Although he didn't give his plan away he did ask about the Flinders Ranges. Both contacts told him that the Flinders Ranges was probably a no-go hinting at heavy Revelationist activity.

They reported there were sympathetic farmers who would report anyone they found on their properties to the church. They also said there were prison farms in the Quorn and Hawker regions.

It was all bad news and Nulla decided to keep it to himself while he thought of his options. Pulling out the maps he spent part of the night looking at properties north of Adelaide and around the Murray River. There had to be a safe place where he could take his people and decided to head north and just see what happens. He wanted to get out of Adelaide first, then they would make up their minds. If the Flinders Ranges was out then he decided to try the Murray River, perhaps near Morgan. He'd decided earlier that Birdsville was just too far for their small group at this time.

By dawn the next morning the three teenagers had returned and were eating breakfast when Nulla came in. He was unshaven and tired, he rubbed at his eyes to get the sleep out of them.

"How'd it go boys, find anything, any signs?" he asked them.

"Nothing, no messages, no people," said Simon resignedly. He slumped back into his chair exhausted.

Luke added, "We saw another pack of dogs though. We had to shoot some. Don't tell Glenda, but they were vicious, they went wild when they saw us. They must've made their home inside the shops, that might be why we didn't see anyone. When we went inside they attacked us. One knocked me over and nearly killed me. There were about twenty of them and some of them were really big." Luke lifted his shirt to reveal a welt on his side but no puncture wounds. Then he showed his arm which was bruised and had been bleeding. Fortunately the boys were wearing their leather riding jackets, even big dogs would have a hard time biting through those.

"Hmm, better get Heidi or Fatima to check that out, you might get rabies from them. Arty, how did you go mate, did you manage OK with your leg?" asked Nulla.

"Yep, all good, Nulla, my leg held up fine, it's sore now though. That was quite a long ride and those night goggles are really awkward. I shot some dogs too, it was pretty crazy." Arthur spoke slowly but now he was getting into his story his voice came to life.

"We weren't even ready for them. They spotted us before we spotted them and they came at us. Look at Luke's arm, they knocked him over, they nearly killed him. Simon and I had to shoot some, then they ran off."

Nulla nodded filing the information away in his mind. "How'd the bikes go? Did they make any more noise than what we expected?" Nulla asked Simon, the more engineer-minded of the three.

"Perfect, Nulla. We need to tell Phil he's done a great job. The bikes didn't make any more sound than a purring kitten and they still had power. He'll be stoked with that," Simon replied.

Nulla had almost finished the debrief. "And did you follow patrolling protocols? Safety and silence?"

Arthur looked at Simon and Luke and they nodded to him to continue. "Yep, we did it exactly as we trained. The night scopes are awkward just like the goggles but they saved our lives." He stopped and looked back at the boys who nodded encouragement to continue. "I wanted to take point and I remembered to take the safety off my Steyr, that's what saved us from the dogs. If I hadn't done all that training in the dark, the dogs would have killed us."

Simon added, "I wanted Arthur up to speed and put him out front. He saved us. The dog that got through was a giant and knocked Luke over before we had a chance to move. Arthur fired and hit a lot of them. The noise frightened the rest of the pack before they got to us. He must have hit four or five of them in about three seconds. I shot the one attacking Luke with my 'special'." Simon smiled as he pulled it out from his shoulder holster to caress it lovingly. "Arthur had to finish off the ones we wounded. It wasn't nice but now we're all blooded. Boss, that was good practice for Arty, thanks."

"And boss," said Luke, "there were no survivors at the centre. We checked everywhere. I guess the dogs ate anyone they caught because there were signs of bodies they'd been eating. Those dogs have taken over the shopping centre and either the people have escaped or they died. I don't suggest we go back, we were too late to save them. I hope Glenda didn't have any friends there." Nulla nodded then directed them to get some sleep. They were leaving that night and they needed to be fresh and alert.

The night was dark, the weather cold and the night vision goggles made everything seem pale. Nulla knew how hard this would be, so he made sure everyone was comfortable wearing their night vision gear.

Every night for three or four hours he had them wearing the goggles inside and outside the house - running, lying down, sighting through their weapon scopes. Both vehicles had a sunroof the dwellers could stand up in and fire from. Right now he had Heidi in the back of Phil's Toyota standing, weapon at the ready and nigh vision goggles on. Glenda was doing the same in his vehicle.

They had their maps and everyone was drilled in the exact route they would take and the alternatives if there was trouble. Heidi had run the map drills and she had done it with night vision goggles at night, and in full vision in the daylight. If anyone became lost or separated, they knew where to meet up. They had backup plans for their backup plans, thanks to Heidi.

Nulla was still unsure of their final destination but said nothing, deciding that their next stop was probably the best time to tell everyone the bad news. He just wanted to get the hell out of the city no matter what, and if they changed plans now, then they would never leave.

Each vehicle and biker had a short wave radio, the boys had theirs strapped to their shoulders and connected to their helmets after some clever electrical wiring by Simon and Phil.

Heidi had devised a series of squelches and clicks so they wouldn't have to talk. Nulla was so impressed that he gave her full reign to teach everyone the sounds. She drilled them diligently before they left. Some nights she made everyone communicate in squelches and clicks only.

Heidi was in her element directing the action once again. "Guys, I don't need an action figure like Charlene, because, as Phil says, I AM an action figure! Action Heidi!" she would announce.

Charlene's spirits were up and she was now taking responsibility for some of the tasks, even telling Simon and Luke what to do. The boys loved it. Their adolescent hormones were riding high as they flirted with the two young women.

Lucy and Annie were just as excited as everyone else. Lucy spent a lot of time with Glenda and Nulla. She fawned over Nulla to the point that Glenda became a little jealous. Nulla never noticed, being so busy with their preparations. Glenda heard what the poor mother had been through and knew her fascination with Nulla would eventually wear off. But all the same, she had her man and she wasn't going to let him get too close to Lucy, not after all the hardship they'd been through.

The four-wheel drives were packed, the trailer was stacked with food, water and fuel, and the motor bikes ran like purring kittens. There was a mixture of enthusiasm and fear in the atmosphere as one by one the dwellers said goodbye to their home and climbed into their appointed vehicles.

Nulla drove out first with the trailer, stacked on top was a covered pen with Fatima's chickens and a rooster, Phil drove the other. Phil was an ex-rally driver, albeit a slow one these days. He was still driving cross-country treks right up to the time of the apocalypse.

Phil said he decided to go with them once he knew he wouldn't have to sit in the back seat. Fatima said she would follow her husband to hell and back if need be, as long as he promised to pull over when she had to go to the toilet. The girls giggled at that while the boys looked at the ceiling and rolled their eyes.

As the convoy rolled out of the garage right on midnight the boys shot ahead on their bikes into position. They pulled onto the main road while Simon took lead position with Arthur, Luke rode rearguard. The convoy was mobile at last and heading out of the city towards freedom - or so they hoped.

Chapter 23

Sundown - Roo's reckoning

The two led their heavily loaded horses and followed the tracks of Riley's truck. An hour before nightfall they heard rifle shots causing the horses to shy. Bongo turned to Roo, steadying his horse.

"Roo, I'll hold your horse while you go and check that out. I bet it's those terrorists shooting up Riley's home."

Sure enough, they saw smoke rising from the direction of the farmhouse. Roo came back from climbing one of the few tall trees and grunted. Bongo looked at him for a moment and said, "Yeah, I knew they'd do that. It's a wonder they took so long to get here. Are they on our tail?"

Roo nodded then tried to speak, "mmm," was all that came out.

"You're doing well, mate, soon you'll be talking so much we won't be able to shut you up."

Roo smiled and pointed his chin towards the hills they were walking towards.

"Damn," groaned Bongo, "more bloody hills to climb. I'm stuffed already and so's the horses. You sure we need to climb to high ground, Roo?"

Roo smiled and nodded, "mmm," he said again and urged his horse forward. He lead the way up into the gully and towards a particularly high rocky outcrop. As he did so Roo pointed to his rifle and then to the rocks.

"Ah, sniping time is it?" asked Bongo, and Roo nodded.

They tied their horses to a felled tree behind the hill. While Bongo watered and fed the tired horses Roo grabbed his weapon, some extra water, and started climbing. He made sure he put the hill between himself and the two Range Rovers heading their way. The Wilsons were following the tracks of their two horses and Riley's truck.

When Bongo finally crawled into position he was exhausted. They drank from their water bottles as the afternoon shadows covered the hideout, just as the two Rovers crawled into sight. Roo nudged Bongo in the ribs and pointed to his double-taped clip. His held up his hands twice, twenty bullets.

Bongo nodded and said, "You're almost out of Gewehr cartridges? I knew that'd happen, you've been shooting too many kangaroos, eh?" He grimaced, "Just save them for the enemy and leave the harassing fire to my trusty AK."

The vehicles were almost directly below when Roo fired and took out the driver of the first Rover. Bongo opened up and peppered the same car till his magazine was empty. As he reloaded Roo took out the second driver. The two cars were now trapped in the killing zone. Roo kept firing until Bongo finished reloading and took over.

Three of Wilson's men leaped from the rear vehicle and raced behind some rocks. They opened fire with automatics forcing Roo and Bongo to scamper back from their position – they had just lost control of the fire-fight.

"Shit!" said Roo frightening the life out of Bongo.

"Bloody hell, Roo, you've got to warn a bloke before speaking like that!" Bongo slipped in a new magazine.

"You're just like a new born, your first word has to be a swear word."

Each time one of them tried to look over the rocky edge a spray of bullets swept around them. Splinters of rock hit their faces and it was Bongo's turn to swear.

Roo suddenly swung his rifle behind and pulled the trigger. There came a roaring echo among the rocks and gully's as a blast of automatic fire came at them in reply. Bongo screamed as a bullet went through his leg and Roo's head was flung back as another ricocheted off the rocks and creased his scalp.

"Hell's bell's!" spat Bongo clutching at his leg while trying to squirm to safety in the tight confines of the small rock ledge. He eventually brought his AK47 to target the track behind them. More bullets hit the rocks above and rained shards of deadly quartz fragments at their heads.

All was quiet for a moment as both Roo and Bongo tried to get into a better position but each movement brought more incoming fire.

"Roo, I think we're stuck. We've got to do something." Adrenaline was pumping through Bongo's system. "My leg's busted I think. I can't feel it. There's blood everywhere. Roo, keep an eye on them while I wrap something around it."

Bongo groaned as he contorted his body around enough to tie his handkerchief over the wound. It was useless and didn't stop the bleeding so he ripped his shirt off piece by piece and wrapped it around his leg. He had lost so much blood that he fainted.

Roo was fighting waves of dizziness when out of the corner of his eye he saw the top of a head move on the track leading to their ledge. He snapped off a shot without having time to aim. He saw an explosion of blood and gore.

One of the men below screamed, "You bastards! I'm gonna kill ya's for that!"

Roo saw Brad scramble up the track firing one of the terrorist's AK47's from his hip. Bullets whipped towards him spitting dust and rock splinters. One hit Roo's arm snapping the bone while another tore a hole in his boot just missing his foot. As though in slow motion Roo awkwardly switched his sniper rifle to his left hand and snapped off a shot at his assailant. He saw Brad flung backwards as though pulled by a rope. His vision was blurring and things were happening in slow motion, but he refused to give up.

Roo was now almost out of Gewehr ammunition and his right arm was useless. The bullet had gone through his forearm fracturing the radius bone, he struggled to ignore the agonising pain. His lip bled where he'd bitten it and the blood from his head wound spread down his face and chest.

In a daze he heard the sound of the Rover starting up so he crawled back to the edge of the rocky outcrop. There was no more incoming fire. As the Rover reversed back up the gully, Roo slowly and painfully raised his Gewehr and sighted carefully. Just before it disappeared around a rocky outcrop he pulled the trigger and collapsed.

Riley's dogs found the bodies in the darkness. He flashed his torch and examined them, he recognised some. Cattlemen from the Flinders Ranges, some had once been his friends. He heard the horses whinnying and, shining the torch, he followed his dogs along the path Roo, Bongo and the two cattlemen had taken.

He saw the two dead bodies, stiff in the cold night air. There came a pained groan and he froze. His three dogs sniffed the air and excitedly started up towards the rocky ledge above. Not sure who it was he decided it best to announce himself, just in case someone took a shot at him.

"Hey, its me, Riley, who's that up there?" he called.

There came a soft voice, "Me, Bongo. Roo too but it looks like he's dead. I can't reach him. You'd better come up and help me, I've lost a lot of blood, and I'm friggin' frozen."

When Riley made it to the rocky ledge he almost fell as his boots slid on the spent cartridge cases. The dogs whined as they licked Bongo's bloodied face while he tried unsuccessfully to shoo them away.

"Strewth, Bongo," Riley exclaimed in shock at what he saw. When he saw Bongo's bare chest, blood spattered face and hands, then his bandaged leg, he pulled the dogs back.

"Here, put this on mate." Riley took his own jacket off and handed it to Bongo, then helped him pull it over his skinny frame.

"How many did we get, Riley, did we get them all? They'll be back if we didn't," said Bongo through chattering teeth.

"Yes, it looks like you got them all. There's two Range Rovers down there and three dead men on the ground plus the two on the track behind you. I don't know how many in the cars though, or if any have run away. We'll look in the morning." He turned to Roo and shined the torch into his closed eyes. Roo blanched and tried to lift his head. The dogs rushed him thinking they were now allowed to help. Roo yelped when one of them stepped on his broken wrist.

"Hey cuz, you decide to drop in unannounced again did ya? You keep doing that and you'll end up hurting someone." His smile was forced and there was a catch in his throat as he spoke. Lifting Roo's head he checked him over but when he moved his arm Roo yelled and out came another swear word, "Shit!"

"Hey cuz, you just learning to talk all over again?" he teased weakly, tears had formed in the corners of his eyes. "I'd better bring some soap with me to wash your mouth out next time."

Riley held back a sob as he helped Roo sit with his head leaning against the rock face. With the strength of an outback cattleman he easily carried Bongo down to the horses. When he came back he examined Roo's wrist and placed a stick along his forearm wrapping it with part of a saddle cloth. Carefully placing him on his back he carried his cousin down the dirt track to place him gently beside Bongo.

"I'm going to light a fire and put you blokes around it to warm up. Then we'll cook some food and have some hot tea, what do you think?" He chatted away all the time thinking of how to get the two away before dawn brought the rest of the Wilson's.

He sent the dogs out to patrol the gully. They thought they were going to hunt kangaroos and raced off barking. The horses were accustomed to dogs and weren't fussed, but they were sore and irritable having struggled as they tried to escape during the fire-fight.

Riley spent some time grooming and settling the horses. Then he removed their saddles and hobbled them so they could forage for food by themselves. He hurriedly made a meal and some hot tea from the stores in the saddlebags and helped his two friends eat. Like a nursemaid he laid them on their saddle cloths and settled them down in front of the fire.

"Bongo, it looks like Roo's got concussion of some sort. He's broken his wrist and lost some blood too. I'm going to grab that Rover down there and put the two of you in it. I'll take you to Katie and the kids. But we aren't out of danger. If one of those Wilson's got away they'll hunt us down, then they'll kill us." He looked at Bongo in the firelight. Bongo nodded, Riley saw he was pale and weak.

"Sure, let's get some rest..." Bongo fell asleep mid-sentence. Riley quickly turned and headed down the track shining his torch to reveal the punctured windscreen and a dead man behind the Rover's steering wheel. He pulled the body out, it was Ferrie, one of the Wilson bully-boys who'd held Bongo while Brad and Greg bashed him senseless.

"You prick, it couldn't have happened to a more deserving bloke." Riley growled as he dragged out another two bodies to make way for his wounded mates. He saw the weapons and ammunition inside and decided to collect as much as he could while he was there.

Riley brought the vehicle closer to the fire and then packed the boys gear in the back. One by one he carried them and placed them inside the vehicle itself. Calling for the dogs to climb in he drove out of the gully and was at his hideaway within the hour.

The old bushman's hut was well hidden among the gully's. Difficult to see unless you walked up to it. But with two four-wheel drives parked beside it there was no way they could escape detection.

With the kids asleep Katie fussed over the two wounded warriors doing what she could to ease their pain. They made up a makeshift bed on the floor for the two wounded men to sleep on, and stoked up the fire. After Katie cleaned and examined Roo's bloodied arm, she called Riley over.

"Riley, hold his arm - here," she showed him exactly where she needed him to place his hands. Roo remained unconscious. "Now hold firmly and no matter how much he screams don't let go. I'm going to set it and then bandage it in place with these two sticks here. You need to hold tight, are you ready?"

"You're not going to pull on it are you? He'll yell the darn place down. You sure you know what you're doing?" Riley's voice was strained and he sounded exhausted.

"I've helped my dad do these sorts of things with the workers and animals. It isn't hard to do, just painful," said Katie matter-of-factly. "If we don't straighten his arm now, he'll have a gammy arm for the rest of his life. It has to be done, Riles, it's now or never. Are you ready?" She grasped Roo's hand and got a good grip, then she pulled.

An hour before dawn Riley was up and setting traps on the approaches to the hut. He knew he couldn't hide their tracks but at least he could upset a few of the Wilson boys if they turned up unannounced. He took the Rover and hid it in one of the side gully's then continued on foot to the scene of the battle. There was enough light for him to track the last cattleman who was lying dead in the drivers seat of the second Rover. He walked around in ever widening circles checking the ground for footprints until he was satisfied no one had escaped.

Seven dead bodies would soon draw the attention of the dingo's, eagles and crows, but he didn't really care. Riley hid the second Rover in another gully then, with the help of his dogs, he walked the two horses back to the hut. He decided to leave the bodies to feed the wild animals in a deep gully only a short distance from where they died.

Riley had a plan to move further into the wilderness, where he knew of another bushman's hut he was sure no one else knew about. An old prospector's hut that was hidden a few kilometres further into the ranges and only accessible by foot. If they came at him they had only one way to go and that would be through him, his traps and now his arsenal of weapons.

The cattleman didn't know it but the Wilson's had troubles of their own. The Revelationist church leaders had called them up to help fight the Birdsville mob. It was part of their responsibility as church members, they insisted. The

Wilson's weren't happy but they had no choice, it was answer the call or lose their privileges. Old man Wilson decided Riley and his cousins could wait.

"Besides," he told his son Jack, now ranting over the loss of his two Range Rovers, "revenge is best served cold."

Epilogue

Fat Boy sat with Sundown, Tricia, Pinkie, Lorraine and Andrew, he'd been crying. They'd been up most of the night watching over Pedro not knowing whether he would pull through or not.

Sundown spoke quietly, "Fat Boy, do you think you can get there and back in time? Tricia said he has about a week at the most. It's up to you, we'll understand if you can't do it."

"Of course I'll bloody do it! He's the only bastard who understands who I am, the only one in my entire miserable life." He blew his nose and rubbed the tears from his eyes. "I need Blondie, she's my disguise, can someone get her?" He looked up as more tears formed.

Tricia got up, she was soon back with Blondie. Blondie went straight to Fat Boy and put her arms around his shoulders, speaking softly to him.

"Of course we'll go, Tricia, I love that old man too. He's the best thing that's ever come into our lives. We'll leave immediately." She stood up and put her hand on Fat Boy's shoulder. "Come on, Fat Boy, time's running out." Turning to Sundown she said, "Can you please ask Harry and Bill to check the bike? We'll go at first light after we've had a quick breakfast and packed some water and spare fuel." She helped a sobbing Fat Boy out of his chair.

Tricia handed Blondie a written note. On it was written the exact medications Pedro needed if he was to survive the infection now killing him. Below, in Bill's scrawling handwriting, was written a list of the parts he needed for the Cessna aircraft still waiting for its repairs.

Tricia looked at Blondie and Fat Boy. Her face was firm but beneath the surface they could see muscles twitching as she tried to hide her emotions. "I don't care how you do it, just do it."

"You do know we might not come back?" said Fat Boy.

Tricia nodded, "Yes, Blondie told me the story. If you have to, then abort and come back. We don't want you two getting yourselves caught and executed. You're part of our family too you know." Her eyes brimmed with unshed tears.

"You don't even know a fraction of who we are and what we've done, Tricia. We'll do this even if we have to kill to do it. Even if we die trying. It's much of a muchness to us."

Sundown walked with them back to their room. "Don't take any chances, just get in and get back to us. Halo and Wiram are preparing to take the dual cab and set up a half-way pit-stop, that's about three hundred clicks. They'll have food, fuel and water waiting for you. They'll escort you back here with your supplies. We'll try to convince our Alice Springs Command mates to swing their ASLAV there to discourage anyone who thinks they should follow you home."

"We've done bad things, Sundown, but this, if we can pull it off, might make up for some of it," said Blondie as she ushered Fat Boy into their room to snatch a few hours sleep before dawn.

THE END

Glossary of Australian words

ASLAV – *Australian Light Army Vehicle, armoured cavalry troop carrier with mounted 7.62 mm machine gun and 25 mm cannon.*

Alice – Alice Springs

Billy – tin to put on the fire to boil water in, for tea making and heating water

Blimey – crikey, strewth, darn, damn

Bloke – man, male, fellow or fella

Bloody – damn or darn

Blowed – confused, no idea, can also mean exhausted (out of breath)

Boofhead – meat head or beef head

Brew – to boil water to make a cup of tea

Brumbies – wild horses

Bullcrap – bullshit, not true

Bushmaster – six-wheeled cavalry armoured personnel carrier with 7.62 mm machine gun.

Comms – communications, radio operator

Crikey – strewth, blimey, darn, damn

Dingo – Australian wild dog

Fellas – fellows, people

Flaming – bloody, damn, darn

Flinders – Flinders Ranges

Football – rugby, like gridiron without a helmet

Four wheel drive – SUV's designed for travel in the desert, all four wheels engage for better traction

Fussed – bothered, worried

G'day – good day, hello

Mate – friend, buddy

Men of high degree – fully initiated aboriginal men with elevated status in their tribe – some would have nangarri, sorcerer or 'medicine men' abilities and training

Mob – mobs, a lot of, usually associated with a group of people and of kangaroos

Nangarri – aboriginal medicine man or sorcerer – see also 'men of high degree'

Needy – horse

Outback – the desert country

Salt-pan – salt covered plain, flat as a saucepan, also called salt-flats because it's flat – the desert has many such salt covered plains

Stations – property or large farm in outback Australia, some larger than Texas

Strewth – damn, darn, crikey, blimey

Stuffed – exhausted

Swags – bed roll, blanket or sleeping bag wrapped in a waterproof canvas

Walkabout – aboriginals would 'go bush' to get back to their roots, sometimes it involved spiritual works as well as for a vacation

Wallaby – small kind of kangaroo

Whacked – hit, smacked

Willy-willy – dust devil, mini desert tornado, whirlwind

Yabbies – fresh water crayfish

Characters - _Sundown Apocalypse: Urban Guerrilla_

House rats / city dwellers Adelaide city - Charlene, Heidi, Arthur, Fatima, Phil, Tony, Lucy, Annie, Abraham, Stacy

Armed Cavalry survivor group - Nulla, Glenda, Luke, Simon

1st Cavalry - Captain Ridges, Sergeant Major Frank Samuels

Sundown's Commando - Sundown, Cambra, Assassin Creed, McFly, Halo, Beamy, Pellino, Bill, Wiram, Chan, John, Donna, Pedro

Birdsville civilians - Tricia, Gail, Lorraine, Billie, Polly, Granny, Pinkie, Jenny, Harry, Lenny, Liam, Danielle, Lulu, Danni, Mel, Andrew, Wilma, Shadow

Scouts - Roo, Bongo

Bikers - Fat Boy, Blondie

Alice Springs Command, Australian Third Army - Major Thompson, Captain Lewis, Sergeant Doff

Arkaroola - Riley, Katie, Elle, Harry

Flinders Ranges - Jack Wilson, Brad, Ferrie, Greg, Joey, Laurie

Crusaders of the Revelations terrorists - General Himmler Army Alpha; Army Charlie: Captain McCarthy, Sergeant Warren, Lance-Corporal Jabba, Emma, Larry; Major Lunney (Deaths Head Commandos); Major Daniels (Stosstruppen - storm troopers)

Thank you for reading the 2nd book in my Sundown Apocalypse series. Please feel free to message me on Facebook - 'LeoNixSundown' or go to my web site and subscribe to my newsletter informing you of my new publications and special deals.

All the best and don't forget to grab the others in the series.

Regards
Leo Nix - January 2017
www.leo-nix.com
Email: leo@leo-nix.com

Books in the Sundown Apocalypse series:

Book One: SUNDOWN APOCALYPSE - Published, 2017

Book Two: SUNDOWN APOCALYPSE - Urban Guerrilla - Published, 2017

Book Three: SUNDOWN APOCALYPSE - Homeland Defense - Published, 2017

Book Four: SUNDOWN APOCALYPSE – Desert Strike - Published, 2017

Book Five: SUNDOWN APOCALYPSE – Special Ops - Published, 2018

If you enjoyed this book please post a review and tell everyone how good it is, thank you.